VICTORIA MALVEY

Fortune's Bride

SONNET BOOKS

New York London Toronto Sydney Singapore

An *Original* Publication of POCKET BOOKS

 A Sonnet Book published by
POCKET BOOKS, a division of Simon & Schuster, Inc.
1230 Avenue of the Americas, New York, NY 10020

ISBN: 0-7434-0334-7

First Sonnet Books printing December 2000

10 9 8 7 6 5 4 3 2 1

SONNET BOOKS and colophon are trademarks of Simon & Schuster, Inc.

Cover art by Alan Ayers

Printed in the U.S.A.

Books by Victoria Malvey

Portrait of Dreams
Enchanted
Temptress
A Merry Chase
Fortune's Bride

Published by POCKET BOOKS

To my friends—
Thanks for all your support & encouragement.
You enrich my life.

And to my bud, Tracy Fobes,
a very special thanks.
You help keep me sane.

ACKNOWLEDGMENTS

My thanks to Pam Hopkins for her
support and guidance.
We make a great team, Pam.

And a special thanks to
Amy Pierpont for her patience and help
in making *Fortune's Bride* even better.
You're the best, Amy.

1

London, England
June 1835

"Give me your hand and I shall tell your fortune," said Lady Alyssa Porter in a low voice, trying to add mystery to her words.

Eagerly, Lady Moore took a seat on the opposite side of the little table and held out her hand. "What can you see, Madam Zora?"

"Ahhhhh," Alyssa drawled, stroking a long nail along the curved line in Lady Moore's palm. "You shall live a long, prosperous life."

Lady Moore's eyes widened as she leaned forward to look into her hand. "You can tell that by simply seeing my palm?"

"Your future is predestined, my lady, and only one trained in reading the signs can foretell what lies ahead for you." Waving a hand, Alyssa sent her many bracelets dancing along her arm. "Luckily for you, I am one such as you need to read your future. Mystical powers have thrived in my family for many, many generations."

"Oh, Madam Zora," whispered Lady Moore breathlessly.

Alyssa held back her smile of satisfaction. She'd obviously impressed Lady Moore with her tale. After three months of perfecting her role, Alyssa had finally arrived. She'd convinced the ton that she was the mystical "Madam Zora," all-knowing seer of the future, and, in doing so, was able to earn enough money to provide for her and her sister. Alyssa nodded once. "Now shall we continue?"

"Oh, continue, please . . . please." Lady Moore scooted forward on her chair. "What of my . . . love life?" she whispered.

Remembering the latest bit of gossip about Lady Moore, Alyssa traced the line on the older woman's palm. "Ah, yes, your love line," she murmured as if caught up in the reading. "You have recently met a tall, dark stranger, haven't you?"

Her mouth dropped open. "Yes!" she finally exclaimed. "How did you know?"

Alyssa smiled slightly. "Your palm reveals all."

"Ohhh," murmured Lady Moore, once again looking intently at her hand.

"I see here your first love has been gone for many years," Alyssa continued.

"My husband, Robert, passed on seven years ago."

Alyssa's coin-laden veil jangled as she nodded sagely. "Which explains the darkness along this line," she said, pointing to the jagged crease in Lady Moore's hand. "But here is where the dark stranger enters."

Lady Moore's expression softened. "Malcolm."

"This man, he treats you well," Alyssa said, watching the woman closely for her reaction.

"Oh, yes," she replied enthusiastically. "He's a dear, but . . ."

"But you still hold your husband close to your heart," Alyssa concluded.

Slowly, Lady Moore nodded. " 'Tis silly of me, I know, but I believe that as long as I remain a widow my Robert will always be with me."

Pointing to three lines on Lady Moore's palm, Alyssa gave Lady Moore the prediction she wanted. "As you can plainly see, your life changes here where three lines entwine as one." She captured Lady Moore's gaze. "If you accept this man, this Malcolm, into your life, you will not be losing anything . . . including the spirit of your late husband. It is your destiny."

A sigh of relief escaped Lady Moore. "My dear Madam Zora," she whispered, dabbing at the corners of her eyes. "You can't know how I longed to hear such a prediction."

Ah, but she could, Alyssa thought, for she'd overheard Lady Moore at a party three nights ago. Folding her hands on top of each other, Alyssa lifted one shoulder. "I only tell you what I read in your hand."

Murmuring her thanks, Lady Moore rose from the seat, making way for the next woman in line.

"Why are there so many men in the study this evening?" asked Ian Fortune, glancing around the smoke-filled room. "Normally most of them are court-ing their ladies on the dance floor."

"But that's just it," replied Peter. "The ladies aren't interested in dancing."

"Impossible."

"It's quite true, Ian," Peter assured him. "All of the women are waiting to speak with Madam Zora."

"Madam who?"

"Zora," repeated Peter. "She's the Gypsy for-tuneteller that Lord Hargrave had at his affair three weeks ago. Ever since Hargrave's party, no event is complete without Madam Zora."

"Who is she? Where did Hargrave find her?"

"According to rumor, she simply walked up and knocked on his front door, demanding an audience. After she proceeded to accurately tell Hargrave's fu-ture, he hired her for his party." A side of his mouth tilted upward. "She claims to be a full-blooded Gypsy."

"And everyone believes her? Just like that?"

Shrugging, Peter glanced around the room. "It would appear that way."

The whims of the ton never failed to amaze Ian. "What parlor tricks does she do?"

"She reads your palm or tarot cards for you," Peter explained. "Two days ago at the Smythe's soiree, she even gazed into a crystal ball."

Ian snorted. "Crystal ball indeed."

"Whether you believe it or not, the fact remains that most of the ladies are convinced that Madam Zora can truly see the future."

"Bloody peahens," Ian retorted, shaking his head.

"Then I should offer my compliments to this Gypsy for having outwitted the elite."

"Indeed you should." Peter gave him a sly smile. "After all she's *your* lady."

"What the devil do you mean by that?" Ian asked with a questioning smile.

"They've dubbed her *Fortune's* Lady."

Bursting into laughter, Ian set down his snifter of brandy. "That settles it, my friend. I believe it's time we learned our fates, don't you?"

"I do," Peter agreed, snubbing out his cigar. "I'm always up for a bit of entertainment."

"Then a Gypsy fortuneteller is precisely what you need," Ian tossed over his shoulder as he strode from the room.

Hurrying after him, Peter called, "May I go first?"

Alyssa watched Lady Pettibone walk away. Another satisfied customer, she thought, holding in her smile. Turning toward the next person waiting, Alyssa blinked once when she saw the two men standing before her. "Oh," she gasped softly, unaccustomed to men seeking their fortune. Quickly, she regained her composure. "You wish to learn your fortune?"

"Indeed I do," answered the slender black-haired man as he took a seat. "Peter Sunley, Viscount of Essex, at your service."

Before Alyssa could even respond, the second fellow stepped forward. "Surely there was no need to tell her your name, Peter. I'm certain she already knows who you are."

Lifting her gaze, Alyssa started at the incredibly handsome man standing behind Lord Essex. The arrogant smirk upon his face did little to detract from his looks. "I tell fortunes, my lord," she replied coolly. "I don't read minds."

"How convenient," the glorious one said, crossing his arms.

The man's attitude was familiar to Alyssa, as she'd often faced disdain since she'd assumed this role as Madam Zora. Yet something about *him* flustered her. The lively gleam in his startlingly blue eyes tugged at her senses. . . .

Alyssa broke off her thoughts and redirected them. After all, she'd been paid well to entertain, not to grow tongue-tied at a handsome young lord. Lifting her chin, she returned her attention to Lord Essex. "Do you wish to have your fortune told or are you simply here to mock me like your friend?"

"Pay Ian no mind," Lord Essex instructed, frowning back at his friend. "He doesn't believe in mystical matters. If he can't touch it or feel it, he doesn't believe in it."

"I already realized that fact."

"And how's that?" Ian asked with a laugh. "Did you look into your crystal ball, perchance?"

"There was no need, my lord. Your attitude alone speaks volumes."

Placing a hand on the back of Lord Essex's chair, Ian leaned closer. "And what does my attitude tell you?"

Rising to the challenge in his eyes, Alyssa tilted

back her head. "That you are well accustomed to having things fall neatly into place."

"What man isn't?" he retorted. "Come now, Madam Zora. Tell me something that only a fortuneteller would know."

"You mock me and then expect to receive my gift of inner sight?" Alyssa clicked her tongue in what she hoped was a dismissing sound. "I think not, my lord."

"As I expected," he returned swiftly. "Your claim of mystical powers seems far-fetched to me, Madam Zora. After all, you continue to address me as 'my lord' when I am untitled."

It took all of her self-control to keep from revealing her surprise at his revelation. With his arrogance and commanding presence, she'd assumed he was a titled gentleman. Shrugging lightly, Alyssa said, "If I had consulted the cards, all would have been revealed to me."

Ian rolled his eyes.

Determined to ignore the impudent man, she turned toward Lord Essex, giving him a smile. "As for you, my lord, since you're obviously a believer, I shall be happy to tell you what awaits you in the future."

Eagerly, Lord Essex shifted forward, holding out his hand. "Miss Hart was kind enough to tell me you were reading palms this evening," he said, nodding toward the blushing girl who was next in line.

The leering note in his voice gave Alyssa her first clue. Cradling his hand, she slowly traced a fingernail along the lines. "You have not yet found the lady of your dreams, my lord."

Lord Essex's eyes widened. "That's true," he replied, awe coloring his answer.

Glancing at Miss Hart, Alyssa saw how the young lady blushed prettily while peeking shyly at Lord Essex. "Yet there are many who would eagerly accept your attention."

"You can see all that in Peter's hand?" Ian nudged his friend. "When was the last time you washed, old man?"

Lord Essex chortled. "Enough, Ian. If you don't desist, Madam Zora will never consent to finishing my fortune." Sobering, he looked at Alyssa. "I apologize for my friend. He means no insult."

"Of course not," Alyssa said smoothly. "Your friend merely mocks me for amusement. I am but a Gypsy sharing my gifts with those who believe in exchange for wages which purchase my food and shelter. Yet, this Ian of yours delights in tormenting me."

Alyssa watched as all of the humor slid from Ian's face, leaving behind a shadow of guilt. Rising with dignity, she faced Ian. "You wish to hear something about yourself that no one else could know, sir?" Without waiting for an answer, Alyssa continued, "You take pleasure in humiliating others." She swept her gaze over him. "It was foolish of me to have mistaken you for a gentleman."

Lifting her chin, Alyssa spun on her heel and walked away.

Shame filled Ian.

The beautiful little Gypsy was quite correct in her assessment. His mockery of her was poorly done.

"You were a bit hard on her, don't you think?" Peter asked, moving to stand next to Ian.

"More than a bit," Ian admitted, rubbing two fingers against his forehead. "I don't know why I was so . . . so . . ."

"Unpleasant? Nasty? Insulting?"

"Thank you," Ian remarked dryly.

"My pleasure." Peter slapped a hand upon Ian's shoulder. "What's gotten into you this evening, my friend?"

"I don't know." Ian felt a bevy of gazes upon him. "I'm quite certain everyone else is wondering the same thing."

"Can you blame them? After all, you did manage to scare off the fortuneteller."

Ian felt another rush of guilt. He'd just been toying with her, but he'd forgotten that true gentlemen threw taunts at each other, not someone lesser than they. "No, I can't blame them," he said quietly. "I shall have to apologize to the Gypsy the next time I see her."

"Apologize?" Peter repeated incredulously. "To a Gypsy wench?"

"No, to a young woman simply trying to make a day's wages," Ian corrected.

Tilting his head to the side, Peter seemed to be considering his response. "If anyone can empathize with the girl, it would be you, my friend."

"Not all of us are born into money," Ian retorted.

Peter gave Ian a pointed look. "And some of us are . . . yet choose to ignore it."

"My father had not a farthing to his name when he passed away."

"The same cannot be said of your grandfather, who is still alive and quite healthy despite his advanced age."

Something inside of Ian twisted. "I do not have a grandfather."

"No, you don't have one you'll acknowledge," Peter corrected.

"Be that as it may, the outcome remains the same, leaving me a man struggling to secure financial success." He looked down at the Gypsy's table. "And it was unforgivable of me to mock those trying to do the very same thing . . . regardless of my personal opinion of their methods."

"If you're set on apologizing to Madam Zora, I believe she's next scheduled to appear at the Covingtons' affair two days hence."

Retrieving the tarot cards the Gypsy had left behind in her haste, Ian tucked them into his pocket. " 'Til then."

2

Though anger drove her forward, Alyssa still took pains to make her way home slowly, taking the most circuitous route to the room she shared with her sister. If anyone discovered her true identity, Alyssa's fortunetelling days would be over and all of her hopes for Calla's future would be destroyed.

Glancing around, Alyssa slipped into her tenant house, stealing up two flights of stairs, and into her room. Calla stood next to the stove, heating a pot of tea, in the corner that served as their kitchen.

"Alyssa," exclaimed Calla, moving forward to hug her sister. "You're early this evening."

"I . . . I was able to slip out," Alyssa murmured, not wishing to upset her sister. Retrieving her shawl, she wrapped it around herself. "I hope you weren't too bored here all alone." Once again, she felt the sting of guilt. Ever since their parents had been killed, she'd struggled to rebuild a life for herself and her sister . . . and she felt as if she was floundering. What sort of a life was it for a fourteen-year-old girl to be left alone in this rented room every night?

"Are you changing the subject?" Calla asked, tipping her head to the side.

Pushing aside her doubts, Alyssa poured herself a cup of tea. "Of course not."

"Come now, Alyssa," Calla scoffed, putting her hands upon her hips. "Tell me what happened this evening."

Sighing, Alyssa gave up her attempt to shield Calla. "Nothing much, truly. There was simply an arrogant fellow—"

"From what you've told me, there isn't a shortage of those among the ton," Calla returned with a smile.

"That's certainly true," agreed Alyssa. "Only this time, I allowed this man's taunts to unnerve me."

Calla's eyes widened. "You?"

Laughing at her sister's disbelief, Alyssa took a sip of tea. "Hard to believe, but true."

"I can't imagine anyone upsetting you," Calla admitted. "You've faced down creditors, sent them packing without batting an eye when they came pounding upon our door."

But none of the creditors were men who sparked a flicker of interest within her. Yet this Ian fellow, with his wicked grin and challenging attitude, had intrigued her from the first moment she saw him.

Lifting one shoulder, Alyssa tried to dismiss her sister's amazement. "I don't know what it was about this man, Ian, but he managed to irk me quite easily."

"He sounds utterly fascinating."

Alyssa laughed at her sister. "How old are you again?"

"Old enough to know that a gentleman who can manage to irk you must be something special indeed."

Something special. The words played over in Alyssa's thoughts as she pictured the stunning Ian in her mind. Shivering slightly, she promptly pushed the image away.

"He was something, I'll grant you, but not something good," Alyssa said tartly.

Drawing her brows together, Calla scowled fiercely. "You're far too picky, Alys. If you don't settle upon one gentleman, you'll never marry."

"Be that as it may."

An exasperated sigh ripped from Calla as she flopped onto a chair. "I don't understand you. You'll never find yourself a husband with that attitude."

"I'm not looking for one, angel. If I were, I would have accepted Mr. Meiser's offer."

"Mr. Meiser?" Calla shivered once. "He was a horrid toad of a man . . . and I thought that *before* I discovered he was our cousin's man-of-business. Anyone who would work for the new earl *must* be nasty as well."

While Alyssa agreed completely, she refused to comment about the distaste she'd felt when her cousin's agent had called upon her and offered marriage. Never once had she considered it, but now, looking around their shabby room, Alyssa wondered if perhaps she'd made a mistake. It was difficult enough to provide for her and Calla, but actually saving enough money to sponsor a Season for Calla now seemed an impossible dream.

Unwilling to burden her sister with her dark thoughts, Alyssa smiled softly. "Mr. Meiser seemed most pleasant when he called upon me, but it didn't change my lack of desire for marriage," Alyssa replied evenly as she took a sip of her tea. "Besides, how am I supposed to meet a gentleman? As Madam Zora?" She shook her head. "Trust me, Calla. The young bloods who haunt these parties are seeking entertainment, not a commitment with a woman whose reputation has been tarnished beyond recognition."

"Your reputation is not—"

"—something I can ever reclaim," Alyssa finished for her sister. "When I became Madam Zora, I gave up any hope of ever being Lady Alyssa Porter, daughter of the Earl of Tonneson."

Shaking her head fiercely, Calla scowled at Alyssa. "That is nonsense."

"Not in the eyes of the ton," Alyssa corrected. "As Madam Zora, I am paid to attend parties, I walk through the streets of London without escort, and I trick notables into believing I am a mystic." She clasped Calla's hand. "But please don't misunderstand me, Calla. Society's misconceptions are perfectly fine with me. Through Madam Zora, I am able to adequately provide for us."

"I know, Alyssa." Calla's gaze lit up. "But I do admit to wishing we didn't have to eat so many potatoes."

Alyssa felt another pinch of guilt. "As do I, but I hope our situation changes. In fact, I hope to save enough money to afford a Season for you in a few years."

"But what about you?"

"I shall be most content retiring comfortably to our cottage in Northumberland after seeing you happily married off to a fine young gentleman."

"That's not a cottage, Alyssa," exclaimed Calla as she wrinkled her nose. "It's more like a hovel."

While her sister was quite correct, Alyssa tried to focus on the positive. "I'll admit it does need a bit of work, but it is the only home our cousin saw fit to leave us after he inherited the title and estate."

Calla reached out, running her hand down a large pile of books stacked haphazardly against the wall. "If only Mama and Papa hadn't gone on that last trip to Africa."

If only, Alyssa agreed silently. Their lives wouldn't have changed at all. She and Calla would still be residing at the Tonneson familial estate, surrounded by caring servants, living a life of ease. But the storm that had dashed her parents' ship against the rocky coast of Africa had destroyed her life as well. "At least we are blessed with lovely memories of them," Alyssa said, hoping to ease the sadness from her sister's expression.

"My memories are somewhat hazy," Calla admitted quietly. "Mama and Papa weren't home very often."

Alyssa felt a flicker of resentment, but pushed it away. "No, they were true adventurers," she said in forced gaiety. "Which is how we've come to possess all of these treasures." She pointed to the masks hanging from the walls, the crystals lining the shelves, and the marble chess set resting proudly on its solitary table.

"Naturally, my personal favorite is my crystal ball," Alyssa said with a smile, this one real.

Calla's mood lightened. "Of course, after all, you are the great and wonderful Madam Zora." Giggling, she curtsied to Alyssa. "I honor your great mystical abilities."

"As well you should," Alyssa pronounced in a grand voice. "If you displease me, I shall have to turn you into a toadstool."

"Could it be a cat instead?" Calla asked hopefully. "I've always wanted to be a cat."

Alyssa smiled at her sister's remark. How simple life was at fourteen.

Preparing for the Covingtons' affair, Ian tugged on his cravat until it was a perfect knot at his throat. It was important he look well-set tonight. After all, he had a little Gypsy to impress.

He smiled into the mirror.

"What are you so happy about?" asked Peter as he strolled into Ian's dressing room.

"Do come in, Peter, and make yourself comfortable," Ian drawled smoothly, lifting an eyebrow at his friend.

"Don't mind if I do." Grinning, Peter sat in a nearby chair, swinging his leg over the arm. "I didn't wish to miss a moment of tonight's entertainment."

"Entertainment?"

"The apology to your Gypsy," Peter murmured with a nod.

Ah, yes, his sweet imposter, who with her large dark brown eyes, olive skin, and thick chestnut hair could have easily claimed Roma heritage. But once

he'd seen the golden streaks in her hair, her slender re-
fined hands, and the innocence in her gaze, he'd had
no doubts about her lack of Gypsy blood.

More than likely, his "Lady" was some down-on-her-
luck peasant's daughter born with quick wit, keen powers of observation, and a large dose of unmitigated gall.

"Surely you haven't forgotten?"

"Of course not," Ian replied, smoothing his hands
down the front of his jacket.

"You do realize, Ian, that an apology is really not
necessary," Peter said, waving his hand in the air. "I'm
quite certain that she's heard other skeptics naysaying
her abilities."

"Perhaps she has, but that doesn't make my actions
any less reprehensible." Picking a flower from a nearby
vase, he tucked it into his lapel. "Who am I to judge
her because she chooses to make her life's wages off
the pampered ladies of polite society?"

"Don't ever let a lady hear you refer to her as pampered or you'll find it difficult to claim one as your
bride."

"Please give me more credit than that," Ian remarked. "I'm not about to make a misstep now, not
when I've worked so hard to achieve all I have. You
know better than most all I've done to position myself
to fulfill my goals . . . *all* of my goals."

"Ah, yes, the valiant fight you took over from your
father to regain your family's fortune and honor."

Slowly, Ian turned to face his friend. "Don't make
me regret having confided in you."

"Come now, old boy, don't get your knickers in a

knot," reprimanded Peter. "I'm hardly mocking you. In fact, I honestly consider your quest a noble one, but even you must admit that you allow your thirst for retribution to consume you."

"Well, pardon my single-mindedness, but it takes a bit of concentration to amass a fortune from a pile of debt," Ian retorted.

"I already told you I find your determination admirable and your idea of acting as an agent between the merchants and the titled gentlemen who have no wish to dirty their hands haggling over money is positively brilliant." Rising from his chair, Peter placed a hand upon Ian's shoulder. "But don't you think it's time to ease up, my friend, and enjoy life a little?"

"I am," Ian said stiffly. "I've been attending numerous social affairs."

"Only because it's time for you to add a suitable bride to your list of acquisitions."

Glaring at his friend, Ian stepped backward. "I fail to see how that has any bearing on the situation. I'd wager half of the men attending these affairs are searching for their bride as well."

"True enough," conceded Peter, his expression sober, "but I don't know of anyone else who plans on tossing their wife's good breeding into their grandfather's face."

The point slammed into his gut. "That is not my plan at all," Ian murmured. No, his plan was to flaunt his wife's good name *and* his fortune as well.

"I must tell you, Ian, I don't understand your dislike of your grandfather."

"Not only did he disinherit my father, but he refused to even acknowledge him as family." Coldness swept through him. "I shall never forget the pain that caused my father."

"I can understand that you're angry about that, but I believe you should also look at this from your grandfather's point of view. After all, your father *did* run off with his serving maid and . . ."

"That serving maid was my *mother*," Ian ground out fiercely, "and I will not tolerate any disrespect toward her memory."

"Now, Ian—"

"Enough!" Ian lifted both of his hands, cutting Peter off. "I value your friendship very much, Peter, and I am asking you to not speak of this again. What I choose to do with my life is my own business."

"I know, Ian. It's just that I worry . . ." An expression of shock spread across Peter's face. "Dear God! I'm starting to sound like my father!" His hand shook as he rubbed it across his forehead. "Sorry, Ian. For a moment there, I must have lost my head. It won't happen again."

The tension inside Ian eased. "I'd very much appreciate that," he murmured, slapping a hand on his friend's arm. "What do you say we go find my little Gypsy now?"

"Most definitely," Peter agreed. "So tell me, my friend, do you see her falling into your lap like a tasty morsel?"

"*Tasty morsel?*" Ian repeated with a laugh. "I said I was going to apologize to the girl, not seduce her."

"Spoilsport."

"Alas, it's true." Retrieving his gloves, Ian began to walk from the room, leaving Peter to follow. "I fail to see the sport in seducing a poor chit who is merely trying to make a living." He paused long enough to toss a grin over his shoulder. "I far prefer lifting the skirts of some of those lovelies parading around as virtuous dames."

"Now you're speaking my language!" Rubbing his hands together, Peter hurried after Ian. "Oh, happy day!"

Laughing with his friend, Ian felt a spark of excitement at seeing Madam Zora once more. The evening ahead played out in his mind as he spun a delightful scenario around his little Gypsy. He could easily picture her astonishment, delight, and appreciation as he offered her his apology.

Naturally, he would accept her thanks and ease his conscience. Then he'd sit back and watch as Fortune's Lady fleeced the darlings of society.

3

The coins on Alyssa's shawl chimed gaily as she drew it around her. Settling back into her chair, she released her breath for the first time that evening. Idly, she stroked her fingers along her papa's crystal ball, wondering at the vague feeling of disappointment swirling within her. She should have been relieved at having been spared the odious company of that Ian fellow. Yet, here she sat, feeling disappointed because he hadn't appeared this evening.

"Is it too late to have my fortune told?"

The crystal ball rocked on the table as Alyssa jerked her hand away and she found herself looking into the very handsome face of the man who had occupied far too many of her recent thoughts.

Scrambling to recover her composure, Alyssa ignored the surge of anticipation as she replied coolly, "I'm not telling fortunes this evening, sir."

Ian looked pointedly at the crystal ball.

"Tonight's entertainment was seeking answers to one specific question."

A grin slashed across his face. "And I imagine your answers were quite imaginative."

"I only told what I saw in the ball," she replied in frosty tones.

"Naturally, they were all delightfully vague." Nudging away from the doorjamb, Ian strolled into the room. "You seem quite skilled at your profession," he continued, his voice light with admiration. "Someone with your quick wit is well suited for fortunetelling."

Remaining wary, Alyssa watched him come closer, wondering at his game this evening.

"Indeed, if a lady asked you if she would find true love, naturally you would respond with a resounding 'yes,' giving her the answer she wanted." Dropping into the chair next to her little table, Ian reached out to touch her crystal ball. "And if someone asked a more specific question, such as where had their grand-uncle Horace buried his gold, you could answer with a pat answer like 'all will be revealed in time.' "

Try as she might to ignore the urge to laugh at his presumptuousness, Alyssa felt a smile tugging up the corners of her mouth. "Are *you* of Roma blood, sir?"

"Not a drop," he replied with a chuckle. "And, I'll wager, neither are you."

His assertion sobered her, making her remember the importance of maintaining her charade. Her livelihood depended on it. "You'd lose your bet," she murmured, her hands tightening upon the bottom of the crystal ball.

The gleam in his blue eyes intensified. "Would I? I highly doubt it."

"So you say," she replied smoothly. "But you are forgetting that I am the one with the gift of sight."

Ian blinked once . . . then burst out laughing.

Well, that certainly wasn't the reaction she'd wanted. Alyssa straightened in her seat, praying she didn't look as off-balance as she felt. "I fail to see what is so amusing, sir," she said in a cool tone.

Reaching out, he tugged on one of her curls. "Then you, my sweet Gypsy, need to look into your magic ball and discover how to get a sense of humor."

"Oh, I assure you I have an active appreciation of entertaining repartee. You simply haven't said anything amusing," she finished briskly.

"So now you've resorted to insulting *me?*"

"One can hardly take offense at the truth."

His smile broadened as he leaned back in his chair, crossing his arms. "You are a clever minx, aren't you?"

"I do relish a good turn of phrase," she replied, enjoying this clashing of wits.

"Ah, but in this instance you shouldn't be so eager to challenge me, as you haven't given me a chance to apologize."

"Apologize?" she murmured, turning the word over in her head. "*You* want to apologize to *me?*"

"Is it that outlandish of an idea?"

"Well . . . yes. I wouldn't expect a gentleman to apologize to someone in . . . in . . . my position," Alyssa finished with a stutter. No one *ever* apologized to a servant, for Heaven's sake!

"As an untitled man who makes his living in trade, how am I any different from you?" Leaning forward, Ian gently clasped her hand. "Like you, I work to succeed at my chosen craft, plying the ton for their business. So, you see, my Gypsy friend, we are very similar creatures, equals in status and situation."

Equals? Her astonishment grew at the very notion. Why would he say something like . . .

Suddenly, Alyssa understood what Ian was doing. While she'd once been innocent to the harsh, sometimes cruel ways of society, her recent dealings with her cousin, as well as various members of the ton, had taught her their tricks well. Polite society liked nothing more than to laugh at a person's weaknesses or naïveté. And now, in the truest tradition of a witty gentleman, Ian was trying to make her the joke.

Indeed, he was simply taunting her once again, yet this time in a far more clever manner than before. Oh, yes, this time he would lure her into believing he considered them equals, seducing her into letting down her guard, only to spring his cruel joke on her, telling everyone that she'd once fancied herself his equal.

It was all too easy for her to imagine him stepping into the Covingtons' study to join the other men and laugh over how the foolish Gypsy wench actually believed that he regarded her as his social peer.

He was mocking her as surely as he had the night she'd first met him at the Hargraves' ball.

This time, however, she wasn't going to let him

upset her and chase her away. No, this time she was going to match him at his game. Slowly, she pulled her hand out of Ian's clasp.

Tilting back her head, Alyssa looked down her nose at him. "Equals? Hardly. I am of Romany descent. The blood of greatness runs through my veins." She sniffed derisively, before repeating, "Equals? Pah!"

The easy smile on Ian's face frosted over, making Alyssa's heart tighten at the loss of his warm regard. If only he hadn't been toying with her . . .

"Perhaps you're right. Perhaps we aren't equals. After all, I present myself honestly to society while you hide behind your Gypsy mask, pretending to be able to see into the future while all you can really see is the money you make off the fools who believe in your tales."

His sharp retort stung. "What I see is that I give people hope, sir. What do *you* do for them?"

"I help them make money." His eyes narrowed. "Which do you think they'd rather have? Hope or financial gain?"

"Both must go hand in hand," she replied, rising to the challenge she heard in his angry voice. "After all, without hope, a person can't even begin to dream of financial reward."

"Ah, here we go again with your pretty phrases that are utterly meaningless," Ian replied with a shake of his head. "If only you were as adept at honesty as you are at deceit."

Her conscience called to her, demanding honesty, but she ignored it. To tell him the truth would be to expose her sister, so she continued boldly onward with her fabrication. "You, sir, wouldn't know the truth if it slapped you in the face," she said briskly.

Both of his eyebrows shot upward. "I beg to differ, Madam Zora. You are no more able to tell fortunes than I am," he said coldly.

"My ancestors—"

"—are undoubtedly as English as mine and I'm quite certain I could prove it with very little effort."

His arrogant response infuriated her, obliterating the flicker of apprehension. "You delude yourself if you believe that, sir. You could never prove my ancestors weren't Gypsies. Never," she snapped.

"Never?" A side of his mouth quirked upward, but his eyes remained cool and hard. "Very well, then, my Gypsy lady, I accept your challenge. I shall expose you, laying you bare until all that remains is the untarnished truth."

Fear scraped inside of her, but she swallowed it back. She'd faced far worse than Ian in the past few months. "You will only look the fool."

Rising to his feet, he strode from the room, tossing one last remark over his shoulder. "We shall see, Madam Zora. We shall see."

From the corner of the darkened hallway, Ian watched the little Gypsy bundle up her crystal ball and scurry from the Covingtons' home like the devil himself was after her. He smothered a chuckle as he realized that in her mind, he *was* the devil.

Heading toward the study to join the other men for a brandy and cigar, Ian felt his irritation toward the arrogant Gypsy fade away only to be replaced by the heady sensation of anticipation. He couldn't wait to see her next move . . . even if it meant being stung by her remarks on occasion. Indeed, his clever Gypsy had an uncanny knack for sneaking under his guard, though it placated him to realize that he annoyed her just as much. No other conclusion could be drawn from her sharp, attacking response.

Of course she'd attacked him. What else did he think she would do? Acknowledge that she was a liar? Hardly, he thought as he stepped into the study. No, he'd enjoy toying with her a bit, but he wouldn't be the one to expose her.

"Ian," hailed Peter from across the room, waving him over to the group.

Pausing only to pour himself a brandy, Ian joined his friend.

"Did you speak with Madam Zora?" Peter asked, his eyes bright. "So? What did she say when you apologized? I'll wager she was stunned."

"You could put it that way."

"Details, old boy. I want details."

"Sorry, *old boy*," Ian murmured with a grin. "There's really nothing to tell other than the fact that my apology did indeed take her by surprise."

Rolling his eyes, Peter settled back. "You're getting to be no fun at all," he complained lightly. "Luckily for you, however, I find it hard to get too perturbed at your staid behavior."

"To what do I owe this good fortune?"

"You should have asked me to *whom* do you owe

this good fortune." Peter lifted his brandy glass in a salute. "Because my present state of mind is due to a bit of advice I received from your lady herself."

"My lady?" Ian broke off as the answer hit him. "Ah, yes, the dear Madam Zora. Fortune's Lady."

"Indeed," Peter agreed. "Your lady told me that I should invest deeply in that saltwater gold mining company."

Ian choked on his brandy. "She did *what?*"

"She advised me that I should follow my heart and invest in the gold mining company like I wanted to . . . despite your advice to pass on the opportunity."

"And you're going to take the advice of a fortuneteller over my sound business recommendation?" Shaking his head, Ian reached out to place a hand upon his friend's shoulder. "You can't think to invest what little funds you have remaining into a scam like mining gold from saltwater."

"Just because I made a few poor investments over the past few years doesn't mean I'm incapable of making my own business decisions," Peter said, shaking Ian's hand loose. "I know in my gut that this is the right thing for me to do and your Gypsy confirmed it. She told me I had to follow my heart."

"Good God, Peter. She probably told five different people they needed to *follow their heart.*" Thrusting a hand through his hair, Ian struggled to contain his frustration. "Trust me when I tell you the Electrolytic Marine Mining Company is *not* a good investment. If you'd like, I can take a portion of your funds and—"

Setting down his brandy snifter, Peter cut Ian off cold. "That's enough, Ian! Do you realize that I sought Madam Zora's advice in the first place because of you? Ever since a few of my investments failed, I started to believe you when you said I didn't have a head for business, even though I have always believed that I can manage my estate quite admirably. Everyone stumbles, Ian."

"That's true," Ian agreed, placing his hand on Peter's shoulder, "but if you stumble once more, Peter, you stand to lose everything."

"I know, but this time I won't fail." Peter's eyes gleamed with excitement. "Don't you see, Ian? Madam Zora gave the same advice to Lord Allerby and he's told everyone he's done quite well with Electrolytic Marine Mining Company. Then there's Lord Hather, who followed Madam Zora's urging and he's made money with the saltwater mining as well." He grinned broadly. "Now, Madam Zora told me to believe in myself, to follow my heart, so I know I won't fail this time."

Peter's unshakable confidence in Madam Zora chilled Ian. He'd failed to realize how influential the Gypsy had become. She did possess power, after all— the power to alter people's lives. "Peter, you must be reasonable. What do we know about Madam Zora? Where did she come from? Who is she? I can tell you she's nothing more than a charlatan. You can't possibly risk your future on her advice." Ian tightened his grasp upon Peter. "It would be madness."

Shaking off Ian's hold, Peter took a step back. "Do

you honestly think it would be madness to believe in someone who has already proven her ability to see into the future? No, Ian, it would be madness *not* to follow her advice."

"Come now, Peter, you know that those gents got lucky—"

"—and so will I."

Frustration rolled through Ian. "Perhaps you will, Peter, but you can't afford to take that risk. Now if you put your funds into—"

Lifting his hand, Peter cut off Ian. "I can handle my own affairs, thank you very much."

Before Ian could say another word, Peter turned on his heel and walked away. "Bloody hell," Ian muttered, before taking a gulp of his brandy.

He'd thought the little Gypsy was handing out harmless advice, but now he realized he'd been wrong. Her prediction for Peter, regardless of how vague, could ruin him financially . . . if he followed his interpretation of her advice. Ian knew he had to stop his friend from making yet another poor investment and losing the last of his inheritance.

But how?

It was obvious that Peter wasn't willing to listen to reason, so perhaps Ian would have to try something unreasonable. Maybe if he discredited Madam Zora, cast doubts upon her ability to foretell futures, then Peter might reconsider his investment.

Ian was more than a little uncomfortable with the idea of destroying her means of support. But now, like it or not, he had no choice.

Madam Zora needed to be stopped before she did any more harm.

"Please place the divan over in that corner," Alyssa asked the servants who were helping her to set the stage for her next performance. "And the pillows can be scattered upon the rug."

"I see you've moved on to garden parties."

Spinning around, Alyssa took a deep breath as she spotted Ian walking toward her. "My ancestors *invented* the garden party, sir. Every celebration Gypsies hold is outdoors."

"I'll allow that your ancestors may have tended to the outdoors as gardeners or farmers, perhaps." He slanted a glance at her. "But I doubt Gypsy traditions ever entered into it at all."

"Why do you persist in bedeviling me?"

"Why do you persist in denying the truth?"

Twisting on her heel, Alyssa offered Ian her back. "I have far too much to do to arrange for this afternoon's entertainment. Please leave me to my preparations."

"Sorry to be a bother, Madam Zora, but what I need to tell you can't wait." He tugged her back around to face him. "I'm afraid your game is up now. While I thought your tales harmless, I now understand that you can grievously harm a person's future."

"Harm?" His words made her stomach clench in fear. "I am a teller of fortunes. I don't control a person's destiny."

"Oh, but you do," Ian insisted. "For example, my friend, Lord Essex, asked you a question last night about an investment he is considering and you told him to follow his heart." Leaning down, Ian frowned at her. "What you fail to understand is his heart is wrong! Because of poor investments, Peter has little money left as is. If he pours his remaining money into the mine, he shall lose everything."

The very thought made her ill. "How can you be so certain of that?" she asked weakly.

"Because making money is what I do. It's what I'm good at," Ian stated bluntly. "I know a poor investment from a sound one . . . and the mine he's been looking at is about the worst investment he could make. He'll lose all of his money, his home, and, ultimately, his pride, if he follows your sage wisdom."

Swallowing hard, Alyssa shook her head. "I didn't tell him what to do. All I encouraged him to be was true to himself."

"Well, he's a bumbler when it comes to his finances, so if he's true to himself, he'll destroy himself *and* his family." Ian clasped her shoulders. "You need to stop making people believe in things that simply aren't true."

His hands fell to his sides as Alyssa twisted away from him. "I can't control what people choose to do with my advice," she said, ignoring the tightness in her chest. "Everyone has a destiny and nothing I say or do will affect their fate."

A heavy sigh escaped Ian. "I will have to stop you then . . . and I'm sorry for that."

"I'm certain your remorse will ease your conscience," she returned coolly. "After all, you're only doing what you feel is right." She turned toward him again. "You're only following your heart," she finished with a frosty smile.

Shaking his head, Ian ignored her remark. "It doesn't have to be this way. If you cease this charade, I will gladly help you."

His arrogance held no bounds! "If you do succeed in banishing me, sir, why would I turn to you for aid?" she asked incredulously.

"Because I can offer you a real job, one that doesn't fleece people out of their money or jeopardize their future." His eyes darkened. "I can offer you a means of support . . . one that doesn't rely on you maintaining this charade."

"Pah!" she spat out, trying to overcome her upset and regain her Roma accent. "You speak of pride and dignity when it comes to your friends, but what of me, sir? Your offer robs me of my dignity. I would just as soon beg in the streets than accept a farthing from you."

He remained silent, looking at her somberly. Finally, he reached out for a moment, before allowing his hand to fall back to his side. "Just remember what I said," he began. "If your situation becomes dire, come to me and I'll help you."

Watching him go, Alyssa remained still until he left the tent, then she allowed her shoulders to slump forward. Dear God, was she truly harming people by her innocent advice? Surely not.

In the case of Ian's friend, her advice would have made little difference in the long run. Of that she was certain. When a person is set upon a course, they need little persuasion to follow through with their plans. Whether she said anything to Lord Essex or not, Alyssa was quite certain that in the end, he would have made the exact same choice.

Breathing easier, she looked around the tented area, satisfied. Inside, she felt an inkling of worry, but she pushed it aside. She'd created Madam Zora, built a new life for herself and her sister, and no one was going to take it away from her.

Not even a man whose words struck much too close to heart for her peace of mind.

The enraptured faces before her made Alyssa pause in her story, drawing out the moment, making them desire more of her Gypsy lore. As a few ladies leaned forward from their reclining positions on the pillows, Alyssa hid her smile and continued, "Then the father warned his son not to fly too high, to remain sensible and in control of his . . ." As Ian stepped into the tent, she faltered for a moment. ". . . his desires," she finished.

Ian lifted a brow at her.

Flushing, she glanced away and forced herself to concentrate on her story. "So, the hapless lad agreed, eager to strap on the wings his father had built for him and fly off to freedom. Oh, how the young man longed to soar along with the birds, to dance on the wind, to kiss the sun."

"Oh, how exciting," whispered Lady Covington, who reclined to Alyssa's right.

"Indeed it was, but once again, the father reminded his son not to fly too high or disaster would befall him." Softening her voice, Alyssa wound the story around the partygoers.

"Off they flew, away from their prison, on the cool ocean breeze." Pausing for effect, Alyssa trailed her hand through the air. "The son flew calmly beside his father until something terrible happened."

The gasps of three ladies nearby rewarded Alyssa.

"The seductive warmth of the sun began to call to our poor lad, beckoning him closer, until he obeyed," she murmured, looking at the sea of eager faces. "Then our poor fellow . . ."

". . . followed the call and when he flew too close to the heat of the sun, the wax that held the feathers upon his wings melted. And, much to the father's horror, he watched his only son plunge to his death into the dark ocean," Ian chimed in as he walked along the edge of the tent, moving toward Alyssa.

4

"So even as the father gained the very thing he thought he wanted most in the world—his freedom—he lost the one thing that made his world whole: his son," Alyssa finished as she moved into a sitting position.

"Therein lies the moral of the story."

"You know Romany lore then, Mister..." she trailed off, offering Ian a chance to supply his surname.

Bowing to her, he answered, "Mr. Ian Fortune at your service, Madam Zora . . . or would you prefer I called you *Fortune's* Lady?"

The flare in her eyes told him she hadn't known his surname. How delightful it was to be one step ahead of this crafty lady. Recovering quickly, his Gypsy murmured, "Madam Zora will be perfectly fine."

"As you wish," he returned, bowing to her once again.

Tucking her bare feet beneath the divan, Alyssa

shrugged lightly. "What I wish is for you to allow me to continue with my tales."

"Ah, yes, your stories of *Gypsy* lore," he said, his voice tinged with sarcasm.

"Tell us, Mr. Fortune," invited Lady Covington as she shifted her position on her pillow. "How did you know the end of the story? Are you familiar with Gypsy lore?"

"Regretfully not, my lady," Ian said with a shake of his head. "However, I am quite knowledgeable about *Greek* mythology." Returning his attention to Madam Zora, Ian smiled at her gasp. "Oh, yes, I'm quite familiar with the story of Icarus and his father, Daedalus. You see, Lady Covington, Madam Zora's tale of Roma lore is, in reality, a Greek myth."

"It most certainly is not!" the Gypsy retorted, her eyes flashing at him. "This story is one that has been passed down from my mother and my mother's mother before that." Flickering her gaze over him, she looked arrogantly disdainful. "You are just a *gadjo* who knows nothing."

Challenged, he pressed the issue. "Then how do you account for the fact that your tale is identical to the Greek myth?"

One shoulder lifted in a dismissive motion. "The Romany people have always wandered the earth. Perhaps the ancient Greeks stole one of our stories and claimed it for their own."

"That's possible," Lady Covington chimed in.

Ignoring the murmurs of agreement, Ian replied, "Possible, yes, but highly unlikely. While Gypsies were merely nomads, the Greeks built a great empire and were considered advanced thinkers and great story-tellers."

"Then perhaps we should add thieves to their list of accomplishments as well," his Gypsy finished.

Her outrageous claim left him speechless. How did one argue with a ridiculously stubborn woman? Shaking his head, Ian gave ground. "We shall have to agree to disagree," he replied politely. "Please, pardon my interruption. Do continue."

If anything, her expression grew more wary. Ah, he knew she was smart. Apparently she didn't need her crystal ball to tell her he might have admitted defeat in the battle, but the war was far from over.

Bidding farewell to Madam Zora and the bevy of ladies before her, Ian then turned on his heel and withdrew from the tent, feeling the weight of eyes upon him with every step.

"I say, Hammond, isn't that your grandson who's bedeviling the Gypsy gel?"

Lord Regis Fortune, Duke of Hammond, glared at the braying fool next to him. "I don't have a grandson."

"Yes, yes," Lord Everett murmured with a wave of his hand, before continuing on blithely, "I know you don't acknowledge him as such . . . but isn't that your Harold's boy? Lord knows, he's your spitting image."

Clamping his lips shut, Lord Hammond refused to even acknowledge his companion's observation, despite the fact that Lord Everett's point was well made. The whelp *did* look like a younger version of him. It would appear that the peasant blood wasn't strong enough to make a mark upon a Fortune, yet the pup's behavior smacked of lower class.

Little surprise there, Lord Hammond thought, sniffing in disgust.

Hadn't he warned his son about the dangers of marrying beneath his class? Yet, his arrogant offspring hadn't listened. No, instead, he'd run off with the serving wench and married her. Hammond still had trouble fathoming his son's actions.

The Dukedom of Hammond had taken a hard blow on that dark day.

Since then, he'd made certain no aspersions were cast upon the Fortune name. Yet now, this young upstart had begun to venture into society and once again the old scandal was beginning to raise its ugly head. Of course, the lad's behavior only fueled the ton's hunger for scandal-related gossip. Undoubtedly it was the boy's unfortunate taint from his mother's side that caused his appalling lack of gentlemanly restraint.

A shiver ran through the duke at the very thought of everyone gossiping about the Fortunes once more and he was left with one conclusion.

He'd have to make certain that the living legacy of his son's mistake went away. For good.

Alyssa's head throbbed as she let herself into her room. Holding back a groan when she saw Calla waiting for her, Alyssa lifted a hand as she set down her satchel. "Please don't ask me how the party went."

Calla's open mouth snapped closed, but only for a brief moment. "Oh, you can't say something like that and then expect me not to ask questions," she said, her eyes sparkling with curiosity. "Something tells me your Ian was involved."

Alyssa scowled at her sister. "First off, he's not *my* anything."

"My, my, aren't we defensive," murmured Calla with a smile.

"Not defensive, annoyed," Alyssa corrected. "Every time I say anything about that Ian fellow bothering me, you immediately begin with your incessant comments about my lack of suitors. How the devil you connect the two issues, I'll never understand."

"You'd understand perfectly well if you'd only listen to me." Flopping down onto their bed, Calla shrugged lightly. "The way I see things, it's only a small skip from anger to grand passion," she finished on a sigh.

Rolling her eyes, Alyssa murmured dryly, "So speaks the voice of experience."

"Mock me if you wish, but I've read enough stories to know about true love."

"Darling Calla, those books you read aren't true to life." Alyssa grinned at her sister. "And even if they were, I assure you, Mr. Ian Fortune hardly cuts a romantic figure."

"Fortune?" Calla whispered, her eyes growing round. "Your Ian's last name is *Fortune?*"

This time Alyssa didn't even bother to correct Calla. "Yes," she answered with a sigh, "it is."

"And the ton calls you—"

"Fortune's Lady," Alyssa finished for her sister, already seeing the wheels spinning in her head.

Calla's eyes rounded. "Then it's destiny," she murmured, pressing a hand to her chest.

"No, it's a sorry coincidence." But from the dreamy look in her sister's eyes, Alyssa knew her denial went unheard. Sighing deeply, she braced herself for more questions about Ian Fortune.

They weren't long in coming.

"What does he look like?"

Sinfully handsome. Alyssa decided her sister was determined enough without knowing that tidbit. "I don't want to—"

"Tell me, Alyssa!"

"Dark hair, blue eyes, tall." Crossing her arms, she gave her sister a disgruntled look. "Does that satisfy your curiosity?"

"Hardly," Calla scoffed. "When you see him, does your stomach get all tingly?"

Exasperated, Alyssa flung her hands in the air. "Yes, all right? What else do you want to know? Would you like to hear that when he looks at me with laughter in his eyes, I get flustered? Or perhaps you'd like to know about how exciting it is when he challenges me?"

"Oh, Alyssa," murmured Calla, a smile upon her lips. "How wonderful!"

"No, it isn't wonderful at all, not one bit of it." Alyssa rubbed at her temple. "Because despite how he makes me feel, I need to stay away from him. He threatens our life, our existence, each and every time he attempts to expose me in public." Sinking down into a chair, Alyssa looked up at Calla. "So, instead of spinning fairy tales about Ian Fortune and me, we'd both be better served if you'd think of ways for me to outwit him."

"I hadn't thought of his teasing in that light before," Calla admitted as she took a seat as well. "If no one believes in Madam Zora anymore, you'll lose your income."

"And we'll lose everything we've fought to regain," Alyssa finished soberly. "I don't say this to make you worry, Calla, but you must realize that I can't spend my time daydreaming about Mr. Fortune."

"No, you can't," she agreed readily. "Indeed, we need to decide the best way for you to outsmart him."

"That's right." Alyssa shook her head at her sister. "Mr. Fortune seems bound and determined to expose me, so we need to anticipate his actions. However, it won't be easy as we don't know what his next move will be."

Frowning slightly, Calla bit her lower lip. "You're right. After all, how will we know what he's planning?"

"I don't know, but I do know how we can find out." Grinning broadly at her sister, Alyssa deliberately lightened the mood. "I am Madam Zora, so let's consult my crystal ball."

Calla's laughter warmed Alyssa, making her believe everything would be all right.

Far north, Isaac Meiser knocked at the door of the Porter sisters' little cottage. He'd been unable to sleep, what with worrying about these two young ladies left destitute. With each unanswered knock, his anxiety mounted.

Walking around the side of the cottage, he rose onto his toes to peer into the tiny window. Cobwebs arched delicately between the sheet-covered furniture. He sank back onto his heels, with a feeling of surprise mixed with dread.

Where had the girls gone?

The nerves jangling inside of him settled downward, forming a hard, cold knot in the pit of his stomach. He didn't know what had happened to the girls, but he would find out. There was no way he was going to live with the dire consequences that had obviously befallen them weighing upon his conscience. No, sir. Not one more day.

And after he found the girls, he would convince the eldest, the charming Alyssa, to marry him. This time he'd make her realize she had no other option but to become Mrs. Isaac Meiser. The thought of having a fine lady as his wife sat well with him.

Determination filled each step as Meiser headed for town to begin his search.

The Gypsy glowed this evening, Ian realized as he stepped into the Treports' drawing room. Watching her stroll around the floor, entrancing everyone with her tales, Ian leaned against the wall, utterly fascinated by her.

The moment she caught sight of him, an odd expression of something akin to triumph flashed across her face. Yet, in a blink, it was gone, leaving behind the cool mask of Madam Zora.

"This evening I have a special revelation for all of

you," she announced, each word dripping with importance. "It has been revealed to me through the magic of my crystal ball that one among you has also been gifted with the sight."

Lady Treport frowned, her brows drawing together. "Sight? Why, I do believe everyone in this room can see perfectly fine."

"Of course, my lady, but the sight I refer to is the inner eye, the ability to see into a person and uncover all the mysteries of their past, present, and future."

"Ahhhh," murmured Lady Treport. Leaning forward, she urged, "Do tell us who it is."

Zora turned her gaze upon Ian. "The seer is none other than Mr. Ian Fortune."

A bark of laughter escaped him. "I fear you have the wrong man, madam."

"Come now, Mr. Fortune," Zora cajoled. "There is no longer a need to hide your gift." Her eyes sparkled with mischievous glee.

Well, two could play at this game. "Perhaps we should test these skills you claim I possess," he replied, stepping forward. "After all, it hardly seems fair that these fine ladies and gentlemen should believe this about me if I truly don't possess . . . a gift."

"Ah, but you see, Mr. Fortune, I *do* have the inner sight, so I *know* if you only welcome your visions and accept your gift, and with proper schooling in the art, then you too will be able to help people."

Fine side-stepping, Ian thought, but it wasn't going to work. "Still, I would feel better if you would volunteer to be my first . . . what do you call us? Customers? Victims?"

Her lips twitched. "I reserve a special name for you, Mr. Fortune."

"One best left unspoken in polite company, I presume."

"Precisely."

Ian couldn't help but laugh at the saucy Gypsy wench. The more he learned about her, it seemed, the more there was to discover. Her keen wit and penchant for secrets intrigued him immensely. "Then we'd both be best served if you would keep your . . . *endearment* for me to yourself." Reaching into his pocket, he withdrew her tarot cards, the ones he'd taken that first night and hadn't yet had the right opportunity to return.

Gasping, Zora pointed to the cards. "Those are mine."

The accusation in her voice didn't affect the grin upon his face. "Indeed they are."

"I want them back," she demanded, holding out her hand. "I've been looking for them. Luckily, I had my crystal ball through which to see the future." Taking a step forward, she repeated her demand. "Please give them to me now."

"Ah, ah, ah." Wagging his finger at her, he walked over to a small table. "Not so fast, madam. First I must read *your* future . . . to practice my gift."

The disgruntled expression that settled upon her face was priceless. "I am not in the mood for a reading."

"I fear you shall have to indulge me, for I've been studying the art of tarot cards and simply can no longer fight this need to tell someone's fortune. And, surely, if anyone can understand that urge, it is you," Ian replied cheerfully.

His Gypsy glared at him, before glancing around, undoubtedly taking note of the fascinated faces eagerly watching them. "Of course I understand the need."

Though he knew he hadn't left her any other path to take, her response pleased him nonetheless. Holding out the cards in the palm of his hand, he met her gaze. "You must cut the cards."

Her hand remained firmly at her side.

"What's the matter, Madam Zora? Not afraid of hearing your own fortune, are you?" Before giving her a chance to respond, Ian assured her. "There is nothing to fear . . . because I don't possess the ability to see people's futures any more than you do."

"But you must, Mr. Fortune, if Madam Zora has seen your gifts," protested Lady Covington.

"All Madam Zora has seen, my lady, is another way to bedevil me and we shall all see proof of that in a moment." Pausing, Ian lifted his brow. "That is, if Madam Zora isn't afraid to have her own fortune read."

Lifting her chin, she accepted his challenge. "What I fear, Mr. Fortune, is the idea of such immense power in the hands of someone so inept at wielding it. You must have proper training before you can hope to understand your gift."

"Then who better to ensure I don't misuse my power. As one trained in the art, you could guide me through the intricacies of fortunetelling, could you not?"

"I'm afraid I don't have the time to teach you."

Her feeble protest told him volumes. "That's hardly a convincing argument, madam. Besides, if you wish, I would certainly be more than willing to pay you for your time." Deciding it was time to play his trump card, he turned toward the group of people watching them in rapt fascination. "Does anyone here want me to read Madam Zora's future?"

As a loud cheer rang out through the room, his Gypsy lady narrowed her eyes upon him, until Ian was quite certain that if she indeed possessed any powers, he would be struck dead in that instant.

He widened his grin in response. "Come now, Madam Zora," he murmured, nudging his hand toward her once more. "Take a chance on fate."

With murder in her gaze, she lifted her hand and cut the cards.

5

Separating the cards into three piles, Alyssa kept her gaze upon His Royal Arrogantness while she shuffled each group before stacking them back together. Automatically, she repeated this ritual three times, careful to use her left hand to separate and stack.

"Why are you only using your left hand?"

She answered confidently, not allowing an ounce of her nervousness to show. "It is part of the ritual as my left hand is closest to my heart."

"Ah," Ian murmured. "A little trick of the trade, eh?"

Alyssa answered that comment with a pointed look.

Once she finished, she handed the deck back to Ian. "I am ready to hear my future," she murmured softly.

Lifting one brow, he sat down at her table and began to deal the cards in a straight line.

Looking down at the table, Alyssa asked, "What are you doing?"

"Telling your fortune," he replied, pausing for a moment before setting out the sixth card.

"Not like that you aren't." She couldn't keep her lips from twitching. "If you wish to read my destiny, perhaps you should use proper placement of the cards."

Ian didn't falter. Instead, he picked up her cue and responded, "This *is* the proper way to tell your future."

"I think not. First you need to form a cross with the cards, then lay four of them around the cross, one card at the end of each point. Then you need to—"

"I thought the Gypsies were a people ruled by emotion rather than structure."

"We are, but—"

"Then wouldn't you say it is far more important for me to place the cards as they *feel* right, rather than in a pattern someone has told me to use?"

Caught, spit, and hung to dry, Alyssa knew Ian had outmaneuvered her. "I suppose it is," she conceded ruefully.

"Very well, then." Setting down the remaining cards, he waved his hand toward the empty chair opposite him. "If you would be so kind as to take your seat, we can glimpse into your future."

Glancing around the room, Alyssa nearly groaned at the avid gazes fixed upon her. Her plan had completely backfired. Instead of shifting focus onto Ian and keeping him far too busy with requests for predictions to pester her, she now found herself fending off not only the attention of the ton, but also Ian's bold taunts.

Well, she was certainly up to the challenge.

Smoothing her brilliantly colored skirts, she lowered herself into the chair, more than ready to match wits with him.

After flexing his fingers, Ian turned over the first card. "Ah, the Six of Cups."

"What does it mean?" whispered Lady Burke as she leaned forward to peer at the card.

Closing his eyes, Ian pressed the card to his forehead. Alyssa almost burst into laughter at the ridiculous action. "The Six of Cups foretells of Madam Zora's generosity," Ian pronounced in a clear voice as he lowered the card and returned his gaze to her.

"I beg to differ, Mr. Fortune," Alyssa said dryly as she ran her fingers over the ornate card. Surrounded by the scrolled border was an image of a page presenting flowers to a child. "This card means that events in my past are affecting my present and future."

Lifting a brow, Ian met her gaze. "While that is true, I am referring to your generosity in sharing your gifts with all of us." Ian's expression grew somber. "And this image tells of how your past actions affect not only your present and future, but those who believe in you as well."

It wasn't difficult to catch his meaning. Nodding, she waved him on. The sooner he finished this mockery the sooner she could return home. "Very true," she murmured softly. "Please continue."

His eyes gleamed as he nodded once, then flipped over the next card. The image of a man laying face down upon a blood-red floor was disturbing enough. The ten swords sticking out of his back gave even Alyssa pause.

"Oh, my," murmured Ian. "That can't be good."

Swallowing her instinctive dismay, Alyssa tried to keep her voice level as she explained, "The Ten of Swords represents trouble and suffering in the person's life."

All teasing slipped from his gaze as he reached out to touch his fingertips to the back of her hand. "Are you in trouble? Is that why you've resorted to doing this?"

Aware of the multitude of gazes upon her, Alyssa forced an expression of disdain onto her face, falling back upon the pretense of Madam Zora to steady her now shaky nerves. "I have not *resorted* to anything, Mr. Fortune. My destiny has chosen me. And as to being in trouble . . ." Pausing, Alyssa shrugged lightly. "Even if I were, I would simply place a curse upon the person causing me trouble and make *him* suffer."

"Ahhhh." His grin had a decidedly wicked tilt to it. "Then I'd best be wary around the all-powerful Madam Zora."

"Indeed," she agreed with a pert nod.

Laughing aloud, Ian looked over at their captivated audience. "Should I stop now in fear of a curse or should I continue?"

"Keep on reading the Gypsy's future!"

"Get on with it, man."

"Don't keep us in suspense."

The urge to roll her eyes at the encouraging calls from the audience nearly overwhelmed her, but Alyssa managed to still the action.

"You heard them, Madam Zora, so onward we go,"

Ian said, as he turned over the third card. "The Magician."

Reaching out, she tapped her finger on the card. "Here is the proof that I am what I say—a gifted fortuneteller."

"Excuse me, but I'm the one telling the fortune here," Ian asserted, sliding the card out from beneath her touch. Tilting his head to the side, he murmured, "And I believe you've completely misread this card. Through no fault of your own, naturally."

"Then how do you explain away that card?" she asked, seeing a perfect opening to convince everyone of her abilities.

"I don't." Ian shook his head. "Don't misunderstand me, Madam Zora. I fully believe that you are a talented magician, well versed in sleight of hand and other tricks meant to fool the senses."

Feeling the mood of the crowd shift from excitement to wariness, she dismissed his assertion. "It is obvious you are unskilled in reading the cards."

"Yes, but might I remind you, I wasn't the one who claimed I could."

There was that sticking point again. Well, she'd backed herself into this corner and it was up to her to get out of it. "Now that I think upon it, my vision was cloudy. It came upon me in the early morning hours, so perhaps sleep still clouded my senses and I misread the signs."

"Finally, you begin to make sense," Ian mocked, the softness in his smile taking the sting out of the words.

"I always make sense," she muttered under her

breath, feeling a bit annoyed at her plan having been thoroughly thwarted. Clearing her throat, she moved to rise from her chair. "Since we both agree, I see no reason to continue with this pitiful reading."

"Well, I think we should continue. I'm finding this most amusing," he protested.

"So happy to be of service."

"Come now, Madam Zora, surely you aren't without good humor. I would expect you to find amusement in my feeble attempts to tell your fortune."

"Oh, do let him continue," urged Lady Covington. "This is quite entertaining."

Left with no choice but to give in gracefully, Alyssa held back her sigh and nodded. "Very well then, Mr. Fortune. Please proceed."

Without further urging, he flipped over the next card. "The Queen of Wands. With her beautiful gift of flowers, she obviously stands for love." The fifth card revealed a picture of two people facing each other with their palms touching. "The Four of Wands. This card stands for—"

"Romance," Alyssa whispered, trying to ignore the jolt inside of her. She didn't believe in tarot cards, she reminded herself forcefully. However, the last card Ian turned over made her question her certainty.

The Lovers.

"How very interesting," Ian drawled, tracing the outline of two naked figures—one male, one female—reaching out toward each other with an angel's hands guiding them together.

The sight of Ian touching the card made her insides tingle with unbidden urges.

"It would appear, Madam Zora, that you are about to meet the one man who completes you . . ." Pausing, Ian reached to clasp her trembling hand within his firm one. "And then you will become lovers."

His voice rang with conviction as his prediction created longings within her that would better suit a young lady with marriage prospects than a penniless girl pretending to be a Gypsy. Closing her eyes, she broke off Ian's intense gaze, only to see vivid images behind her eyelids—visions of Ian kissing her, touching her, holding her.

Gasping, her eyes flew open and she snatched her hand away from him.

She was saved from responding when Lord Hargrave bellowed, "I say, Fortune, are you volunteering for the job?"

"I wouldn't mind filling that position," called out Lord Pettibone.

At the ribald comment, the teasing light in Ian's eyes faded before he pushed to his feet and faced Lord Pettibone. Alyssa could see the anger that vibrated through Ian. "I believe you owe the lady an apology."

The room grew quiet as everyone latched onto the newest exchange that promised fodder for gossip. Confusion darkened Lord Pettibone's expression. "Pardon me?"

"You heard me, Pettibone. I believe you owe the lady an apology," he repeated.

"The Gypsy?"

While Lord Pettibone's astonishment failed to surprise Alyssa, she could see Ian's anger grow.

"Indeed," Ian replied sharply.

"This is not necessary," Alyssa began, only to have Ian cut off her protest.

"It most certainly is." Crossing his arms, Ian glared at Lord Pettibone. "What is it to be? Shall you apologize or shall we step outside to discuss this matter like gentlemen?"

Alyssa held her breath as Lord Pettibone drew back his shoulders in obvious affront to Ian's demand. Finally, Lord Pettibone backed down, offering her a nod. "My apologies, Madam Zora. I spoke before I thought."

"That's quite all right, my lord," Alyssa murmured.

Oblivious to the scene he was creating, Ian continued to give Lord Pettibone a hard stare. "See that it doesn't happen again."

Flushing in embarrassment, Alyssa gathered up her cards, tucked them into her bag, and slipped off her chair.

"The Gypsy is leaving," exclaimed Lady Treport, rising to her feet.

Cringing inwardly, Alyssa spun to face her hostess. "My performance is at an end for this evening."

"But why?" Lady Treport grew petulant. "I paid you for the entire evening."

"And I provided you with entertainment, did I not?"

Frowning, Lady Treport waved toward Ian. "While I have enjoyed myself this evening, I couldn't help but notice that Mr. Fortune was the only one who predicted the future tonight."

"Not so," Alyssa countered. "After all, who predicted that Mr. Fortune would begin to see into the future?"

A look of chagrin passed over Lady Treport's features.

Stepping forward, Ian bowed to their hostess. "Please allow me to compensate Madam Zora as I received great pleasure this evening and would be displeased to imagine it was at your expense."

Lady Treport's hand fluttered against her chest. "Why, Mr. Fortune, that's quite a generous offer. However, I must refuse you." Sniffing lightly, she continued, "Never let it be said that the Treports can't pay their debts."

"I'm confident such a sentiment would never pass anyone's lips," Ian murmured smoothly.

"Very well, then." Gathering her shawl around her, Alyssa dipped into a soft curtsey. "I shall be off now, Lady Treport."

"Madam Zora . . ." Ian began, but Alyssa didn't wait. Instead, she hurried out of the room, wondering how her plan could have gotten so mixed-up.

When the Gypsy didn't even pause at his call, Ian began to step around Lady Treport, only to be pulled to a halt by a strong hand on his shoulder.

"Why don't you join me for a drink?" Peter asked in a jovial voice. "I imagine you could use one after tonight's excitement."

Though his instinct was to pull free from his

friend's grasp, Ian hesitated when he saw the serious-ness in Peter's gaze, so at odds with the smile upon his face. Feeling the weight of everyone's eyes upon him, Ian lifted his hands, shrugging toward the wide-eyed audience. "It would appear that Madam Zora didn't care for my reading. If you remember though, I did try to warn her that she was mistaken in believing I had any sort of mystical powers."

Inside, Ian was fighting against his need to follow the Gypsy. Biting back a sigh, he turned toward Peter. "Lead the way," Ian said, injecting a bright note into his voice.

Down the hall, Peter opened the door to Lord Tre-port's study and stepped aside to allow Ian to enter. The minute Ian walked into the room, Peter rounded on him.

"What the devil are you *thinking*, man?"

Blinking, Ian asked, "Pardon me?"

"All that business with Madam Zora!" Waving his hands in the air, Peter began to pace around the room. "I thought your objective was to find yourself a titled bride."

"It is," Ian replied, wondering where Peter was leading.

"Then you're doing a poor job of going about it," Peter ground out. "You continue to flirt with your pretty little Gypsy in front of all the ladies and soon everyone will consider you of coarse blood. And no man will marry his daughter to you."

His stomach turned at the thought. "Come now. Surely you exaggerate."

"Not one bit. A gentleman does not consort with females of a lower ilk in public."

"Might I remind you my mother was considered of lower ilk, yet she remains one of the finest women I've ever met?"

"I'm certain that's true, Ian, but that's not what I'm saying." Shaking his head, Peter sank into a chair. "My point is that if you wish to capture the attentions of a titled lady, then you need to overcome what society views as your shortcomings."

As distasteful as Ian considered Peter's assertions, the fact remained that he was right. While he would never apologize or hide the fact that his beloved mother had been common, he couldn't forget that he'd long dreamed of marrying a lady of station . . . and flaunting her before his grandfather.

Yet, what would his dream cost him?

Rubbing a hand against his temple, Ian murmured slowly, "To tell you the God's honest truth, Peter, I don't know how I'm going to handle this problem I seem to be having with Madam Zora. Every time I'm around her, I seem to lose control and behave in an outrageous manner. I truly don't know what I'm going to do."

"What do you mean, you don't know what you're going to do?" Peter asked, his tone incredulous. "If you wish to marry well, then what you need to do is perfectly obvious. No more scenes like the one we all just witnessed, no more flirtatious banter with the lovely Madam Zora, and no more focusing solely upon the Gypsy whenever she enters a room." Leaning forward,

Peter rested his elbows upon his knees. "You *must* behave as society expects if you wish to marry a member of the ton."

"I do try to follow proper etiquette, Peter," Ian conceded, "but never at the cost of my self-respect. I need to be my own man, to do as I see fit. I can't simply ignore when someone insults Madam Zora."

"Then don't, but that doesn't mean you have to tell her fortune, for God's sake." An expression of exasperation covered Peter's face. "You were talking about her future lover out there . . . as though you were offering yourself up for the position."

Feeling the sting of Peter's words, Ian curbed his temper, for he also saw the truth in them. "I know I behaved poorly today and I will try to alter my behavior in the future. However, I will not allow anyone to insult Madam Zora nor will I give her a direct cut if she addresses me first, and if that costs me a titled bride . . . then so be it."

The way Peter stared at him, Ian began to wonder if he'd suddenly sprouted horns. "I don't understand you," Peter said finally. "You told me just a few days ago that you'd worked far too hard to get to this point."

"I know, I know." Sinking down into a chair, Ian rested his head against the leather back. "But I didn't realize how different the reality of entering society and securing a bride would be from my imaginings."

"Well, if you're going to succeed at your plan, you'd best get over that feeling as soon as possible and figure out how you're going to handle your little Gypsy."

"I will," Ian vowed . . . despite the fact he had no idea how he was going to be polite to Madam Zora and ignore her at the same time.

"Your cousins have disappeared, my lord."

The Earl of Tonneson waved his beringed fingers. "And this should matter to me? Why?"

Isaac Meiser held back a sigh. "Because they are two young, defenseless, and destitute females."

Widening his eyes, the earl shook his head. "Do you have a point to all of this?"

"Indeed I do, my lord," Meiser replied, trying not to grind his teeth in frustration. Still, he'd learned long ago that he could accomplish far more with the aristocracy if he used his wits. "I'm merely concerned about *your* welfare."

"My welfare?" the earl asked, suddenly alert. "How the devil could those girls affect me?"

"What if someone were to discover you'd left them destitute in the wilds of Northumberland? It would hardly reflect well upon your illustrious name," Meiser pointed out.

Scowling fiercely, the earl rose from his settee and began to pace around the room. "I suppose you're right. Blast it all! Why didn't those two chits have the good sense to stay put in the cottage I'd generously provided for them?"

Glancing around the elaborately decorated room, Meiser compared it to the tiny home he'd seen up in Northumberland. The very shallowness of the earl never ceased to amaze him. However, he remained silent, for he would be able to help the Porter sisters only with the earl's assistance.

"Tell me how to fix this problem, Meiser," demanded the earl as he stopped pacing. "I can't have anyone saying that I don't care for family. It would reflect poorly upon me . . . which is something I must avoid at this delicate time."

"Delicate time, my lord?"

"Yes, yes," the earl replied, exasperated. "I'm only now receiving invitations to the finest homes in England. I can't risk losing the acceptance of society because of two no-account chits."

Though he bristled at the dismissive manner in which the earl referred to his cousins, Meiser again refrained from uttering a word. Instead, he offered a carefully coached suggestion. "I believe it would be in your best interest, my lord, if you were to locate the girls and settle them comfortably in their cottage." Pausing for effect, Meiser finally said, "Of course it would require that you reinstate their monthly stipend, but I'm quite certain you'll see that avoiding the blot to your name is well worth that paltry sum. Though you didn't agree with me the last time I suggested this solution, surely you can now see that it is the only way to save face."

"Just another drain upon me," groaned the earl as he lay back down onto the settee. "Very well then, Meiser. I'm entrusting you to find the girls and put them back in their proper place."

Rising from his chair, Meiser bowed to the earl. "I shall discover the girls' whereabouts as soon as possible."

"That's probably best," agreed the earl. "After all,

there's no telling how much mischief they could get into."

Mischief? Meiser couldn't believe his ears. "I believe, my lord, that your cousins will be far too busy trying to survive to get into much . . . mischief."

"Then you know nothing about females, Meiser. I assure you they don't waste their pretty little heads thinking about such a mundane topic as survival."

Meiser swallowed his distaste and forced himself to smile. "Undoubtedly you're correct, my lord," he murmured, seeing no point in annoying the earl. After all, he'd gotten what he wanted. The earl had agreed to his plan, so Meiser could now dip into the limited resources remaining in the earl's accounts to help him to find the Porter girls.

"If you'll excuse me, my lord, I shall begin my search."

With a wave of his hand, the earl dismissed him without a glance. Ignoring the insult, Meiser strode from the room, concentrating upon the best way to locate the girls.

Of course he had no intention of returning the girls to the little cottage up north. No indeed. In reality, Meiser knew he was now on a search for his future bride.

"I can't believe I let you talk me into doing this."

"Stop complaining," replied Calla with a laugh. "And stop worrying. No one will recognize you."

Looking at the black veil draped over her face, Alyssa had to agree, but she would never admit that to her sister. "This is a foolish risk."

"You've done nothing but talk about me having a

Season, so what better way to prepare me for society than to ease me into it." Kicking at a stone on the path winding through Hyde Park, Calla flung her arms wide. "Besides, it's such a *glorious* day."

Since she couldn't keep from grinning at her sister's enthusiasm, Alyssa was glad for the covering over her face. Sometimes it was a struggle to act like a serious, responsible adult when she wanted nothing more than to join her sister in the joy of the day.

"Though I have to admit, Alyssa, I don't wonder at your reluctance to venture into public today. After all, you have to wear that dreadful outfit so no one will recognize you as the infamous Madam Zora." Calla wrinkled her nose at the mourning dress Alyssa wore. "I vow that dress might have even discouraged me!"

Unable to hold in her laughter, Alyssa chuckled at her sister's comments. "Ah, Calla, you are so good for me," she said finally. "Sometimes I wonder if . . . Oh, no!"

"What?" Calla asked, glancing around. "What's wrong?"

But Alyssa didn't answer. She was too busy fighting back the alarm as she watched Ian Fortune approach from the opposite direction. Of all the rotten luck!

"What is it?"

Drawing back her shoulders, Alyssa grabbed hold of her self-control. "It's him. Ian Fortune."

Calla's eyes grew round. "Good! I'm excited to meet him."

"You *won't* be meeting him," Alyssa said swiftly, astounded that her sister would actually imagine she'd introduce them. Lord, Alyssa had a hard enough time dissuading Calla from focusing in upon Ian now. If she met him, there would be no quieting her.

"I don't see why not. He obviously bothers you and that, in turn, affects me."

"My darling Calla, not everything leads back to you. The only reason I don't want you to meet him is so that there is no chance that he might recognize me."

"In that outfit?" Calla muffled a laugh behind her hand. "Not likely."

Glancing down at her dress, Alyssa tried not to let her sister's comment upset her. And she certainly didn't want to admit that part of her hated for Ian to see her like this . . . even if he didn't know it was she. "We're smarter not to take any chances."

"We won't take any," Calla insisted. "Besides, I deserve to meet him. If he's the reason you wouldn't even talk to me when you got home last night, then I believe I have the right to an introduction."

"*The right?*" Alyssa shook her head. "To borrow your own phrase—not likely."

"Well, I should. Do you deny he's the one who upset you again last night?"

Last night. When he'd read her fortune and told her she would meet the man who completes her . . . and become his lover. A shiver ran through Alyssa as she remembered how images of Ian had danced through her head, keeping her awake all night. The infuriating, intriguing, witty, glorious Mr. Ian Fortune had indeed disturbed her far too much for comfort. She wasn't ready to see him again. Not now. Not when he'd haunted her every thought. And she certainly wasn't prepared to have Calla meet him and increase her sister's desire to spin fairy tales around him.

"See? You can't deny it," Calla said with a triumphant smile. Twisting around, she asked, "So which one is he?"

"Calla, please!" Alyssa exclaimed. Clasping onto her sister's arm, Alyssa glanced at the people strolling by them. "Don't make a scene. We don't want him to notice us."

"You're becoming a dreadful bore, Alyssa," Calla said with a sigh. "Very well, then. Just point him out to me so I can be on my best behavior when he passes by."

Wondering if she was going to regret her actions, Alyssa turned her sister toward Ian. "He's heading right toward us."

A gasp broke from Calla. "You mean your Ian is the one with the dark hair that looks like he walked straight out of a wonderful dream?"

"Yes . . . only he's no dream prince." Alyssa could picture the devilish glint in Ian's eyes all too well. "He's far too . . . untamed," she finished, unable to think of a better word to describe the wildness she sensed inside of him.

"Oooooh, even better." Tucking her arm into Alyssa's, Calla leaned closer. "I had no idea that your Mr. Fortune was so handsome."

"Will you please stop calling him *my* Mr. Fortune?" Alyssa hissed under her breath, not wanting anyone to overhear.

"I don't know why you're worried about him exposing us. He looks far too nice."

"Looks can be deceiving."

Calla shook her head. "Not in this instance. I'm certain of it."

Groaning softly, Alyssa looked at her sister and recognized all too easily the gleam of excitement in Calla's eyes. "Don't even think of doing something foolish," Alyssa warned.

"Foolish? Never," murmured Calla.

Despite her sister's assurance, Alyssa held her breath as they walked ever closer to Ian. The moment they drew abreast of him, Calla collapsed onto the ground in the most dreadful swoon Alyssa had ever seen.

6

Bewildered as to why a lovely young lady would literally throw herself at his feet in such an obvious manner, Ian nonetheless came to her aid. Crouching down next to the fallen girl, Ian reached out to gently tap on her cheek. "Miss? Miss? Are you all right?"

The black crow accompanying the pretty blonde sunk onto her knees as well. "Calla!" hissed the widow. "Get up this instant!"

Ian's head snapped up as the woman's voice tugged at him, the tones in her demand striking him as familiar. Peering closer, Ian tried to see past the black veil draped over the lady's face. But every inch of her was covered in the dark cloth, giving him not even a hint as to her identity.

Opening his mouth to ask her name, Ian snapped it shut as the girl at his feet moaned loudly. His cheeks heated as he remembered the poor chit. Badly done of him to be wondering about a lady's name while her companion lay at his feet . . . even if she hadn't truly swooned!

"Miss," he began again, reaching out to pat the back of the young girl's gloved hand. "Would you like me to—"

"Enough of this, Calla," interrupted the widow.

The girl's eyes rolled back in her head as another loud, dramatic sigh escaped her. Pressing the back of her hand to her forehead, the girl finally fluttered her eyes open. "Alyssa? Is that you?"

A sound of pure frustration erupted from beneath the black drape. "Stop this *immediately*."

Rocking back on his heels, Ian fought back a smile as he watched these two women bicker in hissed whispers.

"Play along," rasped the younger girl from her prostrate position as she flicked a glance at him. "He's watching."

"He's also *listening!*" pointed out the widow, her words vibrating with exasperation.

Ian felt the widow's attention shift onto him.

"I apologize for my sister. Sometimes she is taken with . . . fits and . . ."

"Alyssa!" exclaimed the young girl, pushing up into a sitting position.

". . . is overcome with the need to do completely foolish things," finished the lady firmly.

Sister, eh? Then it was likely that the woman wrapped in black widow's weeds was hardly more than a girl herself. "Quite all right, my lady," he assured her. Rising, he held out a hand to assist the widow to her feet before reaching down to help the younger sister up as well. "Allow me to introduce myself," Ian began, bowing to both of the women. "Mr. Ian Fortune at your service."

Deliberately pausing, Ian waited for the lady to identify herself. "It is a pleasure to make your acquaintance," the widow replied smoothly. "I appreciate your assistance and apologize once more on behalf of my sister for delaying you."

Amazement filled Ian as he watched the woman curl her hand around her sister's arm and begin to drag her away. Why, she wasn't even going to introduce herself!

Pushing good manners to the edge, Ian stepped in front of them, halting their escape. "I'm sorry, but I didn't hear your name."

"I don't believe I offered it."

The black widow's tart response only made him want to discover her identity even more. The feeling inside of him that he knew her, that they'd met before, grew stronger. "Perhaps we could correct that oversight now."

"Her name is Alyssa Porter—Lady Alyssa Porter," exclaimed the girl, "and I'm her sister, Lady Calla Porter."

"Her sister-in-law, you mean," Ian corrected.

"No, my sister."

Frowning slightly, Ian couldn't understand how the two girls could be sisters by birth and still have the same last name when one of them had obviously been married and was now widowed. "How can that be . . ."

"Lady Alyssa Porter . . . Hee . . . Ha . . . Heimel," the lady stuttered.

"Your husband's familial name was Heehaheimel?"

Lifting a brow, Ian smiled at the widow. "Rather unusual."

"I misspoke. My name is Lady Alyssa Porter Heimel, Baroness . . . Greenald."

"Greenald?" Ian turned the name over on his tongue. "Can't say that I've ever heard of that barony."

"My husband's family was from far north," she replied vaguely. "Not many people have heard of it."

"I consider myself among them," Ian murmured, tapping his fingers against his pant leg. "However, that doesn't detract from the pleasure of your acquaintance, Lady Greenald."

"Thank you," she replied. "I wish to apologize for stumbling over my name, it's just that I've only lost my husband recently—"

"—and it was a love match," the younger sister interrupted.

Ian's lips twitched as he saw the widow's fingers tighten upon the girl's arm. "Indeed it was . . ."

". . . which only makes it more tragic . . ."

This time the lady in black plowed onward as if the younger chit hadn't uttered a word. ". . . and since our time together was cut so horribly short, it's still difficult to speak of it. That's also why it's so easy for my sister to forget to introduce me by my married name."

"Perfectly understandable," Ian murmured. And it was. But he didn't believe a word of it. What he couldn't fathom though was why the widow was lying through her teeth. Perhaps she had a scandal in her past she chose to hide beneath her black drapings.

"Yes, that's right," chimed in the smiling blonde at

his side. "My brother-in-law, God rest his soul," she said, pausing to make the sign of the cross, "was killed in a terrible, horrid, simply awful accident when he—"

"I believe we've bored this fine gentleman enough for one day." Stepping to the side, Lady Greenald tugged her sister along with her as she maneuvered herself around Ian.

"Not at all," Ian denied, finding it amusing to watch the young girl dig in her feet. "Perhaps you might enjoy some company as you stroll around the park."

The horrified gasp that came from beneath the black veil was at odds with the expression of pure delight that spread across the young girl's face.

"No!"

"Yes!"

The two women turned to look at each other. "Calla, dear," the widow murmured, though the hardness in the endearment left much to be desired, "you know we can't trouble Mr. Fortune and ask—"

"But we didn't ask, he offered," protested Lady Calla.

"The lady is quite right," Ian clarified, stepping forward and holding out his arm. "It would be my pleasure."

Another gasp sounded beneath the veil. "While I appreciate your offer, I'm afraid we must decline."

"But, Alyssa—"

"Ah, but I insist. Two young ladies such as yourselves should have a proper escort," Ian replied, reluctant to part ways as these two ladies had proved far more interesting than the thought of continuing his daily constitutional alone.

"As a widow, I am well accustomed to escorting myself," Lady Greenald assured him.

"Undoubtedly." Ian offered her his best smile. "Then it shall be a rare treat indeed that you will have company on your stroll."

Offering his arm to the younger girl, Ian couldn't hold back his triumphant smile toward the elder sister. "It would appear that your sister would enjoy the company." His smile spread into a wide grin. "Come now, my lady, and be a good sport. After all, I do have another arm," he finished, offering the intriguing widow his free arm.

For a moment, he wondered if she would refuse his offer, but when the stiffness left her posture, Ian knew he'd won this skirmish.

Slipping her hand around the curve of his forearm, the widow murmured, "It is most kind of you to accompany us."

Ian laughed aloud. "Well, I hardly left you with any choice other than to accept my escort."

"I was trying to be polite," the widow murmured, her vowels rounded in amused tones. "However, I see now my efforts were wasted."

"Indeed. I far prefer tart responses over polite murmurings."

"Then you've picked the perfect companions."

Another laugh escaped him. Before he could respond to the entertaining Lady Greenald, Ian paused as Lady Calla asked, "Are you dreadfully wealthy, Mr. Fortune?"

"Calla!"

Lady Greenald's horrified gasp mingled with Ian's bellow of laughter.

"What *is* it, Alyssa? Why are you always snipping at me?"

"How could you ask such a bold question?" Lady Greenald asked in a low furious voice.

"It's quite all right," Ian assured his companion. "In fact, I applaud Lady Calla her boldness and will gladly answer her question." Not giving the lady in black an opportunity to say anything further, Ian turned his attention to the girl waiting patiently for a reply. "To answer your question, Lady Calla, I consider myself *comfortably* wealthy, not dreadfully wealthy."

Tilting her head to the side, Lady Calla considered his response for a moment. "Comfortably wealthy sounds delightful . . . especially since we're dreadfully poor."

"Calla," groaned Lady Greenald. "We aren't poor, my dear. We're gently impoverished, if you must know, but it is hardly the sort of thing that one speaks about."

"On my honor as a gentleman, your revelation is safe with me." Seeking to ease the lady's discomfort, he confided, "You see, I was born into poverty as well, but my father began a business that I have since expanded and, in so doing, have improved my situation greatly."

"A business, you say? It's funny that you should mention that because my sister—"

Lady Greenald broke into the conversation. "I think that's quite enough about our personal business, Calla. A lady needs to keep a few secrets."

"It keeps her intriguing to gentlemen," assured Ian.

"Well, it's no secret that I hope my sister's business makes so much money that we're able to purchase one of those homes someday," Calla finished, pointing toward the large elegant townhouses surrounding the park.

"Perhaps you will," Ian said encouragingly. "Do you see that gray townhouse next to the brick one?"

"The large stone one?" Lady Calla nodded. "Yes."

"That's my home," Ian told her, unable to keep the pride out of his voice. "That's what all my hard work purchased. I know that most gentlemen feel that one shouldn't dirty their hands with honest labor, but I'll let you in on a little known secret." Bending close, he whispered, "It feels wonderful to know that you *earned* something that beautiful. No one gave it to me, so no one can ever take it away. No, I worked for it and now it's mine."

"And how do you feel about ladies marrying well in order to improve their situation?" Calla asked softly.

Taken aback by the question, Ian hesitated to respond. Finally, he admitted, "I believe it is often a wise path to take. After all, as a gentlewoman, you have frightfully few ways in which to improve your situation other than marriage."

"Not if you're clever," murmured Lady Greenald.

Such a sentiment from a well-bred lady was fascinating. Narrowing his eyes, Ian could barely make out the shape of Lady Greenald's face beneath the heavy black veil. "I suspect, my lady, that you possess far more intriguing secrets than most ladies of my acquaintance."

"Perhaps, Mr. Fortune."

Glancing up from the veil draped features, Ian felt a

surge of disappointment to see that they'd walked the entire path around the park. "Might I escort you home?"

"No, thank you, sir," the widow stated firmly.

"But, Alyssa—"

Walking around to her sister's side, Lady Greenald insisted, "It is best if we part company with Mr. Fortune here . . . rather than at our home."

Lady Calla's eyes widened before she nodded fiercely. "We *can't* have you home."

Yet another secret. Bowing slightly, Ian reluctantly bid his companions farewell. "It has been a most delightful afternoon, ladies. Perhaps we shall meet again."

"Perhaps," Lady Greenald murmured. "Good day, Mr. Fortune."

Tugging her younger sister after her, Lady Greenald strode from the park.

"Now, aren't you glad I pretended to faint in front of him?" Calla asked brightly.

"Calla! Shush! He'll *hear* you!" the widow admonished.

A huge grin split Ian's face as he watched them walk away.

"Calla, what were you thinking?" Alyssa whispered, all too aware of Ian's gaze boring into her back.

"I thought he was utterly charming." Calla's expression filled with pleasure. "In fact, I think he'd be just *perfect* for you. He's amusing and good-natured and completely glorious to behold!" A sigh escaped her. "Perfect."

Unfortunately, Alyssa couldn't deny any of her sister's claims. Ian *was* amusing and good-natured . . . and completely glorious to behold. She'd had a delightful time in his company. "Even if that were true," Alyssa began, not wanting to encourage her sister more by agreeing with her, "the fact remains that Ian Fortune could threaten all we've worked to accomplish. If he found out that Lady Alyssa Heimel . . . I still can't believe I picked a silly name like that . . . if he were to discover that *she* doesn't exist and that I am in fact Madam Zora, he would expose me in a heartbeat and destroy our only means of support."

"But he was so nice," Calla protested.

"He was nice to Lady Greenald and Lady Calla, *not* to Madam Zora!"

This time Calla's sigh lay heavily between them. "Don't you wish that we still were Lady Calla and Lady Alyssa and that Madam Zora had never been born?"

Every minute of every day. Yet Alyssa couldn't speak her thoughts aloud. No, she could never tell her sister that she wished more than anything that she had run into Mr. Ian Fortune when she'd been Lady Alyssa Porter, that he had been taken with her, courted her, and then married her in a nice, neat little fairy-tale package.

There was no use bemoaning a fate that would never come to pass.

Instead, Alyssa said briskly, "Whether I do or do not is irrelevant. All that matters is who we are today and who we will be tomorrow." She lifted up her veil to smile at her sister. "And tomorrow I shall be

Madam Zora!" Alyssa finished in a heavily accented voice.

Responding as Alyssa had hoped, Calla laughed gaily. "Perhaps you will find a way to weave a spell around Mr. Fortune and have him fall desperately in love with you." She sighed dramatically. "Being comfortably wealthy would be lovely."

"I can't disagree with that thought," Alyssa replied. Though, truthfully, Ian's money hardly mattered. It was the man himself who intrigued her far too much for her comfort.

Still smiling after his encounter with the two mysterious sisters, Ian turned on his heel and strolled toward his home. He'd only taken two steps when Peter called out to him.

"I see you've taken to consorting with widows and children now, Fortune," his friend said, staring pointedly after the young women.

Glancing over his shoulder, Ian shrugged lightly. "I merely accompanied them on their turn about the park."

"Who *are* they?"

"The child is Lady Calla Porter and her sister, Lady Alyssa Heimel, Baroness of Greenald."

"Porter . . . Porter," Peter murmured, his brows drawing together in concentration. "Ah, yes, now I remember them. I believe that is the familial name of the Earl of Tonneson. If I remember correctly, the title was recently passed down to Lord Michael Landery. A disagreeable, slovenly fellow if ever there was one."

"Recently?"

"The former earl and his countess were known about town as adventurers. You know the sort. They head off for parts unknown to bring back all types of treasures for museums and collectors. I don't know what happened to them, but evidently they didn't return from their last grand adventure."

"And what of Baron Greenald? Have you ever heard of him?"

"Can't say I have."

"Nor I," Ian agreed, rubbing a finger along his jaw.

"Though there's nothing at all unusual about that. After all, we couldn't possibly know all of the minor peers running about." Peter nudged Ian's arm. "Still, if she is nobility, the widow might suit your purposes perfectly. If you're willing to wait until after her mourning period, she might make a fine bride." Lifting one brow, Peter continued, "And she is certainly far more suitable than your little Gypsy."

"Indeed," Ian murmured, disturbed by the realization that Lady Greenald reminded him of Zora. That he would even compare the two women showed Ian all too clearly that the Gypsy had taken over his thoughts. Shaking his head, Ian tried to loosen the unnerving sensation.

"There you have it, then." Clapping a hand on Ian's shoulder, Peter smiled at him. "This baroness is the perfect solution, combining your odd attraction for the little Gypsy with the respectability of a title. A match made in Heaven."

"I only met the lady today and have yet to see her

face, so don't be marrying me off quite so quickly," Ian murmured dryly.

"Why do you need to see her? I thought that all you cared about was her lineage. Have you gotten particular now?" Peter asked with a laugh. "Next thing I know you'll want to marry for love . . . then God help us all!"

"I shall try not to allow my sentimentality to cloud my better judgment." And even as he said it, Ian prayed it was true.

"That's reassuring." Waving his hand forward, Peter indicated that Ian precede him. "Now, why don't we head to your home and try to uncover who might know more about this widow of yours, eh?"

"I'm quite certain that a few glasses of port will enhance our thoughts," Ian returned, pushing aside his doubts. "Let's be off then, to uncover the mystery of the Baroness Greenald."

7

"**W**hat have you uncovered for me?" demanded Lord Hammond.

"Your grandson . . ."

At Lord Hammond's glare, Jacob Fenwig shifted in his seat. "Rather . . . Mr. Fortune . . ."

"Proceed," Lord Hammond said after one last final glare for effect.

Clearing his throat, Fenwig continued, "As I was saying, Mr. Fortune has apparently entered society for the sole purpose of securing a bride."

The sheer nerve of the whelp amazed the duke. Perhaps there was a good bit of Hammond in his blood, after all. "He's made this common knowledge?"

"It would appear so," Fenwig confirmed. "In fact, there are a number of ladies whose families are in dire straits that would welcome the match."

"Why?" Lord Hammond leaned back in his seat,

awaiting his man-of-business' answer. "Surely they could find a better match than a man who has been disowned."

"Well, as to that, your grace, while you might have publicly disowned your son and his heir apparent, that does not affect the entitled properties nor the title which will automatically pass to Mr. Fortune upon your . . ."

"My death," finished the duke brusquely.

Fenwig swallowed as he nodded once. "So although Mr. Fortune refuses to acknowledge it, there is no denying the fact that he is indeed the Marquess of Dorset."

"And my heir," concluded Lord Hammond as he rose to his feet.

"Of course, you could petition the Crown, but I highly doubt your request to remove Mr. Fortune as your heir would be granted, as he appears to be of sound mind and body," Fenwig concluded.

Clasping his hands behind his back, Lord Hammond stared out onto the lawns that had belonged to his family for centuries. All of this would someday belong to that upstart with peasant blood in his veins. And since it seemed he had no choice in the matter, perhaps it was time he stopped being the fool and took charge of the situation.

"You say my grandson is seeking a bride," the duke said as he turned to face Fenwig.

His business agent's eyes flared briefly. "Your . . . grandson, did you say, your grace?"

"And what of it?" barked the duke. "It appears I have little choice in the matter, so I'd best see to it that the boy is at least trained for the position." Waving his hand, he dismissed his last statement, "No, never mind that. It's probably too late to work with the boy, but at least I could see to it that he marries someone with a pedigree fine enough to overcome his tainted bloodlines."

Leaning forward, Fenwig agreed readily. "That sounds like a fine idea, sir."

"Are there any ladies who have caught my grandson's interest?" the duke asked, rubbing his hands together.

Fenwig's expression grew apprehensive. "None other than a Gypsy called Madam Zora."

"Naturally," Lord Hammond said dryly. What else did he expect from a base-born grandson? Of course it was completely unacceptable that Ian demonstrate even the slightest interest in this Madam Zora person. The last thing he wanted was some Gypsy tramp in his family! The dukedom had already survived one scandal. There was no telling if it could survive another. "I know about the girl. I've seen him exchanging snippets with the Gypsy myself." Shaking his head, Lord Hammond declared, "It appears that I've decided to become involved in my grandson's future just in the nick of time, doesn't it, Fenwig?"

"Indeed it does, your grace," Fenwig murmured.

A wise man always makes the best of a bad situation, Lord Hammond decided with a firm nod.

"Tell me, Fenwig," Lord Hammond began as he sat down again. "Who is on the marriage mart this Season?"

* * *

He had to fight to keep his eyes open.

Standing in the middle of Lord Covington's drawing room, Ian listened to Lady Anne Trent prattle on about her latest visit to the modiste.

". . . and then she proceeded to tell me that the crushed velvet I'd chosen was rose-colored, when I could see that it was, in fact, a few shades darker than a true red rose . . ."

Stifling back a yawn, Ian prayed that Lady Anne would spy someone else she'd rather talk to about her outing. Somehow he didn't think he'd be that lucky.

". . . so my mama told me to simply ignore the modiste since I had a far superior fashion sense and to . . ."

As Peter walked into the room, Ian saw an escape from the deadly dull tendrils of Lady Anne. "As much as I hate to tear myself away," Ian began after he'd interrupted her incessant monologue, "I simply must speak with Lord Essex, so if you'll excuse me . . ."

Blessing good manners that dictated Lady Anne acquiesce to his request, Ian moved away. Unfortunately, he'd only made it a few steps when yet another lady blocked his path. He offered Lady Catherine a faint smile before slipping around her.

"Lord Dorset!"

Lady Catherine's call froze him to the core. Slowly, Ian turned toward her. "Excuse me? What did you call me?"

Hesitantly, she took a step forward. "Lord Dorset," she repeated shyly.

"You have mistaken me for someone else, my lady," Ian said stiffly. "My name is Mr. Ian Fortune."

"Yes, I know," Lady Catherine insisted. "Ian Fortune, Marquess of Dorset."

"Again, my lady, I can only say you are mistaken." Turning on his heel, Ian turned his back on her. Without pause, he made his way toward his friend.

"What's gotten you in a lather?" Peter asked as soon as Ian drew abreast of him.

"Lady Catherine just called me Lord Dorset," Ian ground out, his stomach turning at the title.

"Ah, yes, well that is only to be expected . . . considering . . ." Peter added before trailing off.

"Considering what?"

"Considering that your grandfather has chosen to acknowledge you."

"*What?*" Ian's question echoed throughout the room.

"Good God, man, pipe down," chastised Peter as he glanced around.

Mumbling an apology, Ian urged his friend to continue. "Why would that old bastard choose to acknowledge me now when he's ignored my existence for years?"

"I believe you'd have to ask him."

"Perhaps I will, for I was quite content to leave things the way they were—with each of us despising the other."

Peter leveled a solemn look at him. "You claim to despise the duke, but you can't deny that he's been your motivation to succeed."

"Only because I wanted to prove to him that all of his money and title meant less than nothing to me," Ian exclaimed.

"Oh, I know that," Peter said, lifting a shoulder. "But even you have to admit that you wouldn't have achieved all that you have if not for him."

Ian's head was beginning to pound. "I don't *want* anything to do with the man or his titles," he ground out fiercely. "All my life I've only wanted to prove to him that I didn't need him."

"I know that as well, Ian, but perhaps that's the whole point," Peter said quietly. "While you might not need him, he needs you."

Shaking his head, Ian rejected the idea. "Preposterous. He needs me like he needs a boil upon his backside."

Before Peter could utter another word, Ian turned on his heel and strode from the room.

Head down, Ian hurried down the hall, needing to get outside, free from . . .

"Umph."

Instinctively, Ian reached out to steady the woman he'd run into in his rush to escape the room.

Ah, Madam Zora. The perfect distraction.

"Ian!" gasped Alyssa as she tried to regain her balance, releasing her satchel to grab onto his arm.

Ian's smile was slight and intimate. "I see we've finally gotten past the Mr. Fortune stage."

"No . . . yes . . . You startled me." Praying she didn't look as flushed as she suddenly felt, Alyssa stepped back. "I just finished telling fortunes in the parlor and am on my way home."

"On your way home so soon? I only just arrived a

short while ago; I'd have made an appearance sooner had I known you were here this evening," Ian admitted.

"Well, now you know. So if you'll excuse me . . ."

Bending down, Ian retrieved her colorful bag. "Allow me to walk you out."

"That's not necessary," she protested.

"Shall we stand here arguing over the issue?" He shrugged lightly. "I've nothing better to do this evening, so I'm perfectly willing to indulge you."

Having run up against his stubbornness before, Alyssa was well aware that he would indeed argue the point, then do precisely what he wanted anyway. Even when she'd been dressed as a proper widow, he'd been just as bullheaded. Still, she'd been charmed by his kindness to her sister and his sharp wit. What was the harm in allowing him to escort her outside?

Without another word of protest, she let him lead her down the hall, through the kitchens, and out the servant's entrance. All the while she was aware of the Covingtons' servants staring at them in amazement, though they were all too well-trained to utter a word.

The moment the darkness of night engulfed them in its shadows, Alyssa paused, waiting until Ian drew even with her. "I vow the Covingtons' servants shall be discussing our departure this evening."

"Oh, I'm quite certain they would be able to find juicier gossip if they tried," Ian said, dismissing the idea. "In fact, I'm positive of that fact."

The bitterness in his voice arrested her attention, drawing her in despite her best intentions. "Ian?" she asked softly, placing a hand upon his arm. "Is everything all right?"

Turning his head, Ian stared out into the moonlit gardens. "All right? Now there's a question."

Keeping her eyes firmly fixed upon his profile, Alyssa forgot about her vow to maintain her distance from this man. "Come now, you can tell Madam Zora all."

"Ah, yes, the all-powerful, all-knowing Madam Zora." Tucking a strand of her hair behind her ear, Ian trailed his fingers down her cheek. "You have no idea how lucky you are, Zora. With command of your own destiny, you carve a place for yourself in society. I thought I'd done that as well, but I've found that I can't run from my past."

"No one can, Ian," she said softly. "My present is defined and sculpted by my past just as much as yours is. What you must do is learn to accept what your life has become."

"Simply accept my fate?" Ian shook his head. "I don't know if I can do that."

"If you can't, then you will never find peace in your present-day life." She took a deep breath before suggesting, "Perhaps you should meet with your grandfather to talk about . . . your future."

His gaze sharpened upon her face. "How do you know about the duke?" But before she could reply, he answered his own question. "Then again, how could you not? The news is probably on everyone's tongue this evening. Bloody Lord Dorset."

"I take it you're not pleased with the title."

His lips twisted into a grimace. "No, Zora. I am definitely *not* pleased."

"Then you should speak to your grandfather about it," she said firmly.

"Speak to him?" Ian appeared incredulous.

"How else are you ever going to sort out your past?"

Reaching out a finger, he tipped her chin upward. "I fear, madam, that my past is far too tangled to ever sort out."

Her heart tightened, yet she forced a saucy smile onto her face. "Would you like me to cast a spell for you and unwind the whole mess, then?"

Ian's laugh rewarded her efforts. "If only you could," he said after a moment.

"Ah, forever doubting the power of the great Madam Zora," Alyssa lamented as she gazed up into his face.

Ian brushed back a strand of her hair. "I've suddenly realized I've been mistaken about your abilities. You certainly have a magical way to ease my troubled thoughts."

"With little effort," she added, glad that she'd been able to comfort him with her teasing. "My powers are far greater than that."

Slowly, the smile slipped from Ian's features as he gazed down at her. "I fear you might be telling the truth after all." His head began to dip toward her. "Lord knows, you've bewitched me." And in the next instant his lips claimed hers.

Softly, he brushed his mouth over hers, gently sipping at the edges of her lip. Breathlessly, she parted her lips, wanting more, aching for him to continue.

His breath feathered over her, strengthening the air of passion between them.

A moan reverberated deep in her throat as his fingers tightened upon her nape and his mouth sealed hers with desire. The taste of him intoxicated her and Alyssa pressed against his hardness.

Slipping his tongue between her lips, Ian deepened the kiss into an erotic dance. Emotions surged within Alyssa as the onslaught of Ian's passion swept her away. In that instant, her world became Ian, the touch of him, the scent of him, the taste of him.

Breaking off the kiss, Ian pressed sweet kisses along the line of her neck. "Zora, oh, Zora," he moaned against her skin an instant before he reclaimed her mouth.

Zora.

The name jarred inside of her, making her remember who she was, who *he* was. Remorse filled her, yet she managed to pull away from him, wrenching herself from Ian's arms.

"We can't," she murmured, pressing the back of her hands to her lips. "We *can't.*"

"Zora," Ian began, taking a step toward her with an outstretched hand. As a servant exited from the rear door of the Covingtons' townhouse, slamming the door shut behind him, Ian dropped his hand to his side. "No, you're perfectly correct. We can't. Not here."

But that wasn't what she meant. Alyssa trembled inside as she held back her explanation. When Ian held her in his arms, she forgot that to the world, to Ian, she was Madam Zora—fortuneteller, Gypsy, nomad. Because when he kissed her, he made her feel like Lady Alyssa Porter once more, like a young girl filled with dreams of love and marriage.

But those days were gone . . . and it was best that she remember that fact.

"I must go home," she murmured, reaching out to take hold of her bag.

"Do you have a carriage waiting?"

"No, but I'm well accustomed to walking."

Shaking his head, Ian cupped his hand around her elbow and guided her out to the Covingtons' stables. "While that may be true, you won't be walking this evening."

Ordering his carriage brought around, Ian waited with her as the servants hurried to do his bidding. "This truly isn't necessary," she protested.

But Ian would hear none of it. "I don't want you to walk through these streets alone at night." Glancing down at her, he added, "I'd see you home myself, but I doubt if you'd allow that. You guard your secrets very carefully, Zora."

Indeed she did. If only she'd been as careful with her heart. She looked away quickly in case her thoughts showed on her face.

As if she were a gentle-born lady, Ian handed her up into the carriage and waited until she had settled upon the seat. "Perhaps someday you'll allow me to share a few of your secrets," he said softly.

Remaining silent, she gave Ian a smile as he shut the door and ordered the carriage away. As she stared at the gaily dressed lords and ladies receding from view, Alyssa realized that though she might weave dreams around Ian, any hope of a reality with him would remain forever out of reach. She was no longer one of the ton; she was, now and forever, Madam Zora.

Pressing her hands to her stomach, Alyssa tried to force back the wave of nausea that threatened to overtake her at that thought. Tonight, she'd learned a valuable lesson. Mr. Ian Fortune threatened far more than her source of income.

He had the power to wound her heart.

8

Donning the dreadful black outfit was worth the discomfort, Alyssa decided, when she caught sight of Ian striding toward the blanket where she sat near the pond and watched Calla feed the geese. Though she'd never intended to venture into Hyde Park as Lady Greenald again, she hadn't been able to resist. Indeed, she'd tried to talk herself out of coming to this particular park, but had failed miserably.

Her heart pounded within her breast as he smiled and waved a greeting. Trying to act calm despite the memories of their moonlight kiss, she waved back.

"What a delightful surprise," Ian commented as he came to a stop at the edge of the blanket. Nodding toward Calla, who tossed bread crumbs out to the geese, he chuckled softly. "Lady Calla seems to be enjoying herself."

"She most certainly is," Alyssa agreed, knowing it

was true. Because of their circumstances, Calla enjoyed far too little of these simple childhood pleasures.

"Might I join you, Lady Greenald?" Ian inquired politely.

Gesturing to the blanket, Alyssa issued an invitation, wondering all the while how she could sound so formal when her very breath was lodged in her throat. "Please do."

"I wondered if I might see you here today," Ian admitted.

A flush of pleasure warmed her face . . . until she realized Lady Greenald was simply another part she played. As Alyssa Porter, she had no hope for a future with him. Not now. Not since she'd donned Gypsy garb. "Did you wish to see me for any particular reason?" she asked calmly.

"Yes, as a matter of fact. I wondered if you and your sister might be my dinner companions this evening."

For a moment, she could only stare at him speechless. Finally, she managed to ask, "*Pardon me?*"

"Dinner. This evening," he repeated slowly as if she were hard of hearing. "I thought it might be enjoyable if you joined me—"

"I can't . . . *we* can't," she said, abruptly rising to her feet. "Calla! We'd best be on our way." Bending down, she tugged at the blanket, knocking Ian off balance, tumbling him onto the grass. "So sorry," she murmured in the sweetest voice she could manage. To think he'd kissed her . . . or rather Zora, then invited her . . . as Lady Greenald to dinner the very next day infuriated her.

She knew she had no future with Ian, but she certainly expected better of him!

As soon as Calla ran up, Alyssa grabbed hold of her sister's arm. "We need to hurry home."

"But why?" Calla asked, before automatically shifting her attention onto Ian. "Good day, Mr. Fortune. Did you see the geese—"

"*Now*, Calla." Offering Ian nothing more than a frosty nod, she folded her blanket against her chest. "Farewell, Mr. Fortune."

What the devil had just happened?

Try as he might to sort through his conversation with Lady Greenald, he couldn't imagine what he'd said or done that would evoke such an unpleasant response. One moment the woman was warm and pleasant, yet the very next she was practically spitting her words at him.

Why would the invitation to dine with him cause such a reaction? It was beyond Ian's comprehension. After all, he'd been polite and decorous when he'd invited her. Nothing that should have rattled Lady Greenald.

Now, if she'd been privy to his private thoughts, that might have been an entirely different matter.

It was highly doubtful that the lady would have appreciated being used to overcome thoughts of an all too enticing Gypsy. Rubbing a hand over his eyes, Ian thought back on the restless night he'd had. The sweetness of Zora's lips had haunted him, the image of her in the moonlight had burned in his mind, and the feel of her pressed against him had made him hunger for more, making it impossible to sleep.

What he'd told Zora last night had been nothing less than the truth. He'd tried to put her out of his mind, but something about her—her lively spirit, her intriguing secrets, her captivating wit—struck a chord deep inside of him.

Last night when he'd been torn by his grandfa . . . no, by *Lord Hammond's* pronouncement, Ian had found solace in Zora's embrace. Still, in the harsh morning light, he was uncertain if he could so easily abandon his dreams in exchange for an infatuation with a fortuneteller.

Indecision had driven him from his home in search of the charming widow. Silly, he knew, but desperate times called for desperate measures.

And all he'd gotten for his efforts had been a blatant snub, leading him back to his original question.

What the devil had happened to cause Lady Greenald to become so upset?

Or better asked, *why* did it happen? Perhaps she'd thought him too bold for inviting a widow still in mourning to dine with him. He hoped he hadn't upset her too much as he certainly wouldn't want to add to her hardships. Her life couldn't be easy, what with her lack of funds and raising a younger sister.

Rising, Ian brushed off his pants and took off with new purpose. He would call upon the current Earl of Tonneson immediately to ensure that the ladies received adequate funds in the future. Glancing down, Ian caught sight of his grass-stained pants.

All right, then, Ian amended, he would head over to the earl's residence . . . directly after he changed his clothes.

"Thank you for seeing me, my lord." Accepting the gestured seat, Ian faced the Earl of Tonneson and found it hard to believe that this soft, plump man was related to those two charming ladies in any fashion.

"What can I do for you, Mr. Fortune?" asked Lord Tonneson as he popped a grape into his mouth. "I'm a very busy man."

The words ended up sounding like "I'm a werry weese mam" as the earl tried to speak while eating. Ian didn't know whether to shiver in distaste or laugh at the man's ridiculousness. He did neither. Instead, he focused upon his concerns. "I've called upon you today because I wish to discuss your wards."

"My what?"

"Your wards," Ian repeated. "The two daughters of the former earl."

"Alyssa and Calla?" exclaimed the round man as he sat up in his seat. "You've found them?"

Ian blinked twice. "Are you telling me you'd *lost* them?"

"Not precisely," blustered the earl. "I'd merely . . . misplaced them for a while."

The anger building inside of Ian must have been reflected upon his face for the pale dandy continued to stutter over excuses.

"I'd provided them with a perfectly fine cottage in

Northumberland," protested Lord Tonneson. "They had no cause to leave."

Somewhat mollified, Ian sat back in his chair. "I take it then that you had no idea that Lady Greenald and Lady Calla had arrived in London."

"Lady *who?*"

Lord, the man was as slow-witted as he was soft! Holding in his exasperated sigh, Ian said, "Lady Greenald and Lady Calla . . . your wards."

"Oh-Oh. You mean Alyssa and Calla." Shaking his head, Lord Tonneson frowned. "Though I don't know who this Lady Greenald is."

Since the earl was obviously addled, Ian didn't see any point in arguing. Undoubtedly further explanation would only result in more confusion. "Never mind," he said with a dismissive wave of his hand. "I had hoped that you might know their address so I could call upon Lady Gre . . . er, Lady Alyssa and her sister."

"Can't help you there, but now that I know they're in London, you can be assured that I'll search the city for them."

Lord Tonneson's assurance eased Ian's mind. "If I run into the ladies again, I shall direct them to you, my lord."

"Indeed. I know just what to do with them."

The hard glint that had flickered briefly in the earl's eyes set Ian's nerves jangling again. "Excuse me?"

Shaking his head, the earl smoothed out his expression. "What I meant is that I am eager to set them up in town, to assure myself that they're safe and comfortable."

Indeed he would, Ian thought, as he rose from his chair. In fact, Ian'd make certain of it.

"I don't like to be kept waiting, Meiser," grumbled the earl as he paced to and fro upon the rug. It was the most movement Meiser had ever seen from the earl. "I was visited today by a man, a Mr. Ian Fortune, who told me that my cousins were here in London!"

"*Here?*" exclaimed Meiser. Of all the places he'd imagined the girls would have gone, London hadn't been among them. After all, the girls had never come to town with their parents. Indeed, their entire lives had been spent at the Tonneson country estate, so he thought they'd seek a similar situation.

Meiser had spent the last few days inquiring after distant relatives and the like, thinking perhaps the sisters had sought aid, but never once had he imagined them trying to survive in town. "Why? How?"

"That's what I pay you to find out!" The Earl of Tonneson pointed a pudgy finger at him. "And I want you to find them soon. I don't want any more strangers knocking on my door, requesting admittance, just so that they can insinuate that I've neglected my duties toward my cousins."

In other words, stated the bald truth. Meiser kept that thought to himself. "Yes, my lord. I shall get right on it."

"See that you do, Meiser, or you'll soon find yourself without a position."

But Meiser knew the earl was wrong. With a little luck, he'd find himself with a new bride.

*   *   *

Feeling ill-at-ease in the room where his father must have played as a boy, Ian remained standing as he awaited the arrival of his grandfather, the duke. Ever since Zora had urged him to face his past, Ian had been contemplating this visit, yet he hadn't realized he'd made a firm decision until he'd ended up at the duke's front entrance. Hearing approaching footsteps, Ian turned to face the doorway.

Surprise, recognition, and wariness flashed across Regis Fortune's face, before he stilled his features into cool lines. "When my butler informed me that someone had barged into my home, demanding entrance, I never imagined it was you." One shoulder lifted. "Though given your background, I suppose I should have expected such common behavior."

A sharp retort rose to Ian's lips, but he swallowed it. "I didn't come here to argue with you," Ian said stiffly. "I merely wanted to inform you that your announcement claiming me as your heir is unwanted. I shall never accept the title."

"Good Lord, boy, don't you know you don't accept the title of duke. It's yours whether you like it or not. You were born to it!"

"I was born to poverty, your grace," Ian replied, fighting to remain calm. "But once my father began his business, our financial situation improved greatly. Yet all the while, even when we ate only potatoes at every meal, I knew happiness, love, and security." Flicking a glance around the room, Ian shook his head. "Somehow I doubt my father knew the same as a child."

"How dare you?" the duke rasped. "How dare you come into my home and proceed to tell me what was lacking in my son's life? I loved Harold."

"Until he disobeyed you," Ian said softly, surprised to see pain tighten the duke's features.

"You're wrong. I loved him still, but my duty to my own father and all the dukes before him demanded I cast Harold out for bringing such dishonor to the family name." Clasping his hands behind his back, the duke lifted his chin. "I now see I made a mistake. Instead of allowing Harold to go his own way with the serving wench, I should have shipped them off to Scotland or somewhere in the wilds until you were born. Then I could have claimed your mother was of Scottish nobility. If I'd done that, I could have ensured that you at least received training for your position."

The duke's sheer arrogance astounded Ian. "What makes you believe I would ever have listened to anything you had to say to me?"

"Because you would have been *trained* to do so. I'm certain I could have convinced Harold of the necessity for training."

"Like a favorite dog."

"No, like the grandson of a duke!" Spreading his hands wide, the duke took a step forward. "Don't you realize all I could do for you, Ian? It's not too late for us. If you agreed, I would begin your training immediately and show you all the responsibilities of the dukedom. You'd even be free to give up your demeaning role as merchant."

"Demeaning?" Ian repeated, astounded. "You know

nothing about me if you believe that I find my business demeaning. It has built my fortune, given me purpose, held me together after my father died . . . and my mother succumbed to the loneliness of a broken heart." A harsh laugh escaped him. "I'd no sooner give my business up than I would my memories of my parents."

"Fine, then keep the blasted job!" exclaimed the duke as he pounded a fist against the mantel. "Just accept your responsibilities as the next Duke of Hammond. You're my blood, boy, whether we like it or not. There is so much I could give you."

"There's nothing I want from you."

But even as Ian said the words, he knew he wasn't being completely honest. Deep in his soul, there was a dark longing, a wish that only this man could grant.

To be part of a family again. To have a history, a lineage to look back upon.

Looking at his grandfather was like looking at an older version of himself. There was a bond between them that could be denied, but never broken. If only things had been different and his grandfather had accepted his mother, then there would be more than just blood between them.

But things weren't different. They were simply strangers who happened to share a few facial features and a last name. Ian knew he'd best remember that fact . . . for this cold, hard man had turned away his only son for committing the sin of falling in love with a serving maid.

"There's nothing I want from you," Ian repeated firmly, forcing himself to remember the past and all the pain this man had inflicted upon his parents. "And that includes your bloody title."

The duke flinched, making Ian wonder if perhaps he regretted the past. Impossible, Ian decided. Undoubtedly the duke was merely unused to having his dictates thrown back in his face. Taking one last look around the room, Ian realized that this was the home where his father had grown up, where his mother had come to work as a young girl, where his parents had fallen in love. So many things, so many memories lost because of idiotic notions of station.

"I will never become the Duke of Hammond."

"I already told you, boy. You have no choice in the matter." Pulling back his shoulders, the duke fixed a firm gaze upon him. "And if you refuse to accept the title, then do you also refuse the entitlements? Don't you realize how many people I support on my various estates? If you refuse to accept these responsibilities, what will happen to all of them?" He shook a finger at Ian. "The dukedom is bigger than us, Ian. It's more important than our petty problems or past mistakes."

The tremendous weight of responsibility settled down upon Ian's shoulders even as he tried to escape it. "It's not my concern," Ian said, wishing he could believe it.

"Ah, but it is . . . and you know it." The duke took a step forward. "You feel it, don't you? You feel the pride of generations pulsing through your veins. Deny it all you like, Ian, but you *are* the future Duke of Hammond."

* * *

The duke concentrated to keep his hand from shaking as he took a sip of his brandy. "So what did you uncover for me, Fenwig? Anything? Anything at all? I pay you handsomely to keep me informed," he finished, slamming his glass down on the sideboard.

"Yes, your grace. I've tried my best." Fenwig twisted his hat in his hands. "I followed him from the park . . . where he met a widow and a young girl . . . and on to the Earl of Tonneson's townhouse. He came straight here after that."

"Arrogant pup . . . just like his father."

"And *his* father before that," added Fenwig.

Lifting one brow, he glared at Fenwig. "I beg your pardon?"

"I meant no insult," Fenwig hurried to assure him.

"I should hope not," the duke replied, too distracted by his thoughts to put a bite in the response. Damn, but the boy had been fierce. Not that it would do Ian much good, the duke thought, for he was determined to secure a suitable heir for the title . . . which meant ensuring that his grandson marry someone worthy.

"I do have a bit of interesting news," Fenwig offered, snapping the duke back from his thoughts. "The reason why your grandson called upon the Earl of Tonneson was to inquire after his cousins."

Now that captured Hammond's attention. "Cousins?"

Nodding, Fenwig continued, "Yes, the previous earl had two daughters, sweet, lovely, and well-bred, according to the servants. They told me the present earl set the girls up in the North Country, but they didn't remain there. Apparently, the girls have the wanderlust just like their parents. Today, your grandson remarked that he'd met them here in London."

"Now that *is* interesting," the duke murmured. "The daughter of an earl would be a suitable bride for my grandson, don't you think?"

Alarm widened Fenwig's eyes. "I merely said he inquired after them, your grace. None of the servants said anything about marriage being mentioned."

"If Ian was interested enough to call upon the earl, then I'd say the ladies have already captured his attention. But which one?"

"The younger of the two is only a child, so it must be the elder sister, Lady Alyssa."

Slapping a hand upon Fenwig's shoulder, the duke smiled broadly. "Well done, my man. Track down this Lady Alyssa and find out all you can about her. After I assure myself that she is a proper consort for my grandson, I'll visit the earl and make an offer on Ian's behalf."

9

Laying out the tarot cards, Alyssa let her thoughts settle upon Ian . . . again. She'd calmed down a bit since storming away from him and even felt a bit foolish for her actions. It was perfectly understandable that Ian would invite Lady Greenald to dine with him even though he'd shared a kiss with Madam Zora. After all, Lady Greenald was someone to court, while Madam Zora . . . well, suffice it to say, marriage to a Gypsy would never enter Ian's mind.

It was all so confusing, but in the midst of her chaotic thoughts, Alyssa realized one thing.

She had to push Ian away.

It wasn't fair to either of them to continue these charades. Indeed, Alyssa felt as if she were as guilty of manipulating Ian as his grandfather . . . and that was not acceptable. Tonight, she would find a way to anger him enough so he wouldn't want to spend any more time with her. Though she found the thought utterly depressing, Alyssa knew it was what she had to do.

"I wanted to tell you how much I appreciate your help with Lord Covington."

Shaking loose her thoughts of Ian, Alyssa smiled at Lady Covington. "Thank you, my lady."

"No, thank *you*, Madam Zora," gushed the elderly lady. "Ever since you told him to follow his heart, he's become very enthusiastic about this one particular investment. I haven't seen this much life in him for a long, long time." A pretty flush brightened her well-lined features. "He's become my Edgar again."

"I'm glad," Alyssa answered simply . . . and she was. It pleased her to know that despite what Ian believed, she *did* make a positive difference in people's lives.

Lady Covington's eyes glowed with admiration as she whispered, "Whether you can truly see into the future or not, you've changed my husband because he believes in you." A tremulous smile curved her lips upward. "So, I thank you, my dear."

As she accepted Lady Covington's praise, Alyssa glanced up to see Ian enter the drawing room. The warm smile he sent her only strengthened her resolve. Taking a deep breath, she braced herself as Lady Covington stood and headed for the door.

Making his way toward her, Ian came to a stop next to her table. "Good day to you, Madam Zora."

"It was," she replied caustically, trying not to wince at her rudeness.

His brows lifted. "Am I to take it that my presence has somehow dimmed your pleasure in the day?"

"I have always admired your perception." Aware of the room growing quiet as attention focused upon them, Alyssa began to collect her cards. "I have finished telling fortunes for the evening."

A side of his mouth quirked upward. "That is perfectly fine, for I only came to speak with you, not to listen to your clever tales."

Fighting the urge to respond to his teasing, Alyssa kept her expression cool. "I am paid to entertain the guests, sir, not converse with them on matters other than their fortunes."

A frown darkened Ian's expression. "Zora? What's the matter?"

"Nothing," she said briskly, focusing on packing her bag. "I simply wish to be off for home," she finished, finally lifting her gaze.

Stiffening, Ian glanced around the room. "I suggest we continue this discussion in private."

"There is nothing more to say," Alyssa replied, rising to her feet.

"I disagree." Reaching out, Ian grabbed hold of her arm. "If you'll accompany me to—"

"Release me," she exclaimed loudly, hoping to catch everyone's attention for this final act of her performance. "I . . . I . . . curse you!" she shouted, bringing gasps from everyone in the room. "May . . . may . . . ," she began, searching for a curse to wish upon him, ". . . may a hundred . . . frogs plague you by the week's end."

Ian blinked twice. "A *hundred frogs?*"

The amusement she heard in his voice made her

worry that her plan wasn't working. "Horrid, nasty things that run wild in your home, a home where slimy creatures seem to thrive." The moment those words left her mouth she wished them back, for they only made Ian grin.

"So I'm a slimy creature, am I?"

Ian's laughter wasn't the response she'd wanted. Grasping her bag, Alyssa strode from the room, fully aware of the ton's amused gazes.

In the hallway, she released her breath . . . only to catch it again when Ian strode to her side. "Do you realize what you've done, Zora? By publicly cursing me, you've exposed yourself for the fraud you really are. When nothing amiss happens, everyone will realize that all you are is a magnificent performer."

He was right. She *knew* he was right. But at this moment, she didn't care one whit. Tossing back her head, she gave him her haughtiest look. "And if I am proven right, then you shall be forced to eat your words about my lack of powers."

"Madam Zora, if you are proven right, then I shall eat one of your bloody frogs."

Leaving Ian standing in the hallway, Alyssa headed toward the kitchens, only to pull up short as a gentleman stepped into the hall directly in front of her.

"Pardon me," she murmured, looking up with a polite smile. "I wasn't paying attention to where . . ." Her words trailed off as shock flew through her. Mr. Meiser. How grand, she thought, holding back a sigh. Deciding to brazen it through, she pretended she didn't recognize him. "... to where I was going," she finished.

"Lady Alyssa," he whispered, obviously just as surprised to see her as she was to see him.

"I am Madam Zora, not this ... Alyssa person you seek."

A deep frown furrowed Mr. Meiser's brow. "But you must be ..." He shook his head. "Don't you remember meeting me at the cottage in Northumberland?"

"No, I'm sorry, I don't. I am not the lady you seek," she repeated, before stepping around him and hurrying toward the kitchen. She prayed he'd believed her.

But if she'd looked back, she would have seen the stunned expression upon Mr. Meiser's face harden into certainty.

Her secret had been discovered.

"Oh, Calla," Alyssa moaned as she laid her head upon their tiny, scarred table. "I don't know what we're going to do now, how we're going to live." Tears spilled down her cheeks. "This afternoon I did something unbelievably idiotic and in a few days, no one will ever hire me again."

"Surely it can't be that bad," Calla replied, sitting next to Alyssa.

Seeing the concern upon her sister's face, Alyssa wanted to reassure Calla that everything would be all right, but this time she couldn't summon the words of comfort. Shaking her head, Alyssa said, "I'm afraid it is. This afternoon I tried to discourage Ian once and for all so I ... I cursed him."

Calla's eyes grew round. "You *what?*"

Pressing a hand to her temple, Alyssa tried to rub away the ache building there. "I announced . . . in front of everyone . . . that by the week's end he would be plagued with a hundred frogs."

"A hundred frogs?" Calla squeaked, before a tiny giggle escaped her. "Why a hundred frogs?"

"It was all I could think of at the moment," sighed Alyssa.

Laughing, Calla reached out to clasp Alyssa's hand. "I think that was a perfectly wonderful curse!"

"Oh, Calla, don't you see? Soon everyone will know I'm a fraud and no one will ever want to hire me again."

The smile slid away from Calla's face. "That *is* a problem." Tilting her head to the side, she gazed at Alyssa. "What are we going to do about it?"

"Do about it?" repeated Alyssa. "There is nothing we *can* do about it." Rising to her feet, Alyssa felt the hopelessness of their situation settle around her. "We must simply sit back and wait for the worst to happen . . . then perhaps we should throw ourselves on our cousin's mercy and pray he's had a change of heart." A shiver ran through Alyssa. "Of course, I could always accept Mr. Meiser's marriage proposal."

"Absolutely not!" Calla leapt to her feet. "You aren't going to marry that little toad of a man . . . not when someone like Ian Fortune is falling in love with you."

"But that's just it, Calla. He's not falling in love with me. Not at all." Alyssa allowed her disillusion to spill forth. "And I've been deluding both of us these past few months. My act as Madam Zora barely supports us, so there's no possible way we could ever save enough to pay for a Season for you."

"I don't want a Season!"

A single tear slipped down her cheek as Alyssa reached out to tuck a strand of flaxen hair behind Calla's ear. "You deserve one, though. Even you have to admit that it would be lovely to have new gowns, to never have to eat potatoes morning, noon, and night, to live in a home that actually keeps you warm and safe. You should have all of those things, Calla, and it's my responsibility to see you get them."

Stepping forward, Calla laid her head against Alyssa's shoulder. "I'm such a burden to you."

"No," Alyssa said quickly, wrapping her arms around her young sister. "You are my greatest joy. After Mama and Papa died, I would have been utterly bereft if it weren't for you."

For a long time, Calla was silent. "I love you, Alyssa," she said finally.

"Ah, and I love you as well," Alyssa comforted her sister. "And I promise everything will turn out all right. Somehow, we'll get through this together."

Lifting her head, Calla offered, "I can help."

Guilt plucked at Alyssa, making her wish she'd waited before coming home and pouring out all of her concerns and disillusionment to Calla. There were some things a fourteen-year-old child shouldn't have to deal with . . . and worrying about where they would get the money to live was one of them.

"Calla, please. It isn't your mess to fix. I got us into this situation, and I'll get us out again," Alyssa vowed. "Somehow."

"The earl is *where?*" exclaimed Isaac Meiser, twisting his hands together as he starred incredulously at Lord Tonneson's butler.

"In Bath," the servant replied. "His lordship felt the need for restorative airs after his upset."

His upset? Shaking his head, Meiser rubbed at his temple. If the news that his cousins had been seen in London had been so distressing, Meiser could only imagine how the earl would react to the news that Lady Alyssa was masquerading as the famous Madam Zora. Surely it would be enough to give Lord Tonneson apoplexy.

"Do you have any idea when he'll be back?" Meiser asked, hoping that the earl would return by the end of the week. He needed advice on how to handle Alyssa's charade . . . and the curse she'd foretold. Since he'd left his meeting with Lord Covington, Meiser had thought of nothing else. After all, the ton would be furious at Lady Alyssa once they discovered her true identity and realized she'd been lying to them the entire time.

Meiser's hopes of the earl's speedy return were dashed when the butler replied, "I do not expect his lordship to return until the early part of next week."

"Next week," muttered Meiser. It was Thursday, so there wasn't even time to send the earl a missive.

Thanking the butler, Meiser left the house, praying for wisdom to strike him. One way or another, it was left to him to solve this problem.

She was getting a headache.

All evening long, the members of the ton had been atwitter about the curse. Wagers abounded—wagers on how many frogs would appear, when they would appear, *if* they would appear.

Oh, yes, the ton delighted in the many possibilities.

But each laugh, every speculation, was merely another reminder foretelling the end of her career. Alyssa knew that by this time tomorrow, all of society would realize that she was a fraud. And, much as she dreaded it, tomorrow was also the day she must throw herself upon the mercy of her cousin. She'd decided it was the best course late last night, long after Calla had fallen asleep. Alyssa would only marry Mr. Meiser if she had no other options. Indeed, her cousin seemed the more palatable solution.

The most she could hope for was that the earl would reinstate their small stipend and send them back to their little cottage. Her dreams of a Season for Calla were fading away with every hour that passed.

"Madam Zora?"

Looking up from her table, she saw Lord Essex standing hesitantly before her. "Would you like me to tell your fortune?" Smiling at him, she gestured toward the seat. "I've finished up for the evening, but I'd be more than happy to read your palm before I head off for home."

Shaking his head, Lord Essex braced his hands on the back of the chair and leaned forward. "I don't need you to tell me my fortune tonight. I merely came to thank you." His excitement was clearly visible as he continued, "Because of your advice, I'm going to invest the remainder of my fortune into a company I'd been considering . . . even though Ian advised me against it."

Something inside of her froze. "But isn't Mr. Fortune quite knowledgeable in his business dealings?"

A slight frown marred his brow. "Well, yes, he is, but I *know* he's wrong about this investment. Lord Covington's done exceptionally well with his investment and you confirmed the success of the venture when you told him to follow his heart. You gave me the same advice."

For a long moment, Alyssa remained silent, then she allowed her conscience to win out. "I gave you hope, Lord Essex, but that was all. I can no more see into the future than you can," she admitted softly.

"But . . . but . . ."

Rising, she moved around the table and placed a hand upon his arm. "If your friend advised you not to invest, then I would follow his wisdom. Unlike me, he would never tell you something that might harm you."

"You wouldn't harm me," he protested.

"Not intentionally," she agreed, allowing her hand to drop back to her side. "But if anything I said caused you to go against sound advice, then I was wrong." She smiled at him. "Trust your friend, Lord Essex."

With a sigh, Alyssa gathered her belongings and left the room.

* * *

"I take it you heard everything she said," Peter remarked to Ian, who stood in the entrance to the ballroom.

"Every word," he admitted, still amazed at the Gypsy's generosity of spirit. She didn't have to expose herself in order to save Peter, a stranger, but she did.

When it counted most, she had come through.

Shifting his attention to his friend, Ian asked, "Are you going to listen to her?"

A grimace flickered across Peter's face. "As much as I'd like to ignore her advice . . . and *yours* for that matter, somehow I fear you're both right. After all, it's following my heart that has depleted my family fortunes; perhaps my instinctive reaction is dead wrong."

"Peter, my friend, your gut is always right, but what you need to understand is that you must do the exact *opposite* of what it tells you," Ian said, smiling broadly to take the sting out of his words.

"You're undoubtedly right." Peter sighed lightly. "Then again, you usually are when it pertains to financial matters."

"True . . . and I am right about this investment as well." Seeing his friend's dejected expression, Ian relented. "Still, why don't we head out to the coast and look into the business ourselves. That way we can be certain."

Peter nodded eagerly. "I think that's a sound plan."

"Very well, then." Ian flicked another glance at the door, wanting to follow his Gypsy, to ask her why she'd been so angry at him the last time they'd met, angry enough that she'd cursed him. And set herself up for failure.

The reasons behind her fury eluded him still and he wanted nothing more than to discover why . . .

"Don't just stand here. Go after her."

Peter's command captured Ian's attention. "Pardon me?"

"Go after her!" he repeated, waving toward the door. "It's plainly obvious that you'd like to run after her, so do it. No one will even notice if you leave." A side of his mouth tilted upward. "Besides, this way you can flirt outrageously with her, and no one will be the wiser."

"I don't—" But he did, Ian realized, stopping his protest in mid-sentence. Every chance he got, as a matter of fact. The kiss they'd shared in the garden had been one of the most sensuous he'd ever experienced. He'd wanted to take it further . . . much further. Hell, if she hadn't pulled back he would have . . .

"So what are you waiting for?" Peter asked, slapping a hand on Ian's shoulder. "If you don't hurry, you'll lose her."

Laughing, Ian headed out the door . . . eager to follow his Gypsy.

10

"Why are you looking out the window?" Calla asked for the second time that evening.

Allowing the curtain to fall forward, Alyssa turned toward her sister. "All the way home I had the most disquieting sensation. I felt as if I were being followed."

"You're probably on edge because it's Friday."

"I'm sure you're correct. By tomorrow, everyone will know I don't possess any powers," Alyssa conceded, removing her coin-laden veil and folding it for what would probably be the last time.

"I'll put it away for you," offered Calla, reaching out to take the veil from Alyssa.

Grabbing hold of one of Calla's hands, Alyssa looked pointedly at the dirt beneath her sister's fingernails. "Really, Calla," she chided gently. "You're beginning to look like a street urchin."

They would be returning to Northumberland none too soon.

Ian's hand shook as he poured himself a brandy. Dear God, she lived in squalor. The image of her rodent infested building would forever be burned in his mind. He'd been born into poverty, yet compared to Zora's home, he'd grown up in a mansion.

And after tonight when her curse failed to come true, even the meager amount she earned as a fortuneteller would be taken away from her.

Remembering her generosity toward Peter, he couldn't bear to have her exposed for a charlatan. All he had to do was make the curse come true. Taking a sip of his brandy, Ian turned the idea around in his head. If he ordered a trusted servant to gather a few frogs or toads, then have them released in his home, Zora's prediction would then have come true. And her only visible source of income would be secured.

Draining his glass, Ian realized that he'd worked to expose her from the first, yet now, when he was offered a perfect opportunity to do so, he found he couldn't take advantage of it. Zora had proven herself to be an honorable woman by helping Peter. She deserved far better than to be revealed as a trickster. She deserved to be kissed senseless in a garden filled with moonlight.

Pushing aside the image of her falling into his arms, Ian strode from the room.

He had some frogs to catch.

*   *   *

The morning sun shone brightly upon Madam Zora's building, illuminating the dirt and disrepair that had been partially cloaked by the shadows of the night. Though he would have sworn it impossible, Ian thought the place looked even more disreputable.

Determination hardened within him as he crossed the street. All night long he'd fought with indecision, part of him wanting to forge onward with his dreams of marrying well and the other part recognizing the fire in his blood for a certain Gypsy. By dawn, he knew he couldn't fight his longing for Zora any longer. He would set her up in a cottage nearby and see to her every need ... and together they could explore the depths of passion.

Squelching the heat ignited by his thoughts, Ian stepped into the front entrance. The stale air strengthened his resolve to get Zora out of this place. Looking at the rows of thin, warping doors, he realized he didn't know which apartment belonged to his Gypsy.

Suddenly, a sweet voice calling out a greeting echoed down the staircase. Zora. Though he wanted to vault up the steps, Ian made his way carefully up the stairs, fearful that they might give way at any moment. Just then an elderly woman appeared in the hall.

"Excuse me for my boldness madam, but I was wondering if you might have been speaking to a young lady known as Zora?"

"Don' know no Zora," replied the woman.

The woman's assertion didn't surprise him. He'd never believed his fortuneteller was actually a Gypsy named Zora. "The lady has dark hair and dark eyes and she . . ."

"Ah, you mean—"

"Mrs. Greggs, you forgot your—"

Ian's head snapped around. He smiled at his Gypsy in her plain dress with her hair swept up in a simple knot at the back of her head.

"Is this the lady you wanted?" asked Mrs. Greggs from his side. "Why, that's—"

"Here's your hat," Zora interrupted, her face still pale. "It might rain later this afternoon."

"You are such a dear." Accepting the knit cap, Mrs. Greggs smiled at Zora, then at him. "And this fine gent is lookin' fer you."

Color flooded Zora's cheeks when Mrs. Greggs waggled her eyebrows at her.

"I'll be leavin' the two of you alone, then." She paused to give Ian a stern look. "You be lookin' like a lusty sort of fellow, but you'd best keep it in check. This here's a good gel."

Ian heard Zora's soft groan, and held in his smile. Instead, he offered Mrs. Greggs a solemn nod. "I shall do my best to keep my . . . lusty nature at bay."

"See?" Mrs. Greggs said to Zora who had turned beet-red at this point. "I knew he was a fine gent."

Smiling weakly, Zora remained silent until the front door shut behind her elderly neighbor. Ian could see the panic in her eyes as she turned toward him. "What are you doing here, Mr. Fortune?"

"The name's Ian and I should think it's rather obvious why I came to this . . . place," he finished.

Zora's chin lifted. "It might not be much, but I call it home."

"The hallway belongs to you?" he asked, glancing around pointedly.

"No, but—"

"Then why don't you show me into your flat." He didn't wish to have a conversation here in the blasted hallway.

Alarm flashed over her features, piquing his curiosity even more. "I'd let you in, but—"

"Excellent," he said, interrupting without care for his rudeness. If Zora was nervous, then there was something of her past in that apartment, something to identify who she truly was.

Placing his hand on her elbow, Ian steered her back up the stairs to the apartment door that stood ajar. "Ah, here we go."

"Ian, no, I—"

"There's nothing to fear," Ian reassured her, pausing in front of the door. Stroking his hand down her cheek, he allowed all the feelings he'd pushed away to wash over him. "I'm certain you've realized I'm attracted to you, Zora, and I believe you desire me as well." Slowly, he leaned forward, brushing his lips against her brow. "I'll take you away from this squalor and set you up in a lovely cottage where you can be happy and you won't have to pretend to be a fortuneteller anymore."

Abruptly, Zora stepped back, swatting away his hand. "What makes you believe I would accept such an offer?" she rasped, anger flashing in her eyes. "I'm not a harlot, sir."

"I never said you were." Ian shook his head. "My offer has no conditions set upon it other than the chance to call upon you."

Indecision wavered in her expression. "You would give us all that—"

"Us?" Ian asked, cutting Zora off.

"I mean—"

"Alyssa?"

The soft call froze Ian's blood as he turned to face the young girl framed in the doorway. "Calla?" he rasped, recognizing her immediately.

Calla's eyes flared in alarm as she turned her gaze first to him, then to her sister. Suddenly, the pieces fell into place for Ian.

Snapping his head toward Zora, he pinned her with his stare. "Lady Greenald, I presume."

Her mouth opened as if to respond, but she shut it without uttering a syllable. Instead, she nodded slowly.

Feeling light-headed at the stunning news, Ian reached out to brace himself against the wall. "All this time you've been playing me for a fool," he whispered, wanting to believe he was wrong, but unable to deny the evidence before his very eyes.

"No," Alyssa cried, laying a hand on his forearm. "I didn't intend to deceive you, but—"

". . . you just happened to be walking in the very park in which I take my daily constitutionals and your sister just happened to pretend to faint in front of me and then you just happened to show up and—"

"Enough!"

"Enough?" Snorting in derision, Ian shook his head.

"I hardly think so. Not even close to enough for someone who deliberately set out to deceive me by pretending to be a poor widow. Why did you feel the need to invent Lady Greenald anyway? Did you realize that all Zora could become was my mistress while Lady Greenald might have been able to entice me into marriage?" A bitter laugh escaped. "How you've played me for a fool."

"Please, Ian, it wasn't like that."

"Of course it was," he retorted coldly. "But luckily for me I discovered your game." His stomach tightened as he gazed down into her beautiful, deceitful face. "Perhaps you should learn from your mistake when you pick your next dupe and choose someone less cautious."

"Please, Ian," she said again, reaching out her hand.

But he didn't want to hear anything she had to say. "I suppose I can't blame you entirely. After all, I knew you were defrauding the ton, but I stupidly allowed myself to believe that you were being honest with me." Ian thrust his hands through his hair. "What a dolt I was. Still, you should be congratulated on your fine performance. I'm not usually so easily taken in by an act."

When she flinched, he felt nothing but satisfaction. "What's the matter, Madam Zora? Don't you like to face the truth? I realize you're far more comfortable with lies, but this time there's no veil to hide behind."

"I'm not looking to hide," she said, her quiet dignity so at odds with his fury. "I'd only like to explain—"

Holding up his hands, he cut her off. "I have no wish to hear any more of your lies."

Her eyes filled with tears, but she remained silent.

A maelstrom of emotions raged through him as he watched a tear escape. "No more," he rasped, before turning on his heel and walking away.

Staring down the now empty hallway, Alyssa tried to force her jumbled thoughts into a semblance of order . . . yet the task seemed impossible. Guilt over her deception, longing for Ian's companionship, and sorrow for succeeding in driving him away bombarded her. True, she'd meant to drive a wedge between them, but she'd never imagined she would feel this deep sense of loss once she'd accomplished her goal.

Wrapping her arms around her middle, Alyssa held on to her control, not wanting to break down in front of her little sister.

"Alyssa?" Calla asked tentatively. "Are you all right?"

Alyssa forced herself to smile. "Why wouldn't I be?"

If anything, Calla's concern deepened. "Oh, Alyssa," she murmured, stepping forward to wrap her arms around her sister.

Drawing comfort from Calla, Alyssa held onto her sister. After a while, she pulled away, wiping at the stray tear slipping down her cheek. "We shouldn't be standing in the hallway like this," she murmured. "Scary Mr. Mariachi might wander along."

Calla giggled at the thought as she slipped back into their apartment. Alyssa followed her sister . . . after one last, longing glance down the hallway.

* * *

She'd lied to him! Her deception shouldn't have come as such a surprise, but amazingly, it did. It cut him to the quick to know that all of her concern and tenderness in the garden had simply been part of her act to lower his defenses.

How she planned to use him, he wasn't certain, but that hardly seemed the point. Undoubtedly, he was simply part of her grand plan to deceive the ton. Pain rippled through him at the thought.

Taking his front steps two at a time, Ian heard the voices coming from inside before he even opened the door. What now?

Pushing open the door, Ian skidded to a halt, overwhelmed with shock at the chaos he beheld.

"Where the devil did all these bloody frogs come from?"

11

The question had no sooner left his mouth when one of the slimy creatures hopped onto his boot. Kicking it away, Ian stared at the moist skid now marring the shiny leather. Even as he looked down, two more frogs came hopping by, followed by a shrieking housemaid with a broom.

"Foul beasties!"

Watching his servants scurry around, chasing after frogs of all shapes and sizes and even a few toads tossed into the mix, Ian was speechless. His butler rushed forward, holding a squirming bag that left little doubt as to its contents. "It's a madhouse, sir. Frogs have invaded every corner of the house, from the kitchens up to the bedchambers."

Fixing a stare upon the harried man, Ian demanded, "When I sent you to find some of the buggers, just how many did you bring back?"

"Only ten, sir, just as you asked."

"Then, how do you explain this?" Ian asked, pointing to the foyer where at least a hundred of the creatures were massed.

Shaking his head, the butler shrugged lightly. "I can't, sir. I'm truly at a loss as to where they all came from." His brows drew downward. "Just how quickly do frogs . . . you know . . ."

"Procreate? Reproduce?" Ian asked, unable to hold in his laugh. "I'm not certain, Manning, but I know it couldn't possibly be this quick."

"Then I don't know how to explain it," the butler replied as he tried to straighten his jacket. "Unless the fortuneteller is far more powerful than anyone realized."

"Oh, she's powerful all right. A frighteningly powerful actress. However, what she is *not* is a fortuneteller."

"Then how do *you* explain this?" Manning asked, helplessly pointing toward the green, frog-hopping insanity that now ruled Ian's home.

"I can't at the moment . . . but I will," Ian vowed. "Now gather all the servants and round up these pests."

"Everyone who hasn't fainted or gone running off screaming is already working to capture the nasty creatures." Sighing loudly, Manning admitted, "But I have to tell you, sir, they are slippery little buggers."

"Yes, well, just try your best to—"

"Yoo-hoo! Mr. Fortune!"

Groaning, Ian turned around to see a trio of women standing at the base of his front steps. "Ladies," he greeted them. "It's a bit early in the day for calling."

"Oh, I know, but I assured my friends that you wouldn't mind," Lady Covington replied smoothly.

"Of course not," he murmured, wondering how he was going to get them to leave . . . quickly. "But I fear I shan't be able to ask you in at the moment. You see I'm having a bit of . . . painting done and the workers are literally crawling all over the foyer."

"Oh, but we don't mind at all, do we?" Lady Covington glanced at her two companions, Lady Heath and Lady Weatherstone, who both shook their heads. "We so enjoy your company, Mr. Fortune."

Even if they did, they hadn't come seeking his company, Ian knew, trying to think of a new approach for sending them packing. But just as he decided upon his next tactic, the matter was taken from his hands when a large, dark brown toad hopped out from between his feet.

Stopping on the top step, the creature croaked loudly, before proceeding off the edge of the landing.

"Wonder where that fellow came from?" Ian murmured, hoping to distract the ladies.

But they were not to be deterred.

These formidable matrons had gotten past the most stringent of footmen; they weren't about to allow one lone gentleman to stop them. Ian could see it in their eyes as they took the steps in unison.

"Ladies, please," Ian began, holding up his hands.

"We insist," Lady Covington replied sweetly, her

voice at odds with the steely glint in her eyes. "Everyone who is anyone is simply *dying* to know if Madam Zora's prediction came true."

As the three women took the last step, Ian realized if he was going to stop them, it would have to be by force. It seemed he had no choice. Knowing when he was defeated, Ian stepped to the side. "Why don't you see for yourself?"

Squeals of delight escaped Lady Covington as she beheld the chaotic scene. "I *knew* Madam Zora was the real thing."

"As did I," pronounced Lady Heath, taking a step back as a frog hopped toward her.

"Not a doubt in my mind," Lady Weatherstone added.

Frowning slightly, Lady Covington glanced at Ian. "Though I must admit that the large number of frogs wandering about surprises me. There are most definitely more than a *hundred* frogs here."

"Just lucky, I guess," Ian murmured, thinking about the wonderful morning he'd had so far—first his disillusionment with Zora, then returning home to a frog-filled house. "Just a lucky man," he repeated as a frog jumped from a nearby table and landed squarely on his shoulder.

Looking down at the frog's bulging eyes, Ian sighed as the odious creature croaked at him.

A lucky fellow indeed.

After his noise-filled, chaotic home, Ian found the sounds drifting from the docks soothing. He'd managed to shuffle Lady Covington and her friends out of his home, before leaving his servants to clean up the frogs and heading for the calm of his office. Hell, he was smart enough to know when to seek refuge.

Finding comfort in the order of his books, Ian concentrated on tallying the figures. He'd only finished the first column when there was a knock at the door.

"Begging your pardon, sir," Charles said as he poked his head around the door. "Lord Allerby would like to speak with you."

"Please show him in." Setting down his quill, Ian rose and walked around his desk to welcome his friend. "Allerby," he greeted. "This is an unexpected pleasure."

"Glad you think so, Fortune. I'd hate to be a bother." Allerby pointed to Ian's desk. "And since I see you're busy, I'll gladly call upon you later."

Waving a hand toward the piles of paper on his desk, Ian smiled at his friend. "I'm just calculating the profit Lord Ashton made on a shipment of silk, but it's nothing that can't wait." He gestured toward a chair. "Please, have a seat and tell me to what do I owe this pleasure."

"I've come for your advice," Allerby admitted. "Sunley told me you'd warned him against investing in the Electrolytic Marine Mining Company."

"Indeed I did." Ian returned to his seat. "I find the entire idea ludicrous."

"That's what Sunley said," Allerby murmured, a frown gathering upon his features. "Still, Fortune, you can't deny that many of my peers have made great sums of money from that company, so how could it be a sham?"

"Undoubtedly Mr. Jennings is intelligent enough to pay off some of the first investors . . . not too much, mind you. No, just enough to catch the interest of everyone else. Only after he piques everyone's curiosity and gathers in more investors will the lies be exposed."

Allerby's hand shook as he rubbed his forehead. "You're undoubtedly right, Fortune."

His friend's behavior struck Ian as odd. "You seem most distressed by this situation, Allerby."

"Not distressed, really, merely upset." Allerby clasped his hands together. "I'm simply disappointed that you don't believe in the company. Hell, your instinct for turning a profit is almost legendary in society." His laugh sounded flat. "I just wanted the investment to be solid as I've had a bad turn at the tables and need to recoup some of my losses."

Ian leaned forward, resting his elbows on his desk. "Can I be of assistance?"

"Not unless you'd be willing to take a trip to Bath with me," Allerby replied.

"Bath?" The reason for Allerby's request clicked into place. "Because you'd like to tour the Electrolytic Marine Mining facilities," he concluded.

"Until I see it for myself, I won't be able to put it from my mind."

Allerby's confession didn't surprise Ian at all, for he'd learned during his foray into society that the desire for quick, easy money ran strong in blue blood. "As it so happens, Allerby," Ian began, "Peter and I had already planned to visit the company to see the operation for ourselves. You're more than welcome to join us, of course."

"Splendid." An anxious look flashed over Allerby's face. "Can we head for Bath tomorrow? I know that seems rather hurried, but I doubt I'll be able to sleep until I see the company for myself."

Allerby's request seemed a bit odd, but when Ian considered his current situation, he realized he could use a few days away from town. At least until the furor over Zora's curse coming true died down. Glancing down at the pile of work, Ian decided his peace of mind was far more important. "As luck would have it, tomorrow works fine. I'll send around a note to Peter asking him to join us as well."

"Splendid." Rising to his feet, Allerby offered Ian his hand. "I truly appreciate this, Fortune."

"I'm more than happy to do it," Ian replied honestly.

"We leave tomorrow."

Watching Allerby squirm in the leather chair, the duke grew amused at the man's discomfort. "Are you quite certain?"

"Positive, your grace," replied Allerby, glancing away. "Will you return my markers now?"

Shaking his head, the duke smiled. "Not until your return."

"But you said all I needed to do was arrange for Ian to be out of town for a few days and you'd return my markers that you purchased from Lord Hathaway."

"Quite true," the duke conceded. "However, Ian hasn't been gone for a few days, now has he? When you return from your trip, I shall give you the markers . . . after I'm certain that you didn't mention our little arrangement to Ian."

Allerby's eyes darkened. "Very well, your grace."

Hearing the anger vibrating in the young lord's response, the duke couldn't help but smile.

"Regis Fortune, the Duke of Hammond to see you, my lord."

Choking on his crumpet, the Earl of Tonneson struggled to regain his breath. "For me? Here?" he asked.

"Yes, my lord," the servant intoned.

"Show him in, man. You don't make a duke wait in the foyer, you dunderhead."

Without another word, the butler went to fetch the duke. Clapping his hands once, the earl grinned as he wiped off the crumbs scattered on his vest. It wouldn't do to have a duke see him looking less than proper.

The Duke of Hammond personified the best society had to offer, Lord Tonneson knew, and looking at the regal figure the duke cut as he entered the room, the earl could see that none of the gossip had overstated the man's powerful aura.

"Your grace." Dipping into a bow, the earl straightened and pointed to a nearby chair. "I am honored by your presence."

"Thank you," Lord Hammond replied crisply. "I'll wager you're wondering why I've come to call."

"I must admit I am."

Lord Hammond settled in the designated chair and

crossed his hands over his stomach. "I came to form an alliance between our two houses."

Stumbling backward, the earl thanked Heaven for the settee behind him. "An alliance?" he asked, his voice squeaking on the last word.

"Between your cousin and my grandson."

Frantically he searched his memory, trying to remember if he'd heard mention of the grandson. Not that it mattered, the earl realized. If the grandson of this man had been the devil himself, Lord Tonneson would still have been more than eager to settle one of his cousins upon him. After all, connections were connections. Smiling broadly, he asked, "Which cousin are you inquiring after? Alyssa or Calla?"

"I thought one of your cousins was still a child."

"She's fifteen or so," the earl replied, shrugging off the duke's concern. "In the past, ladies often wed much younger."

The duke cleared his throat sternly, letting Lord Tonneson know he'd made a misstep. "I believe my grandson has an interest in the elder."

"Alyssa." Nodding sagely, the earl tried to make up for his mistake. "As to your offer of an alliance, I believe she would be most amenable to it." Even if she weren't, he'd see to it Alyssa agreed to the match, the earl thought with a smile.

"Excellent," pronounced the duke. "As to the details, I shall have my man-of-business contact yours to draw up a contract—"

"Pardon me, my lord," the butler interrupted.

"What?" snapped Lord Tonneson, not wanting any disruptions.

"Mr. Meiser is here to see you and he is insisting that it is most urgent."

Excellent timing! "Show him in," directed the earl, practically rubbing his hands together in anticipation. "Meiser is my man-of-business, so it might help to move along the contract if he is notified immediately."

"I agree," the duke replied smoothly.

"It's fortuitous that you came, Meiser. His grace and I have come to an agreement between my cousin, Lady Alyssa Porter, and his grandson—"

"Ian Fortune, Marquess of Dorset," supplied the duke.

"Yes, the Marquess," Lord Tonneson repeated, rolling the sweet title over his tongue.

"Very well, my lord. I shall see to the matter immediately." Meiser glanced at the duke, before looking at the earl. "Might I have a word—"

"Perfect," announced Lord Hammond, cutting off Meiser without a qualm. "The sooner the better."

The duke's eagerness caught Meiser's attention. "Do I take it, your grace, that you want me to arrange the terms of marriage, along with inheritance portions?"

"All of it," the duke instructed, waving his hand blithely. "I wish to have the arrangement settled immediately."

That suited the earl perfectly.

"Forgive my impertinence, your grace, but might I inquire as to the reason for such expedience?" Meiser asked hesitantly.

Lifting his brow, the duke answered Meiser's question without hesitation. "Actually, it might be best if I tell you that my grandson has shown some . . . inappropriate interest in a Gypsy wench who entertains at a number of parties here in town."

A curious choking sound came from Meiser. "Do you refer to Madam Zora?" the man managed to croak.

"Indeed I do." Leveling his gaze at the earl, Lord Hammond continued, "Despite this, however, I can assure you that my grandson will make an exemplary husband to your cousin for whom he has already shown an interest."

As if that mattered. Still, the earl managed to hold back the remark. "Very well, then."

Rising to his feet, the duke collected his hat and gloves. "It is settled." Holding out a hand to the earl, Lord Hammond remarked, "It has been a pleasure doing business with you." Glancing at Meiser, the duke nodded in farewell. "I shall arrange for Mr. Fenwig to contact you immediately."

"I shall await your agent," Meiser said in a tight, strangled voice.

As soon as the duke left, the earl dropped his concerned air and smacked Meiser lightly on the arm. "What is the matter with you, Meiser? I thought you were going to get ill all over the duke's Hessians." Doing a little dance around the settee, Lord Tonneson crowed gleefully. "Imagine, me intimately connected to a duke. How utterly delightful . . ."

"My lord?"

". . . how completely marvelous . . ."

"My lord!"

". . . how intensely satisfying . . ."

"Your cousin is Madam Zora!"

Meiser's announcement brought an end to the earl's victory dance. "She's who?"

"Madam Zora," Meiser repeated glumly. "The Gypsy fortuneteller the duke was talking about."

Once again, the earl stumbled backward onto the settee. "You mean to tell me that my cousin has been going to parties pretending to be a Gypsy fortuneteller?"

"That's precisely what I'm saying."

"Blast the foolish wench!" Rubbing at his forehead, the earl tried to sort through the whole mess. "Who else knows about this?"

"As far as I know, no one," Meiser said. "After all, your cousins never had a Season, nor did they spend any time in society. As a result, no one knows what Lady Alyssa Porter looks like. They've only seen Madam Zora."

The earl tapped his fingers against the arm of the settee. "Then this situation is still controllable."

"How, my lord?" asked Meiser, obviously confused.

"Well, it's quite simple, really. All we need to do is sign the agreement posthaste, making certain the duke never meets Lady Alyssa Porter until after the marriage by proxy."

"And by the time the duke realizes that Lady Alyssa and the Gypsy are one and the same, the marriage will already have taken place," Meiser finished softly.

"Precisely!" crowed the earl, slapping his hands together in delight. "See? Everything will be just fine."

"You can't mean that, my lord." Meiser looked a bit

green. "What will happen to your cousin after the duke discovers her true identity?"

"That's hardly important." Waving his hand, Lord Tonneson dismissed his agent's concern. "She'll be the Marchioness of Dorset by then and the duke will have no choice but to accept her or else bring scandal upon his name." He pressed his fingers against his chest, thinking of how society had just begun to accept him. As a relative of the Duke of Hammond, he would be welcomed at all the finest parties. He held back the urge to dance around the room again. "Naturally, I will claim no knowledge of my cousin's shocking activities. Since I've only begun to attend social functions, how could I have been expected to know what my headstrong cousin was up to?"

Meiser's gaze darkened. "It's not right, my lord."

"I'm not asking your opinion, Meiser. I'm instructing you as to your duties." Allowing his hand to fall to his side, the earl scowled at his man-of-business. "If you're unable to perform your duties, perhaps it is time I find myself another agent."

"I'm not unable to fulfill my responsibilities, my lord," Meiser began. "I would like to suggest an alternative, one far easier upon Lady Alyssa." Taking a deep breath, Meiser finished, "I offer myself as her husband."

The earl couldn't believe Meiser's offer. "Are you *mad?*" the earl shouted. "Do you honestly think for one minute that I would turn down the chance to marry my cousin to a future duke and give her to you, a commoner, instead?"

"While I concede my offer might at first appear to be undesirable, I believe if you consider Lady Alyssa's feelings, you will—"

"I don't need to consider anything. She is my ward and will do as she's told or suffer the consequences," the earl replied. "All I need to know is if you are capable of arranging for the proxy . . . or shall I hire another agent?"

12

For the past few days she'd hidden in her rooms, praying a miracle would happen. She should have known better. Miracles didn't happen for people like her. No, she had to fight for everything she got.

And, at the moment, she was fighting with herself, pushing back the urge to run as far and as fast as she could from this horrible place.

Yet here she stood, mere feet from the town house that had once been hers . . . in a previous life when her parents were still alive. Now her greedy cousin resided within the stone-covered walls, undoubtedly counting the resale value of all the furniture inside.

Swallowing hard, Alyssa mounted the steps and knocked once. As the door swung open, she was surprised to see the Porter family butler standing before her.

"Lady Alyssa," exclaimed Giles, obviously stunned

to see her. "Oh, my lady, it has been far too long since you've graced this house."

His warm smile and tear-filled eyes touched Alyssa deeply. "How have you been, Giles?"

Sending a quick glance behind him, Giles shrugged once. "As well as could be expected. But far more importantly, how have *you* been, mistress?"

"I've been having a grand adventure," she said with a laugh, not wanting to burden him with the truth.

Leaning closer, Giles whispered, "So we've heard . . . Madam Zora."

Alyssa felt the blood drain from her face. "Does *he* know?"

"His lordship?" At her nod, Giles continued, "Yes."

Pressing a shaky hand to her stomach, Alyssa expelled a deep breath. "Well, then I suppose there is no reason to call upon him. I'd hoped he might be willing to help my sister and me, but if he knows what I've been doing, he'll want to see me even less than he did before."

"I can happily report that you are most incorrect, my lady."

Hope leapt inside of her, but she squashed it down. "Come now, Giles."

"You doubt my word?" He shook his head. "How could you have forgotten that the walls have ears? Nothing goes on in this house that I'm not aware of. Absolutely nothing." Before she had a chance to respond, Giles reached out and guided her into the foyer. "In fact, the earl has been looking for you, so he will be overjoyed to see you."

"But why—"

Pinching his thumb and forefinger, Giles twisted them on his lips.

Bittersweet memories of Giles keeping her childhood secrets assailed her. "*Now's* not the time to lock your lips, Giles."

His eyes twinkled, but he remained silent. Approaching the room that had once been her father's study, Giles tapped softly on the door, before pushing it open and stepping into the room. "My lord, your cousin, the Lady Alyssa, has come to call."

"Alyssa!"

Wincing at the high-pitched voice, Alyssa would have sneaked back out the door if not for Giles's firm grip upon her arm.

"Welcome! Welcome!" exclaimed the earl. "I've been looking all over for you."

With one tug on her arm, Giles propelled Alyssa farther into the room. He patted her arm in a show of support before he left the room, closing the door behind him.

"My dear Alyssa!" boomed the earl. Hurrying toward her with as much speed as his bulk would allow, he wrapped her in an awkward embrace, before pulling back to press a kiss upon each of her cheeks. "You are looking utterly enchanting."

Glancing down at her threadbare dress and worn shoes, Alyssa wondered if his eyesight was going. "Thank you," she murmured. "You are looking fine as well." Fine and very, very round, she decided, immediately feeling guilty for the uncharitable thought.

"You always were so charming," the earl gushed with a smile.

How could he possibly know, since he'd only seen her once . . . on the day he sent her and Calla packing. However, she wasn't about to say anything that might upset him. After all, she needed his help.

"I'm so thankful you came to see me, my dear. I heard you were in town and I've been ever so worried about you."

"You have?" she asked, unable to believe her ears.

"Of course." Pressing a hand to his chest, he looked wounded by her incredulous response. "You are, after all, my ward. When I'd discovered you'd left the cottage I'd secured for you, I was dreadfully worried until I found out you were safe and sound here in London."

"I came to town to seek employment after our stipend was cut," she said in a sickeningly sweet voice.

"Ah, yes, unfortunate business, that, but it couldn't be helped." Clearing his throat, her cousin waved his hand. "All's forgotten now, though. I'm just so glad you're back where you belong."

Alyssa couldn't help but stare at her cousin. Who was this kind, smiling man and what had he done with her gruff, selfish cousin? "Thank you," she said again, at a loss for any other response.

"I'm especially glad because I have some exciting news for you."

Ah, here's the catch, Alyssa thought, bracing herself. The last time her cousin had "exciting news" she'd found herself relegated to a dreary cottage far away in Northumberland. "News? What sort of news?"

"The best sort." Clasping her shoulders, her cousin beamed at her. "You're to be wed."

It was fortunate he had a good hold on her shoulders for Alyssa was quite certain she would have crumpled to the floor otherwise. "What?" she rasped when she could find her voice.

"I've arranged for you to marry a fine, upstanding, *titled* gentleman."

Alyssa stared at him. Did he honestly believe the fact that this nameless, faceless stranger was titled made a difference to her? Breaking free, she walked on unsteady legs to a nearby chair and collapsed into it.

"I knew you'd be pleased," the earl boasted, rocking back on his heels as he tugged down his vest. "The gentleman comes from an impressive family and will soon become the Duke of Hammond."

Her head shot up at the name. It couldn't be! "Who . . . what is the gentleman's name?"

"Ian Fortune, Marquess of Dorset."

Feeling faint, Alyssa closed her eyes and took several deep breaths.

"Overwhelming, is it?" her cousin asked with a chuckle. "I thought you'd be pleased."

Alyssa shook off her incapacitating shock and sat up straight in her chair. "I can't marry him."

"What the devil do you mean by that? Don't you realize who this man's grandfather is? The Duke of bloody Hammond, is who. Of course you're going to marry the blasted marquess!"

Ah, now *here* was the cousin she remembered. "I can't," she repeated.

His eyes narrowing, the earl leaned forward. "Listen to me, my lady I'm-better-than-everyone-else. The agreement has already been struck, the announcement is coming out in tomorrow's paper, and the duke is pleased with the match. All you need to do is smile and be grateful."

"No."

Enraged, the earl struck out with his hand, sending a nearby vase crashing to the floor. "Is your life as a Gypsy fortuneteller so marvelous that you can't bear to give it up?" he sneered.

Her life as a Gypsy fortuneteller was over. That thought sobered Alyssa as she remembered her purpose for coming to call on her cousin in the first place—to ask for his financial support. If she refused to accept marriage to Ian, then she and Calla would be penniless. If she were the only one affected by this decision, it would have been easy. She would have refused to wed him and left with her pride.

But at what cost came that pride?

If she married Ian, she could provide a Season for Calla. In an instant, her sister's life could become carefree and easy. Calla's biggest worry would be whether to wear her pink dress or the blue one.

And if she refused? If she walked out with her pride intact, then Calla would continue to live in a run-down, filth infested flat, worrying about where their next meal was coming from. When put that way, Alyssa knew she had no choice.

Her only regret was that in saving her sister, she condemned Ian to a life with someone he now despised.

"Does Mr. Fortune know about this?"

"Mr. Fortune? Who in the blazes is that?"

Struggling to recall the unfamiliar title, Alyssa finally said, "The Marquess of Donnelly."

"Of *Dorset*," her cousin replied tersely. "Since you're going to be his marchioness, you ungrateful girl, you'd best remember it."

"Does he know?" she repeated.

Rolling his eyes, the earl sighed in frustration. "I don't know and I don't care. The proxy will soon be signed, so whether he knows or not doesn't make one bit of difference." He glared at her. "Now are you going to act the lady when his grace comes here to meet you this afternoon or do I need to give you more incentive?"

"I have my own reasons for accepting this bargain. All of your pitiful threats mean nothing to me," she informed him coldly.

"As long as you accept, I don't care the reasons." Drumming his fingers on the arm of his chair, the earl shook his head. "Such an outspoken creature. I'll consider myself lucky to be well rid of you."

The feeling is mutual, Alyssa said to herself.

He scowled at her. "And one last thing. The duke, who is a very proper fellow with strong notions about keeping his family free from scandal, doesn't know that you once pranced around London pretending to be this Madam Zora person. So, for your own sake, I'd keep mum about it." His tight smile radiated cruelty. "He might be upset to find out . . . especially since he's already agreed to the proxy."

Dread tightened within her. Her future loomed before her as images of Ian glaring down at her burned themselves into her mind. She'd be married to a man who hated her and beholden to a man who would despise her when he found out about her past.

Only the image of Calla, smiling and finally happy, had the power to keep her panic at bay. All she had to do was keep that in mind and she'd be fine.

Perhaps if she thought that often enough, she might actually come to believe it.

"As you can see, we've used the finest materials to build this factory." Caleb Jennings's smile widened as he swept his arm toward the machines filling the large room. "Our venture here has proven to be most profitable for all of our investors."

"Naturally," Ian murmured dryly.

Stepping forward to stand next to Allerby, Peter gazed around the room. "I'm glad we took the time to come here, aren't you, Ian?"

Ian could practically see the silver pounds shimmering in Peter's eyes. "Indeed, as it gives us an opportunity to look at Electrolytic's ledgers." Turning toward Jennings, he asked, "That is, if you don't mind."

"Of course not," Jennings replied immediately.

The response surprised Ian, but he didn't hesitate to accept the man's offer. "Splendid."

"Unfortunately, the accounting ledgers aren't kept at this location." Jennings tugged down on his vest. "However, I'd be more than happy to arrange a meeting for you to review them at a later date."

Lord, the man was smooth. "Surely you don't expect us to make an investment without first looking into the company's profits?"

"I already told you they were quite high."

"As reassuring as that is, I'd prefer more proof than your word."

"Come now, Ian—"

Peter's protest was cut off when Jennings raised his hand. "No, your friend is simply being prudent," he said calmly. "In fact, I admire a man who is so cautious with his money. It's wise men like you, Mr. Fortune, that we want to be a part of our company." Gesturing forward, he directed him across the room. "If you'll accompany me, I'd be pleased to show you the collectors."

Ian followed Jennings toward a large wooden box. Peering inside, he saw the glitter of large chunks of gold.

"Will you look at that," whispered Peter, his eyes wide with excitement.

"Is it real?" Allerby asked as he leaned closer.

"See for yourself." Reaching into the box, Jennings retrieved the largest piece and handed it to Allerby.

Allerby's eyes glittered as he looked at Ian. "Have you ever seen the like?"

Taking the piece of gold, Ian turned it over in his hand. "As a matter of fact, I have. I recently arranged a trade between an American gold mine owner and a jewelry maker for large pieces of gold such as these."

Jennings stiffened. "Are you implying, sir, that I purchased this gold and placed it in these collectors?"

"I'm not *implying* anything," Ian retorted. "I'm stating it. You, Mr. Jennings, are a charlatan out to fleece my friends."

"How dare you," Jennings rasped fiercely.

"Ian," Peter began, "you really shouldn't be making an accusation without proof."

"I'm holding the proof." Lifting the piece of gold, he held it out to Peter. "Do you honestly believe that there are nuggets like this floating around in the ocean? Allow me to offer proof positive." Ian dropped the golden nugget back into the water-filled collector box and the shining chunk headed straight to the bottom. "See? If it sinks, then why would it be floating in the ocean? It makes no sense."

"Because of the waves," Jennings supplied. "The rocking motion sweeps the pieces of gold up off the ocean bottom and into the surf."

Reaching into the box, Ian circled his hand in the water, creating a strong whirlpool effect, yet the gold remained as it lay. "Admirable try, Jennings, but easily proven wrong." Ian flicked the water from his hand. "Would you like to try again?"

Jennings' expression darkened. "No, I would not. I've wasted far too much time with you as it is and I must ask you to leave now."

Noting Peter and Allerby's expressions of disillusionment, Ian nodded briskly. "Very well," he replied. "I do believe we've gotten all the answers we need."

The clock on the mantel ticked loudly as Alyssa sat across from the Duke of Hammond, waiting for him to speak. After his greeting, he'd said not a word. Instead, he'd settled into the chair opposite her and had simply begun to stare at her . . . and stare and stare and—

"Forgive me, your grace," Alyssa said, unable to stand the silence any longer, "but I'm curious as to your reasons behind this proxy."

Laughing nervously, the earl reached out and grabbed hold of her hand, applying pressure. "Alyssa always did have an odd sense of humor."

"I don't believe she was making an attempt at humor," Lord Hammond said coolly.

"You're quite correct." Tugging her hand out of the earl's grasp, Alyssa shifted out of his reach. "Ever since my cousin spoke to me, I haven't been able to understand why your grandson would wish to marry me."

The duke leaned back in his chair. "You haven't? I thought all the ton knew of Ian's desire to marry well."

That much was true, Alyssa knew, for she'd overheard it at quite a few parties. Still, she couldn't get the image of Ian's furious expression from her mind. "When did you speak to your grandson about—"

"I fail to see what difference the timing makes," the duke interrupted.

She couldn't very well explain without revealing herself as Zora, so she tried a different approach. "When he spoke to you about the proxy, are you certain he mentioned me?"

"Sweet Heaven, Alyssa, must you pester his grace with your incessant questions?" the earl asked in exasperation.

"I don't mean to be a pest, my lord, but doesn't this all strike you as a bit odd?"

"Odd?" The earl shook his head. "I know that marriage by proxy isn't commonly used anymore, but it is still considered legal and binding."

"I understand that," Alyssa said as she turned back toward Lord Hammond, "but what I can't fathom is *why* you are using the proxy. After all, Ian and I are both here in London, so if he wished to marry me, why isn't he here?"

Sputtering helplessly, the earl looked to the duke for a response.

"Because Ian was unexpectedly called out of town and I'm uncertain when he will return." For the first time since she'd met him, the duke smiled. "So as his grandfather, it is only right that I handle this matter for him."

It all made perfect sense . . . but Alyssa couldn't help feeling that something was amiss. Still, she'd known all along that she would accept the proxy. This marriage would enable her to provide a Season for Calla as well as financial security. Despite the costs, she couldn't say no. "Very well, your grace, I shall sign the proxy."

The duke tilted his head. "That was never in question, Lady Alyssa," he informed her. "The proxy is being drawn up by the earl's man-of-business as we speak."

Alyssa couldn't believe his arrogance. "Then what, might I ask, was the purpose of this meeting?"

"I wanted to get a look at you."

Straightening in her chair, Alyssa lifted her chin. "Have you seen enough, your grace?"

Instead of calling her out at her impertinence, the

duke actually seemed to ponder the question. Finally, he gave a brisk nod. "You'll do."

Turning in a slow circle, the duke took in the trappings of wealth his grandson had managed to acquire. Expensive vases sat atop elegant tables near exquisite paintings. The place reeked of class and breeding.

Not at all what one would expect from a serving maid's son.

Walking over to the window, the duke gazed out onto the manicured lawns. It had been three days since he'd met with Lady Alyssa and during that time, he'd been very busy. He'd reviewed the proxy, signed it, and delivered it to the earl for him to look over before Alyssa signed it as well. Now all he had to do was tell Ian of his impending nuptials.

Holding back a smile, the duke turned from the glorious view. With this alliance he'd formed for his grandson, the duke knew that the blot on their family history would be all but erased from the memories of the ton. And if the boy was truly obliging, Ian would produce great-grandchildren for him, and for the dukedom.

Yes, everything was falling into place.

"If you've come to tell me I need to accept your title, you've wasted your time."

Gritting his teeth, the duke refused to rise to the bait . . . however tempting. "I've come on important business, it's true, but not to discuss your bullheaded refusal to accept your birthright."

"Ah, so I take it this is simply a social call," Ian

drawled as he strolled into the study. "Might I offer you a brandy?"

Nodding crisply, Lord Hammond studied the off-spring of his only son . . . and smiled inwardly. Oh, he'd been a fool to ignore the boy for so long. Indeed, Ian would breed the *true* heir. Accepting the drink, he sat in a chair opposite his grandson.

"Shall we exchange pleasantries and pretend that we're a happy family or would you like to get to the point of your visit?"

The boy's sharp wit pleased him no end, but he wasn't about to show it. "Don't be short with me, pup. You should show some respect."

Bowing his head, Ian acknowledged the retort. "My apologies, your grace. You are quite correct. It is hardly the way to treat a guest in my home . . . invited or oth-erwise."

"Quite the charming fellow, I see," said the duke in frosty tones.

At least the whelp had the good grace to flush. Somewhat mollified, the duke continued, "Now as to why I called upon you today—"

Before he could finish his explanation, the duke cried out in disgust, "What the . . . Good God!"

There, right in his crystal tumbler, sat a hideous frog, blinking up at him from amidst the amber liquid.

"Oh, for God's sake, I thought we'd caught all of these buggers," grumbled Ian as he snatched the crea-ture up. Walking over to the window, he raised the pane enough to toss out the offensive frog, then re-sumed his seat. "You were saying?"

"A frog jumps into my glass from nowhere, you nonchalantly pick him up and toss him out the window without batting an eye and you expect me to just continue with our conversation?"

A grin split Ian's face. "That about sums it up."

The duke shook his head in annoyance. Lifting his glass to take a sip, the duke stopped halfway to his lips as he remembered the frog sitting in the brandy.

"Allow me to fetch you a new drink," Ian said, plucking the glass out of his grandfather's hand.

Accepting the fresh brandy, the duke took a sip. "Now if I place the glass upon the table, will another frog leap into it?"

"I can't make any promises one way or the other."

"Then I shall simply have to take my chances." Placing the glass firmly upon the table, the duke tapped his fingers against the arm of the chair. "However, some things can't be left to chance, Ian."

Crossing his arms, Ian settled back against his desk. "We're no longer talking about frogs, are we?"

"I've arranged for you to marry."

Ian's drink sloshed over the side of his glass as he jerked it away from his mouth. "You *what?*"

"Everything has already been arranged," the duke continued, ignoring his grandson's reaction. "The announcement will appear in tomorrow's paper. I signed the proxy in your stead."

"If you believe I'll go along with your scheming for even one minute, you're seriously deluding yourself."

"But there is nothing for you to go along with, Ian. It's already done." Leaning forward, he tried to convince his grandson that this was in his best interest. "The young lady you're to wed is from a good family with a long, respectable heritage. I've investigated her lineage very carefully and it is unmarred by scandal. The Tonneson line is well-respected."

"I don't believe you did this," Ian murmured, thrusting his hand through his hair. "I'll have the agreement invalidated."

"That would mean going through the House of Lords . . . a place where I am quite influential," Hammond added, leaving the implication unspoken. His grandson would find little assistance there. "Don't be so stubborn, Ian. This is for your own good. Lady Alyssa Porter is—"

Ian started in his chair.

"I see you're pleased by the news. As you know, she is the daughter of the former Earl of Tonneson, and she's exactly the sort of woman you should marry. Nothing at all like that Gypsy trash you seemed to enjoy so much."

An instant later, bitter laughter flowed from Ian, the sound jarring the duke to his bones. "You interfering old fool," he rasped. "You don't realize what you've just done."

"I've saved you from disgracing yourself with that Madam Zora person is what I've done."

"Lady Alyssa Porter is Madam Zora."

13

"She's *what?*"

"Alyssa Porter and Madam Zora are one and the same." Crossing his arms, Ian sat back and waited for the duke's reaction.

"Impossible."

"I fear it's not." He narrowed his gaze. "It appears that this time you are captured in your own web of manipulation, *Grandfather*. Didn't you tell me the announcement would be made tomorrow?" Bitter glee filled him as he saw the color drain from the old man's face. Damn the arrogant fool for aligning him with the one woman he never wanted to see again.

"She can't be. I checked her background."

"But did you check her present?" He took a sip of his brandy. "You were so eager to check out her past, to make certain that there weren't any skeletons rattling around, you forgot to look into her current escapades."

A moan escaped the duke.

"I can picture it now," Ian said grandly, spreading his hands wide. "You walking into a ball with my bride by proxy on your arm and introducing her as the newest Fortune bride." He dropped his hands into his lap. "Then everyone looks at her, expecting to see a lady of the highest caliber, and instead they see their little Gypsy fortuneteller, Madam Zora."

The duke closed his eyes for a long moment.

"Perhaps she could have special calling cards made up. They could read 'Alyssa Fortune, Marchioness of Dorset, formerly known as Madam Zora.' " Tilting his head to the side, Ian affected a pleasant expression. "Doesn't that sound wonderful?"

His once pale face growing flush, the duke scowled at his grandson. "Don't be glib, Ian. We'll figure a way out of this mess."

"I don't plan on figuring anything out, your grace." Leaning forward, Ian said softly, "It's not my mess to clean up. And to think you were so eager to keep me from bringing scandal down upon the Fortune name." Rising, Ian smiled coolly down at his grandfather. "Congratulations, your grace, you managed to do it all by yourself."

"You deceived me."

Alyssa blinked once. "I did nothing of the sort," she replied calmly.

The Duke of Hammond paced before her, his hands clasped behind his back, his fury obvious. "You failed to mention your recent . . . occupation."

"You never bothered to ask me any questions about myself," she reminded him. "You and my illustrious cousin had arranged everything between the two of you."

"Humph," the duke snorted.

"I . . . I'll go check on the tea," stuttered the earl before he scurried out of the room, leaving Alyssa to face the duke's anger alone.

"Sniveling pantywaist," scoffed the duke beneath his breath.

Hearing the insult, Alyssa couldn't keep her lips from twitching.

"What's so blasted amusing about this?"

"About this situation, nothing." A side of her mouth quirked upward. "But I found your colorful description of my cousin most entertaining."

For the first time since he'd entered the room, the duke stopped his pacing and stared down at her. "Are you afraid of me?"

She considered his question for a moment. "No. Should I be? If I'm missing something important, please feel free to inform me."

The duke scowled at her. "You've got a sharp tongue, young lady."

"True enough," she conceded, "and it's only bound to get sharper, as I use it so very often."

Lifting his brows, the duke sat down directly across from her. "You'd better learn to curb it," he advised sternly. "The future Duchess of Hammond can't behave in such a manner."

A retort rose to her lips, but Alyssa held it back as

she remembered that the duke would help her and Calla. She couldn't afford to be cheeky.

Lord Hammond leaned back in his chair as an expression of satisfaction settled upon his face. "Very good," he said, his condescending tone making Alyssa grit her teeth. "Now I want to know why the devil you would pretend to be this Madam Zora person when you are a well-bred lady."

Before Alyssa could answer, her cousin peeked into the room. "I've ordered the tea and it shan't be but a moment." He rounded the door, yet retained a firm grasp upon the door handle. "If you need more time alone, I shall—"

"Stop your dithering and come take your seat," ordered the duke. "Your ward is about to explain why she pretended to be a Gypsy fortuneteller . . . and after she's finished, you can tell me why you allowed such nonsense."

The earl paled as he sank into his chair. "I *didn't* allow it. I didn't even *know* about her masquerade," he replied weakly.

Lord Hammond's look of disgust spoke volumes. Turning toward her, he speared her with his glare. "I'm still awaiting my answer."

"As to why I became a Gypsy?" Alyssa unflinchingly met his gaze. "I pretended to be Madam Zora because—"

"She was bored," the earl interjected forcefully.

Stunned, Alyssa listened to her cousin elaborate on the ridiculous tale.

"She's always been a headstrong child and after her

parents passed on, she became a bit wild." The earl gave Lord Hammond a reassuring smile. "But she's ready to settle down now and become a proper wife." He glanced at her. "Isn't that right, Alyssa?"

While she wanted to do nothing more than deny her cousin's claim, Alyssa knew that she'd be wiser to agree. "Yes," she said, forcing the word past the lump in her throat.

Beaming at Lord Hammond, the earl slapped a hand on his knee. "Just as I told you," he crowed. "And now that she's gotten these flights of fancy out of her system, Alyssa will make a fine wife for your grandson."

"Perhaps, but I still need to devise a plan to overcome the inevitable marring of her reputation, once the ton realizes they've been duped." Tapping his fingers against the arm of his chair, Lord Hammond remained silent for a moment. "I believe we should follow Ian's recommendation and hold a ball to introduce Lady Alyssa."

At the mention of Ian's name, Alyssa straightened in her chair. "You've spoken about this with Ian?"

"Of course I have, gel," the duke replied sharply.

"When?" Alyssa asked. "I thought he was out of town and not expected to return in the near future . . . which is the reason for a proxy in the first place."

"He returned to town unexpectedly; however, after a quick visit with me, he was off again." Lifting his chin, the duke paused for a moment, giving her a hard stare. "I don't appreciate having to explain myself."

Before Alyssa could reply to the duke's statement, her cousin leapt into the fray. "Of course not, your grace," he said soothingly as he shot Alyssa a dark look. "I assure you that Alyssa will curb her tongue."

How dare her cousin speak for her! "I have no intention of—"

"Come, my dear Alyssa, don't get overwrought," the earl said, leaning forward to pat her shoulder. "You must remember Calla."

At the mention of her sister, Alyssa stilled, sensing the implied threat. "What does my sister have to do with any of this?"

"I'd say quite a bit, wouldn't you?" he replied smoothly. "After all, she looks to you to set an example . . . among other things."

Alyssa knew all too well what her cousin meant by *other things*. Her sister depended upon her for everything . . . and if she had to bide her temper around these two overbearing men in order to continue to provide for Calla and herself, then so be it.

"Now, as I was saying before you interrupted me," the duke began, "I will host a ball to introduce Lady Alyssa to society as Ian's bride by proxy."

"But the moment I arrive, everyone will recognize me as Madam Zora," Alyssa pointed out.

"Naturally, . . . which is why we'll make that announcement on the invitation."

"S-s-s-surely you jest," stammered the earl.

"Not at all." Lord Hammond smoothed down his vest. "If we inform society before the ball, then there won't be a sense of shock when Lady Alyssa arrives."

Alyssa considered the duke's argument for a moment. "That's true," she conceded finally.

"Of course." The duke's unbelievably arrogant remark made Alyssa smile. "However, I believe we must also be prepared to explain that your mother was of Gypsy descent."

Her smile disappeared. "But my mother was *French*, not Romany."

"Perhaps she used to be, but from this moment onward, she was Romany." Lord Hammond held up his hands to halt Alyssa's protest. "It is the only way to handle this matter." Leaning forward, he hammered his point home. "Think on it for a moment. If you waltz into the affair and tell everyone you doled out advice on a lark, you will garner nothing but ill feelings toward you. Yet, if you announce that you were merely exercising your birthright, no one will feel as if you've swindled them . . . even though you hid your true identity from them."

Though it galled her, Alyssa had to admit Lord Hammond was correct in his assessment. "Very well," she murmured, "though I cannot say I am pleased."

The duke's eyes narrowed. "Are you always this difficult?"

"No, your grace," Alyssa replied sweetly. "I'm usually far worse."

"Then we shall have to do something about that," the duke muttered. "What you need is someone to remind you of the gentler manner befitting a lady of breeding." Snapping his fingers, Lord Hammond exclaimed, "And I know just the lady to do it." His eyes gleamed as he continued, "Tomorrow I shall make arrangements for you to live with my sister, Lady

Eleanor Fortune, in her town house. She can act as your chaperone and your mentor in the feminine arts. I know this is highly unusual, but I don't feel I have any other choice. You must learn to behave like a Duchess, so you will study my sister's every move while under her roof and emulate her behavior." Pausing, Lord Hammond glanced at the earl. "That is, if you have no objection to this plan, Tonneson."

"No, no, your grace."

Alyssa smirked as her cousin tripped over his own tongue in his hurry to agree with the duke's plan.

"After all, without a wife to assist me, I fear I lack the ability to raise two young ladies," the earl added.

No, what her cousin lacked was the willingness to spend one farthing on their care, Alyssa thought dryly, not missing the fact that no one bothered to ask her opinion on the matter. Still, she wasn't about to argue.

"Then it is suitable to everyone." The duke eyed her attire. "Are all your gowns so dreadful?"

Alyssa couldn't help but smile at the question. "More so, your grace."

Scowling at her, the duke tapped his hand against the arm of his chair. "Then the first order of business is to obtain a suitable wardrobe for you."

"And for my sister as well?" Alyssa asked hopefully.

"Certainly. It would hardly do to have you well-groomed and have your sister running about town in rags," Lord Hammond scoffed.

Whatever his reason, if it provided Calla with new gowns, Alyssa was happy. "I quite agree."

Scribbling an address on one of his calling cards, the duke passed the card to her. "Splendid. I shall send a note around to my sister and tell her to expect you tomorrow."

"And what of our things?" Alyssa asked.

Once again, the duke's gaze skipped over her. "Do you possess anything of value?"

"Indeed, I do," she assured him firmly.

Sighing loudly, the duke frowned at her. "Are you determined to be difficult?"

Alyssa simply laughed in response.

Leaving the cool night air to step into her flat, Alyssa realized that tomorrow, she and Calla would leave this poverty behind. In the span of a day, their entire world had changed, she thought, as she made her way up to the small room she shared with her sister.

"Alyssa!" exclaimed Calla as she jumped off the bed they'd shared for the past few months. "Where have you been?"

"I'm sorry to be so late. I know you must have been worried."

"I was," Calla said in a rush. "I didn't know why you were so long."

"Something utterly shocking happened when I called upon our cousin." She smiled at her sister, finding pleasure in the thought of her in satins and lace. "I've some news."

"As do I." Bending down, Calla retrieved a stack of letters from the bed. "All these letters arrived in this morning's post."

"Really?" Taking them out of her sister's hand, she began to peruse the missives, each one of them an invitation for Madam Zora to attend one function after another. "But I'm certain everyone realizes I am a fraud now that the curse didn't come true."

"That's just it, Alyssa, the curse *did* come true!" A happy smile brightened Calla's face as she danced around the shabby room. "According to a letter from Lady Covington, Mr. Fortune's home was positively beset with a horde of frogs. She saw it for herself when she called on him."

All these surprises couldn't be good for a person, Alyssa thought, as she sank into a chair. "But how?"

"I don't know and I don't care," Calla replied with a laugh. "All that matters is we're saved. You can continue to be Madam Zora and I shall continue to sew your costumes."

"We *are* saved, Calla, but not by this news." Clasping her sister's hand, she urged Calla to sit as well. "The Duke of Hammond has arranged for us to go live with his sister in her wonderful town house."

"Why? Who is the Duke of Hammond?"

Alyssa decided to sugar-coat her description of the crotchety duke. "He is a well-mannered, elderly gentleman who shall provide us with new wardrobes and—"

A look of horror swept over Calla's face. "Are you marrying an old duke?"

"No, his grandson." Taking a deep breath, she committed herself firmly to this arrangement. "You know him as Ian Fortune."

Calla's mouth formed an "o" as she gasped in delight. "You're going to marry Ian?" A sigh escaped her. "How romantic. I *knew* he had feelings for you . . . despite that tiff you had in the hallway."

"It was more than a tiff," Alyssa replied, squelching a wave of guilt over her part in deceiving Ian. "I don't want you to have the wrong idea. Ian and I are to be married by proxy. His grandfather made the offer for Ian."

"How *utterly* romantic," Calla said in a breathy voice. "I always knew he was your true love."

Smiling over her sister's sentiment, Alyssa patted Calla's hand. "You are wise beyond your years," she remarked with a laugh.

"True, so true," Calla said, dramatically pressing a hand against her heart.

Alyssa stood and began to pack some of their parents' treasures. "Now why don't you help me with this?"

"All right," Calla said, but she remained seated. "Alyssa?"

Hearing the thoughtful note in her sister's voice, Alyssa paused at her task. "Yes, Calla?"

"I was just curious, but . . ." With her eyes glowing in excitement, Calla had never looked more like a fourteen-year-old girl. "Just how many dresses can I have?"

Laughing gaily, Alyssa knew she'd made the right decision.

14

"Ever since we returned from Bath, you refuse to leave this house," Peter said accusingly, propping his boots on Ian's desk. "You've become a recluse this past week!"

"What I've become is extremely busy." Glancing up from his piles of ledgers, he looked pointedly at Peter's boots. "Do you mind?"

"Of course not," Peter replied, keeping his feet right where they were.

Reaching out, Ian shoved Peter's boots off the desk.

"See? There's a perfect example. You're growing more staid every day."

"Pardon me for not wishing my account books to be stained with the dirt from your boots." Tossing down his pen, Ian leaned back in his chair and gave his friend his full attention. "All right, then, Peter, what is it you'd like from me?"

"Since your esteemed grandpapa is throwing a ball

in honor of your marriage, I thought it would be most amusing to attend with you."

The mention of the duke made Ian's stomach knot. "I already told you I don't want to hear mention of the proxy here in my home."

"Ah, but I didn't mention it, I only remarked upon the ball . . . which naturally led me to recall the reason for the entire affair," Peter remarked blandly.

"Convenient," drawled Ian. "I fear I shall have to disappoint you, as I have no plans to attend."

Peter's mouth dropped open. "You can't be serious."

"Perfectly."

"But . . . but . . ." stammered the normally unflappable Peter. "But your future wife is to make her social debut."

"Bully for her."

"This is your bride-to-be!" Waving a hand, Peter glanced at Ian's desk. "While it's perfectly obvious that she doesn't reside here with you, everyone—including myself—believes it's only a matter of time before you actually wed her." He shook his head. "Though, I must tell you, Ian, by all rights I should still be quite peeved at you for keeping her identity a secret."

Ian still couldn't get past the notion that his grandfather was hosting a ball in Alyssa's honor. "Doesn't he realize that everyone will recognize her?" Ian rasped, disturbed at the thought of Alyssa being publicly mocked.

Grinning, Peter swung his leg over the arm of his chair. "I wouldn't concern myself overly much with that worry. The duke has already addressed the situation."

"How?"

"I take it you haven't seen the invitation."

Suspicions arose within Ian as he pushed back on his chair and retrieved the mound of unanswered invitations piled on his desk behind him. He flipped through the envelopes until he found the one from the duke.

Tearing the invitation open, Ian scanned the note, unable to believe his eyes. Immediately, he imagined the humiliation such an invitation would cause Alyssa. He read it again, hoping the invitation would improve with the second reading.

His Grace, Regis Fortune, the Duke of Hammond, invites you to attend a formal ball in honor of Lady Alyssa Porter, formerly known as Madam Zora, the future bride of his grandson, the Marquess of Dorset.

"Dear God, has the old man gone insane?" rasped Ian. "How could he do this to her?"

True, Ian was still angry with Alyssa, but his raw fury had calmed over the past month. And while he might want nothing further to do with her, that didn't mean his grandfather had the right to completely humiliate her.

"I thought the duke's phrasing a bit rough, but other than that, it is a fine invitation," Peter said from behind him.

Ian barely heard his friend. When he'd tossed the

suggestion to send out an announcement declaring Lady Alyssa Porter to be none other than Madam Zora, he'd never imagined his grandfather would actually do it. "What could he be thinking?"

"I don't know," Peter admitted, "but I can tell you everyone who is anyone will be there."

"That's precisely what I'm afraid of," Ian said grimly, determined to clean up this mess he'd inadvertently created.

"Calla, you need to stand still!"

Hearing the exasperation in Lady Eleanor's voice, Alyssa smiled as she stepped into Calla's room. "I don't believe Calla knows *how* to stand in one spot for longer than ten seconds."

"Then she'll just have to learn," pronounced Lady Eleanor as she gave Calla a stern look. "Or it will mean no treat after supper."

Alyssa decided to give Calla more incentive to stand still. "Which would be quite a shame as I overheard Cook mention she's making a fruit tart for dessert."

Immediately, Calla snapped her shoulders back and stood as still as a statue.

Chuckling, Lady Eleanor winked at Alyssa. "It never ceases to amaze me how well Calla responds if given the right incentive."

"I can still *hear* even when I stand still," grumbled Calla.

Alyssa laughed along with Lady Eleanor.

"Of course you can, darling," murmured Lady Eleanor, patting her gray hair, "which is why I shall cease nattering on about you and focus on fitting you for this gown." Moving over to the modiste, Lady Eleanor began to discuss different design options.

Wandering closer, Alyssa reached out to finger the material draped around Calla. "This shall make a lovely gown."

"Alyssa, I never thought I'd say this . . ." Pausing, Calla glanced around to ensure Lady Eleanor wasn't nearby. ". . . but I think I have enough gowns now. Must I stand here for yet another fitting?"

"Yes," Alyssa replied without a moment's hesitation. "Lady Eleanor has been so kind to us, taking us into her home and making us feel welcome, so if she enjoys ordering new gowns for us, we shall indulge her."

A huge sigh escaped Calla. "I was afraid you'd say that."

"Of course . . . and you agree with me, even if you won't admit it. Neither one of us wants to do something that would upset Lady Eleanor."

Calla nodded glumly.

"Besides, it's only fair that you have your turn with Madam Claire," Alyssa said with a smile. "I was poked and prodded for five days."

Calla scrunched her nose at Alyssa.

"Alyssa, my sweet, why don't you go take a rest?" Having finished conferring with the modiste, Lady Eleanor moved toward them, her lined face curved into a smile. "You want to look fresh for this evening's festivities."

The ball. Alyssa's stomach tightened. "Indeed I do," she murmured, before bidding farewell to Lady

Eleanor and Calla. Shutting the drawing room door behind her, Alyssa hurried up to her bedchamber.

Once in the privacy of her room, Alyssa sank down upon the bed as her nerves danced in an odd mixture of excitement and dread. Tonight she would face the ton as Lady Alyssa Porter, affianced to Lord Ian Fortune, Marquess of Dorset.

Worse yet, she would meet Ian for the first time since he'd stormed away from her. Part of her feared this was all some horrible mistake and the lovely dream she'd lived in this past week would disappear.

She was still uncertain as to *why* Ian would wish to marry her, so she'd feel much better after she spoke with Ian this evening. Then, after she'd reassured herself, she could revel in Calla's happiness.

Ignoring his qualms, Ian strode boldly into White's, almost daring the servants flanking the door to stop him.

"My lord," murmured the doorman, bowing his head in greeting.

Surprise flickered through Ian, but he wasn't about to question his luck. The crinkling of newspapers and quiet murmur of conversation mingled with the scent of fine cigars and imported brandy, creating an atmosphere of gentlemanly refinement.

A foreign world to Ian.

Dismissing his moment's hesitation, Ian marched boldly into the room, glancing around for the duke. Spying his grandfather in the corner, enjoying a private moment with a brandy and the paper, Ian headed directly for him. "What is the meaning of this invitation?"

Eyeing the card in Ian's hand, the duke slowly folded his newspaper, laying it across his lap, before looking up at Ian. "Good afternoon to you too."

"I am far too concerned about your actions to bother with polite exchanges," Ian replied, refusing to feel like an ill-mannered youth.

"The least you could do is take a seat instead of towering over me. Might I remind you, this is a *gentleman's* club."

Waving off the servant who came to see to his needs, Ian took the leather high-backed chair next to the duke.

"There." The duke folded his hands on his lap. "That's much better. At least this way I won't get a crick in my neck when I look at you."

Ian went straight to the heart of the matter. "Why did you deliberately expose Alyssa in your invitation?"

"Expose her?" The duke lifted his brows. "How?"

"By tacking on that line about her former identity," Ian explained. "It will be bad enough when she has to enter that room and people realize who she is . . ."

"Yes, Ian, it will be bad." Leaning forward, the duke lowered his voice even further. "Which is precisely why I chose to add it to my announcement. That way, the gossips will have a chance to talk about her *before* the ball, hopefully lessening their nastiness in Alyssa's presence."

Stunned, Ian sat back in his chair.

"Oh, she'll still have to brazen it out, but that gel's got grit. She'll be fine."

Shaking his head, Ian sought answers to the multitude of questions swirling around in his mind. "Why are you doing this? I thought that above all you wished to avoid scandal. You wouldn't even speak to my father after he married my mother. Yet here you are introducing Alyssa, Madam Zora, to the ton." He shook his head again. "While I applaud your decision, I just don't understand it."

"I handled your father's situation completely wrong, I know that now, but I've learned from my mistake. I won't make the same error twice."

His grandfather's admission left him speechless.

"If I had the chance to go back and do it all over again, I would. At least that way I'd have been able to mold you into a proper duke." Shrugging lightly, the duke met his gaze. "Now the only thing left to do is to ensure you marry well and strengthen your tainted blood with that of a noblewoman. Then I can see to it that any of your offspring receive the training befitting a duke of the realm."

The duke's words squashed the spark of hope inside of Ian. "Foolish me for not understanding your intentions."

"Indeed. I believe I have always made my plans perfectly clear," his grandfather replied briskly.

"Ah, yes, but there is one small matter you forgot in all of your scheming." Leaning forward, Ian stared into his grandfather's face. "You need my cooperation in order to accomplish your goals."

A corner of the duke's mouth tilted upward. "I don't believe that will be difficult, as everyone in society knows of your desire to wed a titled lady. All I did was aid you in your search."

"Listen to me well, old man," Ian rasped. "I will not be your puppet. You can't manipulate me into doing your bidding." He rose to his feet and stared down at his grandfather. "So know this, when you pass on, the title falls to me . . . and I shall enjoy placing a few more stains upon it."

Smiling as the duke blanched, Ian strode from the room.

15

Music swelled from inside the duke's house as Alyssa, Calla, and Lady Eleanor mounted the front steps. Taking a deep breath, Alyssa crossed the threshold.

"Lady Alyssa, Lady Calla, Eleanor," greeted Lord Hammond as he approached them. "Welcome to my home."

"Thank you, your grace," Alyssa murmured. "It is most kind of you to hold this ball."

"Nonsense," he scoffed with a shake of his head. "It's the only logical step in securing you a place in society."

How foolish of her to have thought the duke had any altruistic reasons behind his actions. "Of course," Alyssa murmured softly.

"Then let's introduce you." Reaching for her hand, he tucked it onto his forearm before she could utter a word. "Eleanor, you follow with Calla," he ordered.

"Wait, I—"

"You what? There is no comfortable way out of this mess for anyone, so we must simply brazen it out." The duke stared down at her. "Now, lift your chin and remember you are the daughter of an earl."

Feeling flush from anger, Alyssa returned Lord Hammond's glare. "I was going to ask if Ian had arrived yet."

The duke hesitated for a moment. "No," he finally said.

"Oh," Alyssa murmured, wishing Ian had already arrived. It would be far easier to face the ton with him at her side, she realized suddenly. "I was just wondering."

"Fine," the duke snapped, "now get some backbone and stop looking like you're ready for someone to take a crop to you."

Annoyance flooded her. "There is no reason to—"

"That's it. That's the way I want you to look." The duke nodded once. "Much better."

"I'm happy to have pleased you, your grace," she returned dryly as she kept in step next to Lord Hammond.

A hush fell over the crowd when the duke pulled them to a stop on the top stair. "Ladies and gentlemen, thank you for gracing my home," the duke began. "As you all know, this is a very special night for the Fortune family." Stepping back, he straightened out his arm and nudged Alyssa in front of him. "It is with great pleasure that I introduce the future Marchioness of Dorset, Lady Alyssa Porter."

A dull roar of hushed whispers flew across the room. It was all Alyssa could do to remain standing calmly while everyone spoke about her.

Releasing his hold upon Alyssa, the duke lifted both

of his hands, the movement immediately causing the crowd to quiet. "You all know her as Madam Zora, for when she first came to town, she decided to explore her heritage." He dropped his arms to his side. "Lady Alyssa is of Gypsy descent on her mother's side and fortunetelling is in her blood. Luckily for all of us, she decided to share her gift." The duke paused to look around the room, his gaze touching upon his guests. "I'm quite certain you will all join me in welcoming her to society now that she has decided to accept her rightful place."

For a moment, the room remained silent, causing Alyssa to shift on her feet. Her breath caught in her throat when Lady Covington stepped forward.

"I, for one, bid you welcome, Lady Alyssa," she said in grand tones, knowing full well that as a premier hostess of the ton, her pronouncement would sway many others.

Smiling in thanks, Alyssa curtsied to the grand dame. "My thanks, Lady Covington."

And as everyone else pressed forward to welcome her, Alyssa glanced over at the duke, noticing his satisfied smile. She lost sight of him as people swarmed around her.

"Was your mother raised by the Gypsies?"

"Did she teach you the art of fortunetelling?"

"Will you still tell our fortunes?"

Feeling a bit like a unique specimen in the zoo, Alyssa struggled to answer all of their questions. It was a challenge as she mingled the truth with fabrications, weaving a complex tale that she prayed she'd remember tomorrow.

* * *

Drawing on his cigar, Ian lounged upon a garden bench, watching the couples waltz past the brightly lit windows. He hadn't intended to come to his grandfather's house, but he found that he couldn't stay away. Not that he hadn't tried. Even his work, a pastime he usually lost himself in, couldn't take his mind away from this party, from Alyssa's introduction to society as his future wife.

His future wife.

Lord, he'd tried to ignore that idiotic proxy his grandfather thought to force upon him. Ian intended to petition the courts to declare the agreement invalid, but he simply hadn't gotten around to it yet. A man couldn't neglect his business, after all, and he'd already spent far too much time away from his books because he'd been looking into the Electrolytic Marine Mining Company for Peter and Allerby.

How ironic it was that while his grandfather had indeed arranged for a titled lady to wed, he'd unwittingly chosen the one woman who had deceived him. Though he'd never intended to marry for love, he'd certainly expected that there be trust between him and his wife. A gentleman had the right to expect *that* much, didn't he?

Ian's thoughts skittered to a halt when Alyssa stopped in front of a window, gazing out into the garden. Though he knew the shadows hid him from her view, he still wondered if she could somehow sense he was there. As he watched, her shoulders lifted and released as if she'd taken a deep, calming breath.

But it was her expression that called to him.

For only a moment, she allowed her smile to fade,

giving him a glimpse into her true feelings. A quick peek was all he got before she took another bracing breath, smoothed her features, and turned around once again.

Yet that moment was all he needed to shake him to his core.

His bold Gypsy had looked . . . defeated.

Without conscious thought, Ian tossed down his cigar, grinding it out beneath his boot heel, and began to stride toward the town house.

She felt like screaming.

Instead, Alyssa turned toward the window, staring out into the dark night. Catching sight of the glow from a cigar, she wished she might join that gentleman in his solitude, escaping the unending questions just for a moment. It seemed the ton still couldn't get enough of her. Not that Alyssa could blame them. For if she'd heard Lord Hammond's colorful story about someone else, she would have been fascinated as well. As soon as the duke left her side, the gossips had descended with their thousand and one questions. Was her mother truly a descendant of a powerful Gypsy? Did she know her curse had come true? Why had she cursed her own husband-to-be?

But the worst question by far was "Where is the Marquess of Dorset?"

How could she answer that one? Oh, Lord Dorset is simply unable to attend. Or perhaps she should give them the truth—that she had no idea where Lord Dorset was at present.

Oh, yes, that response would receive a wonderful reaction.

"My lady?"

Recognizing Lady Alridge's voice, Alyssa sighed once, before fixing a pleasant expression onto her face and turning to face the woman. "Lady Alridge," she said smoothly. "How are you this evening?"

Just then Alyssa became aware of a flurry of whispers rushing through the ballroom. "Oh, my dear Lady Alyssa," murmured the woman beside her. "He's come. He's here."

Who was here? Alyssa wondered, glancing around. "I'm not certain who you're speaking of, Lady Alridge," Alyssa returned, praying she didn't sound as horribly bored as she felt.

"Why, your future husband, of course."

Anticipation rushed through Alyssa as she watched the large crowd part like the Red Sea before Moses as Ian approached her. She hadn't realized until this moment just how much she'd wanted him to come this evening.

"Good evening, my lady," he murmured, holding out his hand.

Flustered, Alyssa gave him her hand, watching in disbelief as he pressed a kiss to her palm. The last time she'd seen him, he'd been glaring at her in anger, then he'd had his grandfather arrange a proxy, now he was acting as if nothing amiss had ever happened between them. Confused, Alyssa found herself uncertain of how to address Ian. "My lord," she returned finally, unable to stop her voice from cracking.

Straightening, he smiled at her. "Please forgive me my tardy arrival," he said in a slightly raised voice. "I meant to be here to claim the first dance."

She was too surprised to answer.

"While I missed that opportunity, I am pleased to see that I've arrived in time to claim this waltz," Ian continued brightly.

Her heart raced as Ian escorted her onto the dance floor and pulled her into his arms.

For Alyssa, the night had suddenly become magic.

16

*B*reathless, Alyssa waltzed around the room, held safely within Ian's embrace. Though she didn't want to ruin the rapport between them, she was unable to remain silent any longer. "I was hoping you'd come this evening," she murmured with a shy smile.

Glancing down at her, he admitted, "I hadn't planned on attending."

"Why did you, then?" she asked, further confused by his response.

"I don't know." His jaw tightened as he looked away. Exhaling, he returned his attention onto her. "Even after I'd arrived, I had no intention of claiming a dance . . . yet I couldn't bear to see you looking so defeated," he admitted softly.

Defeated? Alyssa didn't understand what he was talking about until she remembered what she'd been thinking as she'd looked out the window. "You were in the garden just now," she murmured.

His eyes flared in surprise. "How did you know?"

"The same way you knew what I was feeling."

"My, aren't we the perceptive pair," he said with a smile.

Alyssa said the first thing that popped into her head. "Perfectly matched."

His eyes flared once again, but this time with a surge of heat. Dropping his gaze onto her mouth, Ian pulled her closer to him, sending shivers of yearning down Alyssa's spine.

Desire, fierce and hot, flickered in his expression as his arm tightened around her even more. "Alyssa," he murmured in a low husky voice.

The sound of her name upon his lips made her catch her breath. Unmindful of the eyes fixed upon them, she tilted her head back, leaving her neck exposed to his hungry gaze.

The music ended and yet Ian didn't release her. He devoured her with his gaze and Alyssa eagerly welcomed his attention.

Loud clapping made them both blink. "Join me in welcoming my grandson, the Marquess of Dorset, to my little affair this evening," boomed the duke.

Ian's expression froze in an instant, the ice on his face extinguishing the desire that had lain there just moments before. Stiffening, he stepped back, allowing his arms to drop from around Alyssa.

She reached out to him, but Ian took another step backward, increasing the distance between them. All of his attention was fixed upon the duke, who stood at the edge of the dance floor. The tension between the two men was palpable, until finally Ian broke the silence. "No need to welcome me, your grace. I simply came to claim a dance. I have no intention of staying." Glancing at Alyssa, he amended his reply. "That is, I am most disappointed that I will be unable to remain, but other obligations demand my presence."

It was a pitiful excuse and everyone in the room knew it.

"Excuse me," Ian murmured politely, bowing to Alyssa, before turning on his heel and marching from the room.

"You were *marvelous!*" crowed the duke in an uncharacteristic display of excitement.

Even in the dark interior of the carriage, Alyssa could see the gleam in Lord Hammond's eyes. "How so?" she asked quietly as they made their way back to Lady Eleanor's townhouse.

"The way you handled yourself tonight spoke well of your breeding." Settling back against the cushioned seat opposite her, the Duke nodded firmly. "I'm confident everyone believed my tale about your wanting to explore your Gypsy heritage, so now you appear to be exotic rather than deceitful."

"Thank you . . . I think," Alyssa murmured. Since Lady Eleanor had taken Calla home earlier in the evening, Alyssa decided to use this moment of privacy with Lord Hammond. "I don't understand some of the things Ian said to me this evening."

Lord Hammond stilled. "Such as?"

"He told me he hadn't been planning on attending this evening, but I don't understand why, as this ball was in honor of our marriage by proxy. It was as if—" She broke off as the truth of the situation struck her. "He never agreed to the proxy, did he?"

For a moment, the duke hesitated. "Don't be ridiculous," he scoffed.

But the duke's hesitation had spoken volumes, drowning out his protest. Her stomach lurched as she absorbed this blow. "You arranged this proxy without even speaking to him," she whispered, guessing accurately. "Why did you do it? And why, for Heaven's sake, did you choose me?"

Alyssa was uncertain if the duke was even going to answer her. Finally, he broke the silence. "I was simply helping to guide him on making the best choice. When I approached you, I'd already ensured that your background was impeccable."

"So you made the offer without consulting Ian, hoping to force his hand. But you had no idea that I was also Madam Zora because you'd investigated my past, but not my present." Suddenly, everything made sense. "Ian told you that Lady Alyssa Porter and Madam Zora are one in the same, didn't he? That's how you knew."

"He didn't simply tell me," the duke ground out. "No, he lorded my mistake over me."

To be referred to as a mistake stunned Alyssa. "Well, bully for him," she retorted.

"I find your rudeness most unbecoming," the duke

informed her coldly, as the carriage rocked to a stop in front of Lady Eleanor's town house.

"And I find your lack of respect for your own grandson reprehensible," Alyssa said boldly.

Uncaring of the duke's response, Alyssa clambered out of the carriage. She ignored Lord Hammond's order to stop as she made her way up the front steps. Because of his machinations, Ian had once more been deceived. This time, however, she wouldn't be a party to it.

"If you try to back out of the proxy, you destroy any hope you have for your sister."

Freezing upon the top step, Alyssa turned to face the duke, unable to believe the threat he'd just issued. After learning the lengths he'd go to force Ian to his will, she didn't know why anything would surprise her.

"You have no choice in the matter," Lord Hammond informed her. "While you are annoyed at present, I know you'll see the logic in my plans once you calm down. A marriage between you and my grandson fulfills everyone's needs. You gain the security you long for and he marries a lady of title. It is the perfect solution."

Drawing her shawl about her, Alyssa gazed down at the duke. "I will not be a part of your attempts to bend Ian to your will."

"Go ahead and cling to your ridiculous notions of honor, Lady Alyssa," the duke said, scorn dripping from every word. "You'll find honor makes a poor meal indeed. So before you thoughtlessly toss aside the offer to marry my grandson, you might consider what life will hold for you."

Though the thought of once again being penniless

made her blanch, she would not, could not, be party to the duke's schemes. Ian deserved better. *She* deserved better.

Drawing back her shoulders, Alyssa projected a calm she was far from feeling. "Then I shall resume my life as Alyssa Porter."

"And how will you support yourself? Will you become Madam Zora again? Or do you hope your cousin will have a change of heart and decide to reinstate your monthly stipend?"

How could she possibly respond when she didn't know any of the answers to his questions? Holding her head high, she walked into Lady Eleanor's house.

What had he been thinking?

Draining the last of his brandy, Ian poured himself another snifter full of the potent stuff. By dancing with her, he'd all but declared that he did indeed plan on completing the proxy and claiming her for his wife in more than just name. No, he admitted as he gazed into the amber liquid, just by attending, he'd given his seal of approval on the Duke's plan.

If only he hadn't been drawn over to the house. If only he hadn't seen her expression and felt the need to respond to it, to help her. If only . . .

Setting down his brandy, Ian thrust a hand through his hair. He knew better than most that life was made up of "if only's," and there was no use in looking back. He'd battled through a thousand questions, all of them beginning with that useless phrase, after his parents had died. Still, he'd succeeded in building a comfortable life for himself. He'd formed wonderful plans for the future and had worked hard to see them to fruition.

And he'd accomplished all of his goals . . . except for one.

Now Alyssa stood in the way of fulfilling his last dream. Even if he'd never learned of her perfidy, Ian wouldn't accept her as his bride. She was part of the duke's plan to rule his future. If he accepted Alyssa, Ian knew he'd lose in his power struggle against his grandfather. Still, despite all of this, he seemed compelled to protect her.

Reaching for his brandy, Ian brushed away a frog that leapt onto the sideboard. Yet another wonderful mark the Gypsy had left upon his life.

Taking a long swallow of the strong drink, Ian hoped that temporary comfort lay within the amber depths. Picking up the bottle, he walked over to his chair, settling in comfortably. Suddenly, the sound of knocking echoed throughout the room. Yet, when he bid the servant to enter, no one answered.

Rising from his chair, Ian walked over to the door, opened it . . . and found the hallway empty. With a shrug, Ian returned to his chair and took another sip of his drink when he heard the knocking again.

This time he realized the knocking was coming from the left side of the room. Putting down his glass and the bottle, he walked over to the windows and peered out into the night. Alyssa stood there, still wearing the ballgown she'd had on earlier.

"What the devil?" he muttered, thrusting open the

window. "What are you doing out here at this time of night?"

"I needed to see you," she whispered. Holding up her hands, she directed him. "Now, please help me inside."

Shaking his head, Ian stepped back. "I shall let you in the rear door if you'll—"

But the stubborn woman had already grasped the edge of the window and was attempting to pull herself up and into his house. Frustration ripped through him as he gave up the notion of talking sense into her. Stepping forward, he bent down and grabbed hold of her waist, lifting her inside the room.

As she thanked him for his assistance, Alyssa smoothed down her skirts. When he'd first seen her this evening, her appearance had stunned him. He'd always known she was attractive, but dressed in her finery with her hair caught up in an intricate knot and her body encased in silk, Alyssa was breathtakingly beautiful.

And she'd traipsed through the streets of London dressed like this.

Concern spread through him, making his tone sterner than he'd intended. "What possessed you to come over here in the middle of the night without an escort?"

"I needed to see you."

"And it couldn't wait until morning?" he asked, incredulous.

Placing her hands on her hips, Alyssa gave him a shake of her head. "Obviously I didn't feel it could."

Her disregard for her own safety astonished him. "I

can't think of anything important enough to risk life and limb."

"Life and limb?" Alyssa laughed softly, a pretty sound that sparkled through the room. "I simply walked down a few streets. Nothing perilous, I assure you."

"I beg to differ," he retorted, taking a step closer to pluck a twig out of her disheveled hair. "Criminal elements roam the streets at night."

Exasperation echoed in her sigh. "Please, Ian, I don't wish to argue about whether or not I should walk through the streets of London. I came to discuss the proxy."

Taking a step back, Ian retrieved his glass of brandy. "Ah, yes, the proxy."

"I thought you'd asked your grandfather to approach me," Alyssa said softly. "He told me you were out of town on business and that was why he was making the offer instead of you."

Ian leaned back against his desk. "That wily old bastard," he murmured.

"It struck me as odd that you would have your grandfather negotiate the proxy, but when I asked him if you'd agreed to it, he assured me you wished to marry me." Clasping her hands in front of her, Alyssa met his gaze. "I believed him. No, that's not quite true. I had doubts, but I ignored them because I *wanted* to believe him."

Her statement tugged at him. "Why did you want to believe my grandfather?"

"Because of what it meant to me and Calla. If I were to marry you, all of our financial problems would be over. Calla could receive the Season she deserves and I would be content in marriage." Alyssa shook her head. "I'm so sorry, Ian, that I allowed my selfishness to blind me to the truth."

Oddly enough, Ian felt a vague sensation of disappointment when Alyssa had admitted to wanting to marry him for his money. Pushing the unsettling feeling aside, he reassured her. "Don't blame yourself, Alyssa. My grandfather can be most persuasive when he so chooses."

"At least I discovered his deception before it was too late to correct matters." Alyssa smiled for the first time since he'd hoisted her through the window. "While I've agreed verbally, I haven't yet signed anything. I shall simply refuse to sign the papers when your grandfather sends them to me. Please be assured that any threat of a proxy is over."

"It's over?" Ian asked, stumbling over the question. Shaking himself, he cleared his throat. "I mean, yes, of course, the proxy is no longer a threat."

"Tomorrow afternoon, I shall attend Lady Wirth's tea party and announce that Lord Hammond was mistaken and there is no proxy agreement between us."

"But you accepted his introduction this evening," Ian pointed out. "How will you explain that?"

Biting her lower lip, Alyssa remained quiet for a moment. Finally, she snapped her fingers. "I shall simply tell the ladies that the duke was suffering from a Gypsy spell and I was going along with his delusions in order to help him break the spell."

"And what of your financial situation? How will you address that problem?" Ian asked quietly.

The smile upon Alyssa's face died. "I fear that problem will not go away quite so easily."

"It would if you allow me to offer you aid." As soon as the words left his mouth, Ian saw Alyssa stiffen. Raising his hands, he warded off her anger and clarified his statement. "I'm not asking you to become my mistress. I am merely offering you financial assistance."

"While I appreciate the offer, I can't possibly accept it," she replied firmly.

Crossing his arms, Ian tried to wear down her stubborn refusal. "Pride can't place clothes upon your back."

To his surprise, a smile played upon her lips. "Your grandfather said something similar to me this evening."

Her comparison left him cold. Straightening away from the desk, he allowed his arms to drop to his sides. "The hour is too late for agreeing upon a solution. I shall call upon you tomorrow to see if we can reach an agreement."

"What you mean is you are hoping I will accept your help in the morning," Alyssa remarked with a laugh.

"Precisely." Clasping her elbow in his hand, Ian propelled her toward the door. "Now I shall have the carriage brought around and escort you to your townhouse."

"But I . . ."

Pressing a finger to her lips, he reminded her of the last time they'd had this same argument. "I allowed you to walk home the last time, so I believe it makes it my turn to win this disagreement. Why don't you simply allow me to call the carriage?"

Alyssa pulled his finger away from her mouth.

"Very well," she conceded, "because you're quite right. It *is* your turn to win this disagreement."

Laughing, Ian headed off to have the carriage brought around.

"Alyssa, darling, if you'd wanted your egg scrambled, why didn't you order it that way instead of mashing your hard-boiled ones?"

Glancing down at her plate, Alyssa was surprised to find a mess of yellow and white bits of egg spread across her plate. "I'm sorry, Lady Eleanor," she murmured, retrieving her napkin to swipe at the tablecloth. "I'm afraid I was woolgathering."

"Quite all right," Lady Eleanor said with a reassuring smile. "Everyone needs to lose themselves in their thoughts every once in a while." Leaning back as a servant took away her breakfast plate, Lady Eleanor began to leaf through the stack of letters set off to her right. "Calla and I plan to tour Kew Gardens today. Would you care to join us?"

"Actually, I was planning on attending Lady Wirth's tea," Alyssa replied, keeping her response vague. After all, Lady Eleanor's loyalties undoubtedly lay with her brother, Lord Hammond.

"That sounds delightful." Holding out more than half the missives, Lady Eleanor explained, "These are all addressed to you, Alyssa."

"Me?" she squeaked as she accepted the letters. Opening them, Alyssa was stunned to find invitations to the finest parties. "These are all invitations."

"I imagined so," Lady Eleanor replied offhandedly.

"But . . . but . . . why?" Helplessly, Alyssa shook her head. "I know that last night helped rebuild my reputation, but I certainly wasn't expecting this."

"Whyever not?" Lady Eleanor set down the letter she was reading to give Alyssa her undivided attention. "Even as Madam Zora, you commanded interest, but now that you are both a Gypsy fortuneteller *and* a well-bred lady, you've become the darling of society."

Too stunned to speak, Alyssa listened to Lady Eleanor.

"I'm quite certain that everyone who is anyone will vie for your favor." Lady Eleanor leveled a serious look at Alyssa. "But I must warn you, with great popularity comes great responsibility."

"I don't understand," Alyssa replied as she continued to open the invitations.

"What I mean, Alyssa, is that one ill word from you and a person could find themselves ostracized." Rising to her feet, Lady Eleanor smiled gently down at Alyssa. "A favorite of the ton wields great power over the reputations of others." She patted Alyssa on the shoulder. "Now if you'll excuse me, I'd best see if your sister ever plans on rising today."

Murmuring a farewell, Alyssa remained seated as shock rippled through her. Of course, she thought, a method for securing her future had been right in front of her the whole time . . . but she hadn't seen it. Now that she did, she wouldn't waste a moment to act upon it.

Eagerly, Alyssa rose from the table, retrieved her bonnet, and hurried from the house.

* * *

"Are you *threatening* me?"

Alyssa smiled over her cousin's incredulous question. "That is such an unattractive word," she said politely. "I prefer to think of it as incentive to provide Calla and me with a few basic necessities."

"The amount you are demanding will certainly purchase more than just basic necessities," the earl exclaimed as he gathered his robe about him. "First you call upon me before I've had a chance to dress, then you proceed to threaten me." Pressing a hand to his chest, he sank into a chair. "Surely this can't be good for a person."

"Come now, dear cousin. There is no need for dramatics." Alyssa tugged on her gloves. "If you'd given Calla and me what we deserved from the very start, there would have been no need for this unpleasantness. It is unfortunate that I was forced into this situation, but that doesn't mean we can't overcome our circumstances." Strolling over to the large desk that had once been her father's, Alyssa trailed her fingers along the wooden edge.

A sly look sharpened the earl's features. "What if I only give you half the sum you're requesting?"

"Then I shall only be forced to speak ill of you half the time," Alyssa replied with a laugh. Moving around the desk, she settled into the leather chair behind it. "This morning I received numerous invitations to many different affairs. I find myself one of the darlings of the ton," she informed her cousin blithely. "And that's when I realized how everyone was listening to my every word last night."

"So if you chose, you could destroy a person's reputation in the matter of one afternoon," the earl concluded glumly.

"Precisely," Alyssa replied with a bright smile. "And as luck would have it, I'm attending Lady Wirth's tea this very afternoon." Leaning forward, she placed her elbows on the desk and stared at her cousin. "Which is why you shall have the papers *unconditionally* awarding me the monthly stipend I requested brought around to Lady Eleanor's home this afternoon before I leave for Lady Wirth's affair."

"But . . . but I don't know if Meiser will be able to draw the papers up that quickly," protested the earl.

"Then you'd best give him added incentive," Alyssa said with utter disregard for her cousin's distress. After all, he'd left them up in Northumberland to rot without a sou to their names. Pushing to her feet, Alyssa stared down at the round man. "As long as you continue to support Calla and me, no one will ever know that you once refused to honor your duties as our guardian."

"That's . . . that's blackmail," shouted the earl.

Smiling lightly, Alyssa headed toward the door. "Another unpleasant word. As I said, I prefer to think of it as incentive."

Struggling to his feet, the earl clutched his robe about him. "If I can't add a clause stating that you must refrain from speaking about me, how do I know you'll keep your end of this arrangement after I give you the money?"

"You don't," Alyssa informed him calmly. Pausing

by the door, she glanced back at her red-faced cousin. "You shall have to accept my word . . . and hope I honor it."

The moment Ian walked into his great-aunt's drawing room, Alyssa flew at him with a huge smile brightening her expression. "I've done it!" she exclaimed, clasping his hands between hers.

"Done what?" he asked, smiling over her exuberance.

"Found a way to ensure Calla and I never have financial worries again."

Stunned, Ian looked down at Alyssa. "How did you accomplish that?"

"It was quite simple, really; and the solution had been in front of me all the while." She squeezed his hands. "After I received a stack of invitations this morning, I realized I could now force my cousin to honor his duty toward me and Calla."

"How?" Ian asked again, aware he was repeating himself.

"I threatened to destroy his reputation by telling everyone that he wouldn't honor his responsibilities toward us and that he'd tossed us, two poor innocent females, into a cottage in the wilds of Northumberland to fend for ourselves."

He couldn't help but admire her spirit. "Well done, Alyssa."

Laughing, she released her hold on his hands and, flinging her arms wide, she spun around once. "I feel so free . . . for the first time in so very long."

His breath caught in his throat as he watched her

joyful abandon. It was as if the Alyssa he'd come to know had evolved into this exotic, sparkling, enticing creature before him. Clearing his throat, Ian forced himself to stop staring. "I'm pleased for you."

"As well you should be," she replied with a laugh. "All that is left to do is to announce that we never had a proxy agreement and then you shall be free as well." Wrapping her arms around her waist, she looked at him. "Then we will both be able to marry for love instead of convenience."

"Indeed," Ian murmured, wondering at the odd sensation inside of him.

"This evening I shall attend the Allerbys' ball. Will you be there as well?"

Ian shook his head in confusion. "I'm afraid I don't understand, Alyssa. If you're going to announce that there is no proxy this afternoon, why would you want me to attend a ball with you this evening?"

"Not *with* me, Ian," she replied, smiling at him. "That's the whole point. If you attend as well and ignore my presence, it will only strengthen my denial of the proxy."

Seeing the logic in her idea, Ian nodded in agreement. "I shall be most pleased to attend the Allerbys' ball this evening . . . and pretend you don't exist."

She beamed at him. "Splendid."

As the music stopped, Alyssa glanced toward where Ian stood against the far wall of the Allerbys' ballroom. Ever since he'd arrived an hour before, she'd been aware of him, yet every time she'd looked at him, he'd been conversing with someone. It was as if Ian didn't even realize she was at the ball.

"Thank you for the dance," murmured her companion.

Forcing her attention back to her dance partner, Alyssa returned, "It was my pleasure, Lord Willowby."

The gentleman bowed and stepped away. "I do believe you've made another conquest, Alyssa," murmured Lady Eleanor.

"Hmmm." Tipping her head to the side, Alyssa tried to catch another glimpse of Ian through the crowd.

"But then, you're truly not interested in anyone other than my grand-nephew, are you?"

"No, I . . ." she began, still distracted. Suddenly, Lady Eleanor's remark sunk in. "What did you say?"

Laughing gaily, Lady Eleanor snapped open her fan. "You heard me perfectly well."

"I know, but what I don't understand is why you'd make a remark like that." Alyssa prayed her cheeks weren't reddening. "Why, Ian hasn't even asked me to dance."

"Yes, but his very absence makes me wonder if perhaps he isn't working a bit too hard to avoid you," Lady Eleanor remarked, fanning herself slowly. "His actions are *very* telling, my dear Alyssa."

"You're imagining things, my lady," Alyssa returned, yet part of her hoped Lady Eleanor was correct in her assessment. Using the pretext of fixing one of the ribbons on the sleeve of her gown, Alyssa peered through the milling crowd to glance at Ian.

It surprised her how difficult it was to avoid him. She longed to approach him, to let him know she'd made her announcement about the proxy at Lady Wirth's party this afternoon, to share all her news with him. Worst of all was wondering if he missed her company as well.

But this wouldn't do at all, Alyssa decided firmly, gathering her emotions in hand. She had so much to rejoice in. Why was she acting so dreary? All she'd dreamed of was now a reality. Calla would have her Season, their financial troubles were over, and she was free from worry. By all rights, she should be celebrating, not moping over a man who'd made it perfectly obvious that he had no wish to marry her.

Taking a deep breath, Alyssa turned toward the gentleman next to her with a broad smile. "Lord Weatherstone, how delightful to see you here."

Immediately, the handsome gentleman faced her with an answering smile. "My lady," he murmured, lifting her hand to press a kiss upon the back of it. "Might I have the honor of this dance?"

Feeling her mood lighten, Alyssa nodded firmly. "I would be delighted."

He couldn't take his eyes off her.

Watching Alyssa waltz around the room, Ian felt his chest tighten with an odd emotion . . . an emotion alarmingly like jealousy. Immediately, he dismissed the notion as utterly ridiculous.

Undoubtedly, it was simply surprise at seeing Alyssa reveling in the attention being heaped upon her. It was as if someone had lit a candle inside of her, for she glowed.

"Why don't you ask her to dance instead of standing here watching her?" Peter asked bluntly as he moved next to Ian.

Shaking his head, Ian forced himself to look away from the fascinating sight. "I don't know what you're talking about, Peter. I'm merely enjoying my punch and watching the dancers."

"One dancer in particular."

How could he deny the truth? Instead, Ian simply changed the subject. "Is that Jennings over there?" he asked, nodding toward a group of men off to their left.

Narrowing his gaze, Peter peered at the men. "I do believe it is."

"I wonder what he's doing here," Ian said, not really caring one way or the other. All he'd wanted to do was distract Peter from his pointed questions about Alyssa. Ignoring the urge to look at her again, Ian kept his gaze locked upon the men. "I see he's speaking with Allerby."

"Allerby? I thought you'd convinced him that the Electrolytic Marine Mining Company was a fraud."

"As did I." Now Ian's curiosity was piqued. "Why don't we stroll over and join the discussion?"

"Why don't we," Peter replied with a grin. "I do so enjoy to hear you argue."

"I don't argue." Glancing back at his friend, Ian corrected him. "I simply disagree in a firm, yet controlled manner." They joined the group. "Good evening, gentlemen."

Ian watched with satisfaction as Jennings paled.

"Mr. Fortune," the older man said, his voice tight. "I didn't expect to see you here this evening."

"I can say the same," Ian returned before giving Allerby a pointed look. "I must say I am quite surprised to see you speaking with Jennings."

"Don't worry, Ian," Allerby rushed to tell him. "I was just telling Jennings that I had no further interest in his company."

"Indeed, he was," Jennings agreed with a smile that didn't reach his eyes. "You must have quite the influence, for none of these men are interested in partaking of a fine investment in Electrolytic."

Crossing his arms, Ian settled back on his heels. "Then I admire their business sense because your company, Jennings, is a bad investment."

"How can you say that when many gentlemen have already seen a great return on their investment?"

Ian didn't recognize the smaller man standing beside Jennings. "Have we met, sir?"

"No." Bowing in deference, the man made the appropriate introductions. "Forgive my rudeness for not introducing myself immediately. Mr. Arthur Ryan at your service."

"Mr. Ryan is the president of Electrolytic Marine Mining Company," explained Jennings. "He runs the day-to-day operations."

"While you solicit the investors," Ian said to Jennings. Nodding once, he complimented the pair. "You have quite a convincing scheme. I'm quite certain you've managed to swindle a number of gentlemen out of their money."

Stiffening, Ryan glared at Ian. "How dare you, sir."

"Quite easily," he returned smoothly. "And I shall advise anyone who asks about your company to seek a more solid investment."

Before Jennings had a chance to respond, Ian nodded to the other gentlemen. "If you would excuse me, I believe I'll retire to the study for a cigar."

"Allow me to join you," Allerby said without hesitation.

As he headed for the library, Ian glanced back to see Jennings and Ryan standing by themselves as the other enlightened gentlemen wandered away.

"That was most enjoyable," Peter remarked as he accompanied Ian and Allerby to the study.

"Indeed it was, but I'm certain that's not the last we've heard of the Electrolytic Marine Mining Company," Ian said, unable to stop himself from taking one last glance at the dance floor. Alyssa was out there again . . . with yet another partner.

Bloody hell, Ian thought with a scowl, did the blasted woman intend to dance with everyone in the room? Everyone, that is, but him.

Maybe he'd have a drink along with that cigar.

Stepping into Lady Eleanor's foyer, Alyssa handed her shawl to the footman. Her feet ached from so much dancing, but her heart felt light . . . lighter, in fact, than it had in years.

True, most of the gentlemen had asked her questions about their future. One had even tried to get her to read his palm while they danced. Still, it did little to lessen her enjoyment in the evening.

"Lady Alyssa."

Lord Hammond's call shook her from her reverie. "Your grace?" she asked in surprise as he stepped from the front parlor. "It is rather late for a visit."

"This isn't a social call," he corrected. "It's business." Stepping into the foyer, he beckoned her toward the parlor. "I need to speak with you."

Sighing, Alyssa preceded the duke into Lady Eleanor's parlor.

"I've brought the proxy to be signed," he announced after he'd shut the door behind him. "This will only take a moment then you can be off to your chamber."

"I've changed my mind."

The duke froze. After a moment, he found his voice. "Don't tell me the rubbish I heard from the gossips is true?" His features tightened into a fierce scowl. "I know you wouldn't have announced at Lady Wirth's that there wasn't—nor would there ever be—a proxy."

"But that is precisely what I did, your grace," Alyssa replied in a voice far calmer than she felt inside.

"I thought we had an understanding." Lord Hammond tossed the papers down onto the table.

"As did I," she murmured as she tugged off her gloves. "But then I discovered that you'd lied to me."

Leaning his hip against the table, the duke gave Alyssa a steady look. "I assume you've been speaking with Ian."

"Very astute, your grace," she murmured.

"What I fail to see is why you won't sign the proxy."

Lord Hammond's statement left her speechless.

"After all, a marriage still suits your needs along with Ian's, and while he might not have asked me to arrange the proxy, it is a well-known fact that he has been seeking a titled bride."

Alyssa lifted her chin, meeting the duke's gaze. "That does not give you the right to arrange his life for him," she said coolly.

"No, but the fact that he is my heir *does* give me the right to ensure he marries well," the duke asserted.

It amazed her that Lord Hammond actually believed that nonsense. "How utterly ridiculous."

"I didn't ask your opinion, Lady Alyssa," he replied coldly. "I am merely telling you that one way or another I shall arrange for my grandson's marriage. If you don't sign the proxy, I'll simply find someone else who will. So, why not be the one to benefit?" Straightening away from the table, he gestured toward the papers. "One signature and you will become the future Duchess of Hammond."

Slowly, Alyssa reached for the proxy. Picking it up, she read the first few paragraphs . . . then tore the papers in half. "I don't believe that will ever happen."

The duke shook his head. "You foolish girl," he said, a pitying note coloring his voice. "Do you honestly believe your refusal will stop me? All you've done is postpone the inevitable."

"Perhaps," she agreed, "but at least I won't be your pawn."

His lips twisted into a sneer as he turned and left the room.

Lord Hammond's determination seemed unyielding, so Alyssa knew she had to warn Ian.

This time when Ian heard the knocking, he walked directly to the window. Pushing it open, he braced his hands on the sill and leaned out. As expected, Alyssa stood beneath the window. "This is getting to be a habit, Alyssa," he murmured with a smile. "Shall I expect you to arrive in this fashion every night? If so, I'd be more than happy to arrange for fresh tea when you come to call."

Holding up her hands, she couldn't help but smile at Ian's jesting. "Be silent for just a moment and help me into the room."

"But of course, my lady." Reaching down, he lifted her through the window. As soon as he'd settled her onto her feet, he tilted her chin up. "I believe I've made myself quite clear on how I feel about you traipsing about London alone."

"And I believe I've been equally clear when I assured you that I'll be perfectly fine," she scoffed.

"Of course you will. After all, you are the all-powerful Madam Zora."

She bristled at his mocking tone. "I was powerful enough to cause . . . *that!*," she finished triumphantly, pointing to a frog that sat upon his mantel.

"Come now, Alyssa, do you honestly think I believe

for one moment that you have any mystical powers whatsoever?" he asked with a laugh, picking up the frog and tossing it lightly out the window.

A chagrined smile curved her lips. "Everyone else seems convinced." Shrugging lightly, she continued, "I thought perhaps you might be as well."

"There's hardly a chance of that, as I was the one who—" Breaking off his admission, Ian cursed himself for revealing so much, hoping Alyssa hadn't been paying close attention.

"*You* released frogs in *your own house?*" she asked in a whispered tone.

Ah, his clever Gypsy had indeed caught his misstep. "Just a few," he admitted.

"Why?"

Her question deserved an answer. Shrugging self-consciously, Ian said, "Call me foolish, but I couldn't take away your only means of support even if I didn't understand why you felt the need to curse me." The frog he'd put outside began to croak loudly. "But I don't understand where they all came from. I only had ten or so brought to my house, yet there were hundreds of the beasts filling my home the next day. Since I know frogs don't reproduce that quickly, I can only conclude that others had the same idea and let a few frogs loose as well."

Alyssa's lips twitched. "Were there really *hundreds* of them hopping about?"

"At least." Pointing to another frog as it crawled beneath the sideboard, Ian continued, "As you can tell, there are still a few roaming about. I vow if I can't put an end to this problem and catch all the pests, I'll have to find a new residence."

"One that is frog free," Alyssa added with a smile.

Laughing, Ian agreed. "Precisely." Mellowed, he leaned back against his desk. "What can I do for you, then?"

"It's what I can do for you," she countered, moving close enough so that her skirts brushed against his legs. "I came here tonight to warn you."

Arching his brows, Ian didn't even try to conceal his surprise. "Warn me? About what?"

"Your grandfather's plans," she replied, looking down at her hands. "When I arrived home this evening, Lord Hammond was waiting to see me. He'd brought the proxy for me to sign."

"I take it he was unhappy with your refusal to sign the papers." It was all too easy for Ian to picture his grandfather's anger at having his plans thwarted. Smiling, Ian murmured, "Ah, I wish I'd been there when he learned his plan had failed."

"But that's just it, Ian. While he knows I won't sign the proxy, he's bound and determined to find someone who will. He said he'd find a way to see you well married with or without my cooperation." Reaching out, Alyssa placed her hands upon his arms. "He truly means it, Ian."

"I can deal with him," he said, trying to ignore the racing of his blood at her nearness.

"Be wary of him, for he's most convincing in his lies," she warned. "Please, Ian. You must trust me on this."

Her gaze, dark and earnest, burned into him, willing him to believe her. To have her so close, so soft, overwhelmed him. All evening he'd wanted to do nothing more than to claim a dance, to pull her into his arms and feel her against him.

And here she stood before him in the quiet solitude of his home. All of his thoughts and desires solidified into one—one burning thought that was too powerful to resist—he needed to touch her, taste her. Wrapping his hands around her waist, he guided her closer, until she pressed against him, her womanly softness melding perfectly with his aching body.

"Ian," she whispered, her soft breath brushing over his face.

Gazing down into her eyes, Ian felt a rush of pure need flow through him. Her cheeks flushed and her lips parted as he pressed her into him once again. Longings, so long suppressed, leapt upward, needing to be free.

And Ian couldn't deny them any longer.

Groaning softly, he captured her lips beneath his. The touch sent a shiver through him and he deepened the kiss. With a soft sigh, Alyssa raised up onto her tiptoes and wound her arms around his neck, shifting their bodies into an even more intimate position.

Ah, how she fit perfectly against him.

Ian tightened his arms, accepting what she offered without hesitation. Hunger, raw and wild, pulsated through him. Parting her lips with his, he delved inward, the taste of her making him crave more.

Slanting his head, he explored her mouth, reveling

in their passion. Her hands moved up to clasp his head, her fingers entwining with his hair. The erotic feel of her nails scraping over him intensified the desire within him.

Shifting his mouth downward, Ian pressed open-mouthed kisses along the slender line of her neck. "Alyssa," he rasped against her nape.

As desire filled him, Ian continued his downward path, over the delicate curve of her collarbone and onto the sweet slope of her breasts. Needing more, he nuzzled against the low bodice of her gown. Arching back within his embrace, Alyssa offered herself up to him, withholding nothing, and he willingly accepted everything she gave him.

Sliding one hand up her waist, over the luscious curve of her breast, Ian curled his fingers along her bodice, tugging slightly to free the delectable, feminine flesh within.

The lush ripeness of her nipple strained forward. Groaning deeply, he closed his mouth around the point, drawing the tip between his lips. Alyssa clutched his hair as a soft moan escaped her.

Desire pounding through him, he slid his hand downward to cup her bottom, tilting her up into his hardness. Rubbing himself against her, Ian was rewarded with another sweet cry of passion.

Lifting his head, he gazed down at the magnificent sight before him—Alyssa lost in glorious abandon.

"Ian," she moaned softly, tugging him toward her again.

Eagerly, he recaptured her lips, tasting deeply of her

cravings that so perfectly matched his. God, how he wanted her.

Breaking off the kiss, he followed the path downward once more onto the supple wealth of her breasts.

"Oh, Ian."

Her urgent whisper sent a shiver along his spine, invoking images of Alyssa spread in passionate welcome upon his bed. Tightening his hand upon the sweet curve of her hip, Ian lost himself within her.

17

A haze of desire clouded all but the pulsing need to find a place to lay Alyssa down and make her completely, irrevocably his. Forever.

Forever.

The word clamored through him, jarring him back into reality. Lifting his head, Ian gazed down at this beautiful, sensual woman in his arms . . . a woman who had been hand-picked for him by his grandfather.

Loosening his clasp upon her, Ian shifted backward. "No," he whispered softly.

"Please, Ian," she murmured in a husky, passion-laden voice.

The urge to lower his head, to again taste desire upon those incredible lips, nearly overwhelmed him. It took all of his self-control to clasp Alyssa by the shoulders and shift her away from him. "We can't do this, Alyssa," he said softly. "If we do, we'll be playing right into the duke's hands as if we were his puppets and he was pulling the strings."

Twisting away from him, Ian could see Alyssa adjust her bodice and gather herself inward. "You're quite right, of course," she returned, her voice cracking slightly. "I don't know what came over us."

"It's late, we're both tired, and our emotions have been tested today. We probably just got caught up in the moment." Lord, that excuse sounded pitiful even to his own ears.

"Yes, that's probably it," she agreed a little too quickly.

An awkward silence stretched between them until finally Ian cleared his throat. "Wait here and I'll have the carriage brought around."

"Fine," Alyssa said as she wrapped her arms around herself.

Ian fought the urge to pull Alyssa into his arms and offer her comfort. Instead he forced himself to walk from the room to order the carriage.

It only took him a few minutes to arrange. Pausing outside the door, he took a few calming breaths before he stepped back into the room . . .

And found it empty.

He knew immediately what had happened. His little Gypsy had decided to find her own way home.

Without hesitation, Ian vaulted out the window to follow her.

She knew she'd taken the coward's way out, but she couldn't face that horrible awkwardness between them. If she'd waited for Ian to return, he would have murmured a few stiff phrases before bundling her into his carriage and exchange polite nothings with her. No, she just couldn't bear that.

Not after a mind-shattering kiss like the one they'd just shared.

She'd lost herself in Ian's embrace, endangering her peace of mind. His kisses had robbed her of her ability to reason, leaving her heart open and vulnerable. She wouldn't allow herself to feel anything deeper for Ian, because she knew he would never forget her lies. True, she'd deceived him in order to protect her sister, but the fact remained that she'd woven a web of deceit and he'd been caught in it.

Turning into a darkened alleyway, Alyssa realized that she would be just fine in the future . . . even if it didn't hold Ian. After she'd settled her sister, Alyssa would choose someone for herself. Someone kind and generous and who never argued with her.

But why did that sound so deadly dull?

Lost in her thoughts, Alyssa slowed to a halt, trying to make sense of the conflicting emotions racing through her. The scrape of a footfall in the alley ahead of her immediately put Alyssa on guard. Calling herself a fool for not staying alert on the streets, she forced herself to focus on her surroundings. In all the times she'd come down this alley in the dark, she'd never run into anyone else. Nerves jangled as she spun on her heel and began to retrace her steps back to the main street.

As she headed back down the alley, Alyssa heard the footfalls behind her increase in volume and speed . . . as if the person were running after her. Alarm crashed through her and without sparing a glance backward, she lifted her skirts and began to run in earnest.

"Come back, Madam Zora!" the man behind her called.

But she didn't hesitate. Instead, she increased her speed.

"I must speak with you." The man's voice sounded more winded, giving Alyssa hope of outrunning him. "You have such great mystical powers and I need you. I'll take care of you."

Rounding the corner onto the main thoroughfare, Alyssa didn't slow at all. As the sound of the footsteps stopped at the end of the alley, she felt a rush of triumph. Her elation was short-lived, however, when a moment later she heard them start up again. This time more faint, but growing louder by the minute.

Panic clutched at her already aching chest as Alyssa fought to run faster. The footsteps grew closer and closer, and her hope of escape began to fade away as the man closed the gap between them, so close she could hear the rasping of his breath.

Obviously she wasn't going to be able to outrun him, so she only had one option left to her now.

Go on the attack.

Spinning on her heel, Alyssa swung around with her hand fisted, aiming for the man's face. Luck was on her side as she hit the man's nose square on, hurting her fist. As the man bent over, holding onto his now bleeding nose, Alyssa began to run in the opposite direction.

"*Damnation, Alyssa.*"

Ian! Turning on her heel, she raced toward him to throw herself against him, seeking shelter in his arms.

"I've been over this a thousand times," groaned Alyssa, rubbing at her tired eyes.

"Then let's make it a thousand and one." Ian paced before her, his hands clasped behind his back. "I just want to make perfectly certain that you didn't leave anything out."

"No, I believe we've discussed the fact that I behaved like a ninny more than enough," Alyssa retorted. "It was foolish of me to be afraid when it was just someone trying to speak with Madam Zora."

"You shouldn't dismiss my concerns so hastily. After all, I've expressed my concern about you walking home many times."

"I *knew* you wouldn't be able to resist bringing that up!"

A side of Ian's mouth tilted upward. "So glad I didn't disappoint you."

"I appreciate your concern, Ian, but I believe tonight's fright was simply a result of my overactive imagination. I'd been woolgathering when I heard the footsteps and I foolishly panicked." She smiled ruefully. "I'll wager I frightened the person following me almost as much as he scared me."

"You're probably right," Ian conceded, "but I'd feel

better if you'd accept my escort to functions for the next few days."

Pressing a hand to her suddenly warm cheek, Alyssa wondered at the odd mixture of dread and excitement filling her at the thought of spending time at Ian's side.

Lord, she hoped she wasn't making an even bigger mistake.

"There's something I need to discuss with you, my lady." Clasping her hands in her lap, Alyssa looked across the table at Lady Eleanor.

Eleanor set down her fork and pushed aside her breakfast plate. "Yes, dear?"

"There is no proxy," Alyssa said in a rush.

Lady Eleanor lifted her eyebrows. "Pardon me?"

"I'm not going to sign the proxy with your grand-nephew."

"I'm sorry to hear that," Lady Eleanor murmured softly.

"Calla will be as well."

Nodding sagely, Lady Eleanor agreed. "Indeed she will. Your sister thinks very highly of Ian."

"I know she does," Alyssa replied. "And she's also grown very fond of you, my lady."

"The feeling is mutual, I assure you."

"Calla will miss you quite a bit."

"Miss me?" Lady Eleanor frowned at Alyssa. "But my dear, I'm not going anywhere."

"No, but we are." Taking a deep breath, Alyssa smiled at Lady Eleanor. "Now that I am no longer going to become a member of your family, I'm certain you will wish us to find more suitable lodgings. I appreciate your hospitality and hope—"

"I wish nothing of the sort," Lady Eleanor interrupted. "Before you and Calla came to live with me, I often found myself at loose ends, bored with the parties and unending soirees." Her hand shook slightly as she took a sip of her tea. "I wish you would reconsider, Alyssa, for I would truly miss you. Please . . . please stay."

"Of course," Alyssa returned in a rush of relief. "I just didn't wish to be a burden."

Rising, Lady Eleanor walked around the table and gathered Alyssa into her arms. "A burden?" She gave a shaky laugh as she released Alyssa. "Never."

Joy flooded Alyssa as she realized that here in this kind woman's house she had found a home.

"I appreciate your allowing me to join you on your morning stroll," Ian said as he escorted Alyssa down the stone path.

"Usually, I have my maid accompany me." Smiling absently at a passerby, Alyssa tried to tamp down the happiness inside of her. Ever since her talk with Lady Eleanor, Alyssa had felt so free, so joyful, that she'd bordered on being giddy.

And it was far too easy for her to get excited over the smallest things. From the moment Ian had called for her this morning, she'd felt like giggling in pure joy. Yet, she couldn't look too deeply at Ian's reasons for calling upon her. Ian was simply concerned for her safety, she reminded herself firmly. This was *not* a courtship. For the first time since he'd called upon her, Alyssa met Ian's gaze. "Isn't it odd how we've become friends of a sort?"

"I suppose it is," Ian admitted. "It was inevitable once we'd begun to work together to outsmart my grandfather."

"True, but I think I show great forbearance in my dealings with your family."

"My *family?*" Ian exclaimed beneath his breath as he nodded at Lord and Lady Atherton. "I'm not the one claiming Gypsy forefathers."

Grinning, Alyssa refused to concede the point. "Might I remind you that it was *your* grandfather who gave me a Gypsy heritage?"

"Everything always comes back around to him, doesn't it?" Ian shook his head. "Perhaps I should thank you for your tolerance."

"I believe a good bout of groveling and begging will suffice," she replied airily.

Laughing, he reached down and plucked a tulip from the border garden, before dropping onto one knee before her. Ian held out both of his hands, palms up, with the flower laying across them and his head bent in supplication.

"My lady, might I beg your—"

"*Ian!*" Alyssa hissed, noticing the attention they were drawing. "Everyone is staring at us."

He lifted his head to look at her. "Then you accept my—"

"Yes, yes, I accept," she replied, willing to say anything to get him back on his feet. Picking up the flower, she reached down to tug at his arm. "Now please get up, Ian."

When he rose, she tucked her hand around his arm

and, holding on tightly to her flower, enjoyed the rest of her walk.

"I say, Hammond, isn't that your grandson over there?" asked Lord Witherspoon, squinting at a couple strolling and laughing along the footpath.

"I believe it is." The duke replied, noting that his grandson and the impertinent Lady Alyssa were far too engrossed in each other. "Interesting," murmured Lord Hammond.

"Pardon?"

At Lord Witherspoon's question, the duke gathered his thoughts . . . and took advantage of the God-given opportunity that had just fallen into his lap. "It's nothing, really," he said with deliberate nonchalance. "I'm simply happy for my grandson."

"Happy? How so?" asked Lord Witherspoon as he eased back on the reins. "I thought my wife told me you were under a misguided Gypsy spell when you believed there was a proxy between your grandson and Lady Alyssa."

"Indeed I was," the duke admitted readily. "But you see, all worked out for the best. My grandson doesn't want *me* to offer for Lady Alyssa." Leaning forward, he patted his horse's neck. "My grandson is an old-fashioned sort and he wanted to ask Lady Alyssa to be his bride himself."

Lord Witherspoon's reaction pleased the duke. "So Mr. Fortune—"

"I believe you mean Lord Dorset," the duke corrected.

"Ah, yes. Of course. *Lord Dorset* is going to ask Lady Alyssa to marry him?" The duke could feel Lord Witherspoon's excitement.

"It's true," Lord Hammond agreed. "A formal announcement is imminent."

"Might I share the joyous news with Lady Witherspoon?"

"I wouldn't think of excluding her," the duke returned with a broad smile. After all, Lady Witherspoon was one of the biggest gossips in all of London.

Lady Alyssa might have refused to sign the proxy, but she certainly didn't seem to have any qualms about spending time with his grandson. Despite her protests, it was perfectly clear to him that she wouldn't mind becoming the next Marchioness of Dorset.

All she needed was a little prodding in the right direction. Perhaps once she became accustomed to the idea, Lady Alyssa would settle down and accept Ian as her husband.

"Ian, you sly devil, I should have known that you would come to your senses," Peter remarked as he lit his cigar.

"Pardon me?"

Peter blew out a puff of smoke. "I said you finally came to your senses and are going to ask Lady Alyssa to be your wife."

Choking on his drink, Ian glanced around Covington's study to see if anyone overheard Peter's remark. "I'm doing nothing of the sort."

Peter's brows lifted. "That is not what Lady Witherspoon is saying."

"I believe I would know if I were planning on marrying Alyssa . . . regardless of what Lady Witherspoon says," Ian replied dryly.

Shrugging lightly, Peter explained, "Then you'd best let everyone know your intentions for Lady Witherspoon is telling all of the ton that she heard about your upcoming nuptials from her husband who heard it from—"

"Let me guess," Ian interrupted, holding up both of his hands. "My grandfather."

"Precisely."

"That meddling old man," Ian muttered under his breath as he tamped out the end of his cigar. "Excuse me, Peter, but I need to speak to Alyssa."

"About this latest rumor?"

"Yes," Ian remarked as he set down his snifter.

"What I don't understand, Ian, is why you don't just marry the girl," Peter said firmly. "After all, she fits your needs perfectly. More than perfectly, in fact, because you're *attracted* to her."

Thankful that the study was nearly empty, Ian turned toward his friend. "And precisely how do you envision my wedding day, then? Will my grandfather stand next to me on the altar, directing everything from there, or do you think he'll be kind enough to wait until after I marry Alyssa before he continues to manipulate my life?" He shook his head. "I will not allow him to control my future."

"Personally," Peter began, "I think you are doing

exactly that by refusing to do what's best for you just to spite him."

"How can marrying someone he hand-picked for me be in my best interests?"

Shrugging, Peter waved his cigar. "How, indeed."

"Excuse me, Conover, might I cut in?"

Smiling, Alyssa stepped away from Lord Conover and into Ian's arms. "Good evening, Ian."

"And to you as well, Alyssa," Ian replied, twirling her away from the disgruntled young lord. "I apologize for cutting in, but you haven't sat out one dance, so you left me with no option." He eyed her. "You've become a diamond of the first cut."

"What a lovely compliment, Ian," she said with a laugh.

Ian's hand tightened upon her waist. "I meant it, Alyssa. Once again, you've become the darling of the ton."

"Only because they still consider me exotic. This evening alone I've had five requests for me to read palms," Alyssa said, not deluding herself for a moment. "Yet I admit that I am having a delightful time, regardless."

"Wonderful." Tipping his head to the side, Ian asked, "Tell me, Alyssa, do you still enjoy to argue?"

"With you?" She smiled up at him. "It remains one of my greatest joys, Ian."

"Then I am about to make you immensely happy, Alyssa, because we need to argue."

"Here?" she asked, looking around the Covington's ballroom. "Now?"

"Yes . . . and quite loudly too." Bending closer, he imparted the news he'd just heard from Peter. "So I believe the best way to convince everyone present that we are not planning to wed is if we argue publicly."

"Argue about what?"

Ian pressed his lips together for a moment. "What if I pretend to take offense to the fact that you danced with Lord Conover twice."

"I didn't realize you'd noticed," she murmured softly.

"Well, I did," he returned gruffly. "Then you can announce that I have no claim upon you and you remain free to dance with whomever you please." He paused for a moment. "How does that sound?"

She smiled briefly, before fixing her expression into a furious scowl. "You have no right to tell me who I can and can't dance with," she stated loudly.

"I'm merely offering advice," he replied in an equally booming tone. "People will begin to talk if you dance with any gentleman more than twice."

"That is none of your concern." Pulling from his arms, Alyssa stood amidst the dancing couples, fully aware of the gazes fixed upon her. "You have no claim upon my time."

"I am well aware of that," he returned sharply. "I was simply trying to be of help."

"You can help me if you keep your opinions to yourself." Gathering her skirts, Alyssa turned on her heel and marched away, leaving Ian standing alone in the middle of the dance floor.

For a minute, he looked around the room before he too spun on his heel and walked away in the opposite direction.

Everyone remained silent, obviously stunned by the delicious bit of gossip that had just unfolded before their very eyes.

"Amazing how heated a lovers' quarrel can become, isn't it?" Stepping forward, the duke addressed the gaping crowd. "Allow me to apologize for my grandson's public display. He's still young and obviously hasn't learned to channel his passions." Lord Hammond tugged at his cravat. "And if this little display proved anything, it showed me just how passionately he and the Lady Alyssa feel for one another."

Murmurs of agreement rippled through the crowd as they exchanged youthful tales of passion-filled days gone by. Satisfaction filled the duke as he successfully spun his own angle on Ian's fanciful display.

"You were wonderful, Alyssa," Ian announced as he approached from the far end of the garden.

"Shhhh." Pressing a finger to her lips, she glanced back at the Covingtons' town house. "I don't know if we're alone and I wouldn't want anyone to realize we were simply pretending to be angry."

"You're a bit too late for that," said Peter as he stepped down off the terrace and onto the garden path.

Moving next to Alyssa, Ian frowned at his friend. "What the devil do you mean?"

"The moment you stormed from the room, your grandfather stepped forward and declared your argument a lovers' spat." Peter tugged on the cuffs of his jacket. "It was a clever ploy, actually, for everyone readily believed him." Shaking his head, he smiled at them. "Next time I would suggest arguing about something *other* than how many men your lady has danced with," Peter murmured. "Your disagreement reeked of jealousy, Ian."

Even in the dark, Alyssa could see Ian flush. "I should have thought our display through a bit more."

"Well, whatever you decide to do in the future, I would suggest you make it a good plan, for half the ton has you wed and bed before the end of the month."

This time it was Alyssa's turn to grow warm. "What shall we do, Ian?"

"Perhaps you shouldn't do anything at all," Peter suggested. "After all, the old boy will soon tire of the game if you don't play."

"You've never spoken to Lord Hammond, have you?" Alyssa smoothed her skirts. "He's *determined* to see Ian married to a lady he deems suitable."

"Alyssa's right." Thrusting his hand through his hair, Ian began to pace. "We need to do something drastic, something that will convince the ton that we have no plans to marry." He slanted a grin at Alyssa. "It's a pity you can't call upon some of your Gypsy magic to make this problem go away."

Ian's jest caught her attention. "Perhaps I can," Alyssa murmured softly. "What if I publicly curse you again? If I call a plague upon you, surely no one will mistake the argument that would ensue for a lovers' spat."

Grasping Alyssa by the shoulders, he placed an exuberant kiss upon her mouth. "You're brilliant!" he exclaimed.

Her lips tingled from the touch of his, making it difficult for her to remain focused on the discussion. "T-t-thank you," she stammered. "I do try."

"Where will you be tomorrow?"

Regaining her calm, Alyssa replied, "Calla and I will attend Lady Atherton's musicale in the afternoon."

"Excellent," Ian said, satisfaction deepening his voice. "I shall attend as well. After I arrive, we can argue and you can curse me."

"It's a pity I'll be unable to see this outing," Peter drawled as he sat down on a nearby bench. "It certainly promises to be quite entertaining." He looked toward Alyssa. "Precisely what do you plan on calling down upon Ian's head this time? Since I shall miss all the amusement, I'd be grateful if you'd indulge my curiosity."

"I'm not certain, but I'll think of something suitably bothersome before tomorrow," she promised with a smile.

Crossing his arms, Ian rocked back on his heels. "Why do I suddenly feel apprehensive?"

"Because you're an intelligent fellow," Peter countered.

"At times," Alyssa quipped, smiling at Ian. "At times."

18

While Calla bounced excitedly on the seat next to her, Alyssa fought the urge to join her. This afternoon should prove to be most amusing.

"When is the singing going to begin?"

Forcing a smile onto her face, Alyssa turned toward her sister. "As soon as everyone has had a chance to partake of the refreshments and has found a seat."

"Oh. I do wish they'd hurry," Calla said under her breath. "I can't wait to hear Lady Covington's daughter sing."

Alyssa held back a laugh. She'd been to enough parties to know that good breeding didn't guarantee a good voice. "When I invited you to attend with me today, I'd forgotten you'd never been to a musicale before."

"Well, I haven't, so I'm very happy to be here."

Shifting on her seat, Calla tried to see who else had come to the affair.

"Calla." Alyssa leaned closer to correct her sister. "It isn't polite to be craning your neck around to—"

"There's Ian!"

Straightening, Alyssa turned to look around the room for Ian. "Where?"

"By the door." Rising to her feet, Calla began to wave. "Ian! Over here!"

Unused to polite society, Calla had no idea what a stir her shout had created. Always eager for the next on-dit, everyone in the room quieted and turned to watch Calla, who stood on her tiptoes, waving at Ian.

Undaunted by the avid attention, he strode toward them, simply ignoring the onlookers. Alyssa's breath caught in her throat as she watched him approach. So handsome, so gentle with her sister, so very much a gentleman.

Thoughts of what he expected her to do this very afternoon caused her stomach to flutter with excitement. She'd been awake half the night, trying to decide upon a fitting curse.

"Calla," he called in greeting. Clasping Calla by the shoulders, Ian leaned forward to kiss both of her cheeks. "What a wonderful surprise," he continued, pitching his voice loud enough so everyone in the room could overhear him. Releasing Calla, Ian turned toward Alyssa.

"My lady," he said stiffly.

Lifting her chin, Alyssa stared at Ian down her

nose. "Sir," she said, her voice chilled. "I didn't expect to see you here."

The lack of welcome in her statement made everyone in the room aware of her displeasure. "I wasn't aware I needed to send my daily itinerary to you."

Hoping she appeared suitably upset, Alyssa glared at Ian. "It is only fair, since you seem to feel you have the right to dictate with whom I may dance."

"True, but no one ever said anything about being fair. You are a *woman*, after all," he pointed out.

"Not an ordinary woman," Alyssa reminded him coolly. She knew that Calla watched her with a wide, inquiring gaze, but, not wanting to taint Calla's reaction, Alyssa hadn't told her sister about this staged argument. Lifting both her hands, she glared at him intently. "I curse you, Ian Fortune."

Everyone around them gasped, before eagerly leaning forward.

"Go on," Ian murmured, a smile playing upon his lips. "What shall be my fate this time? I fear I'm still bothered by those pesky frogs, so I'd prefer if you chose something a bit less offensive this time around."

"Oh, don't mock her, Lord Dorset," reprimanded Lady Covington. "The more you anger her, the worse your fate will be."

"Words of wisdom," Alyssa remarked, lifting her brows at Ian. "When the sun rises for the second time, you shall awaken to discover a gaggle of geese invading your home."

Ian's curse was joined by a chorus of shocked

gasps. Leaning closer, he whispered, "Geese, Alyssa? Couldn't you have picked something else? Those blasted birds are nasty."

This time it was her turn to wear a satisfied smile. "I know."

The cake slipped from the Earl of Tonneson's fingers and landed in his lap. "She did *what?*"

"Cursed Mr. Fortune again," Meiser reiterated, wishing it weren't his job to report this distressing news back to the earl.

"The idiotic twit!" Brushing the crumbs off his vest, the earl sat up on the chaise. "Doesn't she realize how she mocks this entire family with her foolish actions?"

Eyeing the earl's food-stained vest, Meiser wisely remained quiet.

"We need to do something, Meiser." Tapping his booted foot against the gleaming floor, the earl glared at Meiser. "You're my man-of-business. You think up something to do that will get us out of this mess."

What mess? Meiser wanted to ask. But it wasn't his job to ask questions. No, all he needed to do was remain focused upon the task at hand and find a solution.

One that would help Lady Alyssa.

"I have a plan . . . though I warn you it is somewhat unorthodox," Meiser said finally.

"Go on, man."

"We make the curse come true, then you can speak to Lady Alyssa and ask her to cease from pretending to be Madam Zora."

The earl scowled at the suggestion. "And this will help me . . . how?"

"It will maintain Lady Alyssa's credibility and, in doing so, reflect favorably upon your family."

Rubbing his chin, the earl considered the proposal. Finally, he nodded once. "Very well, then," he muttered in a low, grumbling voice. "See to it."

"This was not one of your better ideas," Ian complained as he shoved a hissing goose into a nearby crate.

Flapping her skirts wildly, Alyssa directed another goose toward Ian. "I thought I was most clever in my curse."

"No, we wouldn't be standing in this park rounding up these blasted creatures if you'd been clever." Ian reached for the goose and tossed it into the crate as well.

"Damn!" Jumping back from the box, Ian rubbed at the fleshy part of his thumb. "The bloody bird just bit me."

Alyssa burst into laughter.

Immediately, Ian rounded on her. "You find this amusing, do you?" he murmured, his voice low. "I doubt you would enjoy it quite as much if we switched positions and you had to toss the vile beasts into that crate."

"Oh, do stop your whining, Ian."

Grinning wickedly, Ian approached her. "Whining, is it?"

"It most certainly is," she replied, backing away from him. "A most unappealing characteristic in a gentleman."

"Then it's well-suited for my current frame of mind,

for I'm not feeling much the gentleman at the moment."

Smiling, Alyssa continued to step backward as Ian advanced. "At this moment? Pardon me for my boldness, my lord, but when *do* you feel like a gentleman? I've yet to see a time when—"

Lunging forward, Ian made a grab for her.

With a shriek, Alyssa shifted out from beneath his hands and began to run across the park lawns. Lifting her skirts, Alyssa dodged away from Ian, darting left, then right, to escape him. One misstep sent Alyssa spilling onto the ground.

In an instant, Ian was by her side. "Are you all right, Alyssa?"

"Help me up," she said, holding out her hand.

The moment he curled his fingers around hers, Alyssa yanked hard, pulling Ian onto the ground next to her. Dissolving into giggles, she tried to lever herself up, but Ian tugged her back down. Alyssa twisted within his grasp, trying half-heartedly to break free, but Ian held her firm. Rolling on top of her, Ian straddled her hips and held her hands above her head, effectively caging her attempts at freedom.

"I've got you now."

Laughing, Alyssa arched upward, trying to knock Ian off, but he had her pinned.

"You are at my mercy," he announced with a grin.

At his mercy. Suddenly, she grew aware of their intimate position. The laughter faded away as she watched Ian's expression shift from gleeful triumph into sensual awareness.

No longer did his hands hold hers down. Instead, his fingers entwined with hers, creating an intimate touching of fingertips to palms. The heat from his body radiated into her, making her burn to experience the passion she'd found in his embrace. Her gaze dropped to his mouth as Ian slowly began to lower his head.

19

Alyssa angled her head to receive Ian's kiss. Oh, how she wanted to get lost within his embrace once more, to taste—

"*Quack!*"

Alyssa jumped at the sound as a nearby duck broke the spell. Straightening as if he'd been poked with a hot iron, Ian shifted off Alyssa. "Please forgive me. . . ." he said stiffly.

Trying to ignore the embers of desire still flickering within her, Alyssa sat up as well. "It would appear, sir, that we were both carried away."

"Indeed." Rising to his feet, Ian held out his hand to help her up.

"Isn't this where we started?" she asked, unable to hold back a small laugh.

"I believe it is. Perhaps this time you can refrain from pulling me onto the ground."

"No promises," she replied. "It is such a tempting possibility."

"Come on, Alyssa." With one pull, Ian helped Alyssa to her feet. "We'd best get these mangy beasts into my house before dawn. I wouldn't be surprised if some nosy old gossip stops by on her way home from a party."

"Nor would I," Alyssa agreed, looking at the crate. "We only have one problem, Ian. Two geese hardly make a gaggle."

"I don't care. For Heaven's sake, I don't even want these *two* damn birds in my home. The thought of a whole flock of the creatures makes me cringe."

Tilting her head back so she could look into Ian's smiling face, Alyssa warmed at the realization that for tonight at least they were acting like . . . a couple— without hints of animosity or anger between them.

Unfortunately, it wasn't real.

"I'll grab this end of the crate and you . . ."

". . . will carry it all by myself," Ian finished, altering her suggestion without pause. Hefting up the crate, Ian glared at the squawking birds. "If one of you beasts pecks at me, I'll hand you off to my cook and serve you for dinner."

The morning sun was beginning to peek over the horizon when Ian and Alyssa walked up his front steps. "Just in time," he remarked as he heard a few carriages rumbling down the lane. "It sounds as if everyone is beginning to head for home."

"I can hear them as well," Alyssa agreed, listening to the noise from the street.

Frowning, Ian tried to pinpoint the sounds. "No, that racket isn't coming from the steet. It's coming from . . ." Dread filled him as he turned toward his door. ". . . inside my house."

Setting down the crate of protesting geese, Ian pushed open his front door to discover bedlam . . . again. Stunned, Ian stepped into the foyer to find his servants chasing a flock of geese. Even his normally staid butler ran after a bellowing goose. With a final lunge, Manning grabbed the bird by the neck, cutting off the bird's protests in mid-squawk. "Got you," he crowed proudly as he secured the bird against his thoroughly rumpled jacket.

"What the devil is going on here?" Ian demanded, unable to believe his eyes.

Handing off the goose to a nearby servant, Manning brushed at his stained vest. "It happened again, sir," he said with as much dignity as he could muster. "I was in the kitchen having a spot of tea when I heard this horrible racket out in the foyer. When I came to investigate the sound, this is what I found."

Staring at the goose droppings now staining his floor, Ian shook his head in disbelief. "How did this happen?"

Beside him, Alyssa shook her head and pressed the tips of her fingers to her lips, but he could see from the sparkle in her gaze that she was having trouble holding in her laughter.

"So happy we can provide adequate entertainment for you," he murmured under his breath.

She burst out laughing.

A smile played upon his lips as he watched her dissolve into mirth. Lord, how had this happened? Before Madam Zora, his life had been organized and well-managed, but each day had blended into the other. Yet whenever he was around this woman, he never knew what would happen, so he eagerly anticipated each day, every moment.

But could a man live in bedlam without eventually going completely insane?

Taking a deep breath, Ian pushed aside the disturbing question and concentrated on the situation at hand. "Manning, wake up more servants and have them help you round up these birds."

An hour later, Ian and Alyssa stood in the middle of a now empty foyer. Looking down at her skirt, Alyssa smiled ruefully. "I'm fortunate Lady Eleanor enjoys to shop, for I've completely ruined this gown."

"I'm looking a bit rumpled myself," Ian said, brushing a feather off his jacket. "But at least we have this situation under control."

"Hallo! Is anyone home?"

Ian groaned softly as he turned to face Lady Covington and her two friends who, with an amazing sense of timing, stood on his doorstep.

"What were you saying about having things under control, Ian?" Alyssa murmured softly.

"I do hope you don't mind that we stopped in, but as we passed by your lovely home on our way home from Pettibone's ball we couldn't help but notice that the door was wide open." Fluttering her hand against her chest, Lady Covington smiled at Ian. "Naturally we simply *had* to stop in to see if something was amiss."

"Naturally." Forcing a polite smile onto his face, Ian began to make his excuses. "As you can see, I just returned from Lady Smythe's soiree." He glanced at Alyssa. "My great-aunt asked me to escort Lady Alyssa home this evening and . . ." He trailed off, uncertain of what excuse would justify Alyssa standing alone with him in the foyer of his home without an escort.

". . . we needed to stop here before Mr. Fortune brought me home so that he could retrieve some papers that Lady Eleanor asked him to review," Alyssa finished with a smile.

"Perfectly understandable." Lady Heath sent a knowing look to her companions. "And most . . . convenient."

Tapping her fan against her cheek, Lady Weatherstone murmured, "And yet there is a peculiar crate with two geese in it on your front steps."

"Geese . . . just like the curse called for," Lady Covington pointed out.

"Of course it's not because of the curse," scoffed Lady Heath. "Lady Alyssa specifically called for a gaggle of geese to invade Lord Dorset's abode. Two measly fowl in a crate hardly fulfills the curse." Turning back toward Ian, she smiled at him. "Though I admit to being curious as to why these birds are here. Perhaps you might indulge my curiosity, Lord Dorset?"

All three ladies leaned forward, eagerly awaiting his response. Struggling to come up with an explanation that sounded reasonable, he hesitated for a moment before offering a reason. "I'm not certain why that crate is there," Ian said smoothly. "Perhaps my cook ordered the geese for dinner this evening and the birds were mistakenly left by the front door instead of the rear entrance."

Disappointment dimmed Lady Covington's expression. "That does sound logical," she agreed.

"Though I can't help but wonder why there are . . . droppings on the floor." Peering closer, Lady Weatherstone nodded firmly. "In fact, they look like *goose* droppings."

Clicking his tongue, Ian looked around the foyer. "I see I shall have to get after my servants. While I have no idea what those spots are, I can assure you they are not—"

At that moment, a loud squawking echoed down the long corridor leading toward the kitchens. Flapping its wings furiously and bellowing indignantly, a lone goose burst into the foyer, fluttering past in a hurry to escape its captor. An instant later, a harried servant with marks covering his face, marks that looked suspiciously like goose pecks, followed behind the bird.

Glancing at the three ladies, Ian saw them taking in the ridiculous scene with avid gazes. "I believe that goose must be for tonight's dinner as well," Ian said firmly, hoping the ladies would let it go at that.

He should have known better.

"Perhaps it is the curse after all!" exclaimed Lady Covington, her excitement apparent.

And with that, all three women began to chatter about Alyssa's power. Leaning closer to Alyssa, Ian murmured, "Wonder what they would have said if they'd wandered by an hour ago?"

The brilliant smile she gave him made Ian's chest tighten, making Ian wonder if perhaps Alyssa didn't possess a little bit of gypsy magic after all for she'd certainly entranced him.

"Lady Covington's sense of timing amazes me," Ian admitted as his carriage headed toward Lady Eleanor's town house. "I only hope that she believed the story about us needing to stop off at my home."

"If you're concerned about my reputation, don't be," Alyssa assured him with a smile. "As Madam Zora, I am forgiven indiscretions that would ruin another."

"But you're not Madam Zora any longer," he pointed out. "And as Lady Alyssa Porter, I'm quite certain your reputation can be damaged."

His concern touched her even if it was unnecessary. "I'm positive I shall go unscathed by this evening's events." She thought back on all that had happened. "Speaking of this evening's events, who do you think put all of those geese in your house?"

Ian shook his head. "I don't know."

"Obviously it was someone who wanted to ensure that my curse came true," Alyssa said, "but I don't know who would benefit from that fact."

"Nor do I."

"Then perhaps I should curse you again and we'll see who comes to complete it," Alyssa said with a laugh.

Ian's expression grew contemplative.

"I was only jesting," she told him.

"Of course, but what you said has a certain logic to it." Ian leaned forward, placing his elbows upon his knees. "It would help us uncover who wishes to see the legend of Madam Zora live." And who was pursuing her through the dark of night, Ian thought.

"Perhaps you're right." Alyssa nodded firmly. "Very well, I shall curse you again tomorrow."

Eyeing her, Ian straightened. "Precisely what are you planning to do?"

"Don't worry, Ian," Alyssa said with a wave of her hand. "I shall think of something."

"That's what worries me," Ian muttered.

20

"*Boils*, Alyssa! Did you have to pick *boils*?"

Shrugging lightly, Alyssa sat down in a chair opposite Ian and watched his Aunt Eleanor apply a glob of red paint to Ian's forehead. "I thought it was an original curse. After all, I'd already called enough plagues into your home. I had to come up with something different."

"True enough," Ian agreed, lifting a mirror to gaze at the blotches now covering his face. "I still have frogs hopping about. But you should have thought of another curse, Alyssa, one that required someone *other* than me to make it come true." Squinting into the reflective glass, Ian groaned. "I know you're trying, Aunt Eleanor, but I look like I have blobs of paint stuck on my face. Those marks look nothing like boils."

"I think they look fine," Alyssa offered, even though she thought the splotches looked nothing like boils.

"Maybe if I keep the curtains drawn and my face partially hidden." Warming to the idea, Ian expanded upon it. "I could tell everyone I'm too self-conscious and have no wish to be stared at."

"Good luck with your curse," Alyssa said, rising to her feet.

"You're not staying to help me convince the old gossips that these boils pain me?"

"I'm afraid I can't, Ian," she said cheerfully. "I have other obligations this evening."

"How convenient."

Ian's dry tone made her laugh. "Yes, I rather thought it was." Walking over to Ian, she patted him on the shoulder. "Sorry about the boils, Ian, but I suppose this is what happens when you spend time with a Gypsy."

Finding an empty chair near the hallway, Alyssa sat down to enjoy her punch. All evening she'd had the feeling that everyone was looking at her . . . yet she didn't know why. Perhaps she simply needed a moment to collect herself.

Sipping on the punch, Alyssa heard light footsteps echoing down the hall.

". . . I tell you, Melisante, Lord Dorset looked positively dreadful today. There wasn't an inch of his face that wasn't covered in boils."

"Boils? Oh, the poor man. Whatever happened?" asked Melisante.

"Madam Zora is what happened."

Peering around the corner, Alyssa saw Lady Elderbury and Lady Hockle pause in front of a mirror. Lady

Elderbury patted her hair. "Did she curse him yet again?"

"Indeed, she did!" Lady Hockle confirmed. "Yesterday at Lady Winterbury's musicale."

"What did he do to offend her this time?"

"Who knows?" Lady Hockle said with a wave of her hand. "It seems as if he merely has to look at her and she curses him."

Smoothing her bodice, Lady Elderbury said, "I suppose we should be thankful that she hasn't turned her evil eye upon us."

"Indeed." Stepping away from the mirror, Lady Hockle nodded at her reflection. "Shall we rejoin the party?"

"Let's do . . . before we miss something interesting," Lady Elderbury agreed with a laugh.

Setting down her punch, Alyssa rose and hurried into a nearby alcove, feeling like a pariah. All evening people had been avoiding her company or giving her wary looks, but now at least she understood why. Everyone feared she would curse them with dreadful boils or slimy frogs if they annoyed her.

Just lovely.

"Excuse the interruption, my lady, but I was wondering if I might speak with you for a moment?"

Glancing to her left, Alyssa smiled at Lord Wirth. "Of course, my lord," she replied easily. At least here was one person who didn't seem afraid of her.

"I needed to ask your advice on a very important financial matter," Lord Wirth whispered, looking around him.

"Then you'd be far better suited to speak with your man-of-business," she replied as gently as she could. Still, her days of dispensing advice were over. "I'm certain he's far better suited to advise you on financial matters."

Lord Wirth rubbed at his forehead. "But I've already spoken to him and he believes the company I wish to invest in is a sound investment."

"Then I'm afraid I don't see the problem," Alyssa murmured. "Surely you trust your own agent."

"Yes . . . but I also implicitly trust the gentleman who advised me against investing."

Lord Wirth's glum tone touched Alyssa. Reaching out, she laid a hand upon his arm. "I believe you should follow your heart's desire, not allowing anything or anyone to sway your opinion. As long as you stay true to yourself, everything will work out for the best."

Relief sent Lord Wirth's shoulders sagging forward. "Thank you, Madam," he whispered, bending down to press a kiss upon her hand. "I appreciate all your advice."

"You're quite welcome, my lord." Alyssa's smile remained firmly in place as Lord Wirth walked away.

Behind her, Alyssa heard a soft rustling behind a large floral arrangement. Peering through the flowers, Alyssa tried to see who was hiding there. Suddenly, a glove-encased hand shot out and grabbed hold of her wrist.

Yelping in alarm, Alyssa jerked her arm back, breaking off the contact. Immediately, the hand withdrew behind the blooms. "Who's there?" she demanded.

"My lady?"

Gasping in surprise, Alyssa whirled around. "Lord Wirth," she murmured, relief softening her voice. "Thank Heaven it is you."

"I heard you cry out and came to make certain you are well."

"There is someone in the corner . . . and he tried to grab me," Alyssa stammered as she stepped closer to Lord Wirth.

"I say, come out of there now!" Moving closer, Lord Wirth bent down and shifted the huge floral piece aside. Alyssa held her breath as he stuck his head around the arrangement. After a moment, he turned to face Alyssa once more. "Whoever was there must have slipped out the door into the garden," he replied briskly. "I shall gather up a group of gentlemen to aid me in finding—"

"That won't be necessary, my lord," Alyssa said hastily, not wishing to cause a scene. "I was simply startled, but I'm certain the man didn't mean me any harm. Perhaps he overheard me speaking to you and decided he wished to ask me a question as well."

A skeptical expression shifted upon Lord Wirth's face. "If that were the case, the chap could have approached you like a true gentleman."

"Very true," Alyssa conceded, "but the fact remains that he didn't. Regardless, I would greatly appreciate it if you would keep this incident between us."

"It would be an honor to hold your confidence." Bowing to her, Lord Wirth pressed a kiss upon the back of her hand.

"Thank you, my lord," she returned, dipping into a small curtsey.

"Might I be of further assistance?"

Pushing the upsetting incident from her mind, she forced herself to dismiss her concerns. "I would greatly enjoy a dance."

With a laugh, Lord Wirth offered her his arm and escorted her back into the main ballroom.

"No, Ian, I won't do it."

Tea sloshed over the rim of his cup as he set it down abruptly. "What do you mean you *won't* do it?"

Pouring herself a cup, Alyssa leaned back in her chair. "I won't curse you again," she asserted firmly. "Ever since you came down with the boils a few evenings ago, people have begun to avoid me as if they're afraid that if they displease me in any fashion, I'll curse them." Setting her cup down, Alyssa leaned forward. "Please understand, Ian. I'm trying to build a life for myself and Calla. If the ton grows to fear me, some of their apprehension might spill onto my sister as well."

Though he might not have liked the answer, Ian could certainly see her reasoning. "I do understand, Alyssa, but you must curse me . . . just one last time . . . in order for us to uncover who fulfilled the curses." He saw the indecision upon Alyssa's face and pressed harder. "This will be the last time. I promise. Then you can announce that you will no longer be telling fortunes or issuing curses."

"That should alleviate everyone's unease," Alyssa agreed.

"Indeed. And we could point out that the only one

you ever cursed was me." Tapping his fingers against the arm of the parlor chair, Ian outlined his plan. "You will say I'm to be plagued by a herd of swine."

"*Pigs?*"

Alyssa's astonishment made him laugh. "Don't concern yourself, Alyssa. No one will set pigs free in my home. This time I shall lie in wait and watch to see who comes to fulfill the curse."

"But why pigs?"

"Someone would be hard pressed to get them into my home unnoticed," he explained.

For a long moment, Alyssa remained silent, before finally nodding her head. "Very well," she conceded, "but even if this plan doesn't work, promise me this will be the end of the curses."

"You have my word."

"I believe we've accomplished our goal," Alyssa whispered in the darkness of Ian's foyer.

"Our goal?"

"In convincing the ton that we have no intention of marrying."

"Oh, *that* goal."

She wondered at the dark tone in Ian's voice. "Is something the matter?"

"No," he replied softly. Clearing his throat, he added, "I believe you're correct though, for I haven't heard mention of my grandfather coming up with any further schemes. Perhaps even he's given up."

"Only on me." Shifting on the stair, Alyssa peered at Ian through the dimness, trying to see his features.

"It seems unlikely that your grandfather will be swayed from his intent to see you well married."

"Interfering old bastard," Ian muttered.

Allowing silence to fall between them, Alyssa listened while the grandfather clock chimed the early morning hour. "It is a shame you don't get along with your grandfather," she said finally. "He is, after all, family."

"By blood only."

She had to concede that point. "That's true," she murmured. "It surprises me that Lady Eleanor could be his sister."

"Me as well, even though I'd only seen her a handful of times as a child. My father always spoke well of her."

"How could he not? She's a delightful woman." Wrapping her arms about her knees, Alyssa thought of all the changes Lady Eleanor had made in her life. "Calla and I adore Lady Eleanor. Thank you for sharing her with us."

Ian shook his head. "There is no need to thank me, Alyssa, as I can't lay claim to her."

"But she is your *family*, Ian," Alyssa insisted. "Don't you want to be part of a family again? There were times after my parents died that I felt so alone, even though I still had Calla." Reaching out, she placed a hand upon Ian's arm. "But ever since your family entered my life, everything has changed for me. I've changed."

"Yes, you have," Ian agreed softly. "But you still sneak off in the middle of the night."

Lightly, she swatted at him. "I'm being serious, Ian. Don't you ever wish to be part of a family again?"

He remained silent for so long, Alyssa didn't think he planned to answer her. "Yes, I do."

"Then you should come around more often to call upon Lady Eleanor. I'm quite certain she would love to see you." Looking away, Alyssa smoothed her skirts. "And you could even try speaking with your grandfather."

Ian's bitter laughter was precisely the reaction she'd expected. "How could you suggest something like that when you know how manipulative he is?"

She countered his question with a question. "Have you ever thought that perhaps he is trying to control your life simply because he wishes to be a part of it?"

"If that is true, he has certainly picked a poor way of demonstrating it."

"There is no denying that, Ian, but what if he doesn't know any better? After all, the duke treated your father just as poorly, so perhaps he simply doesn't know how to forge a bond." Turning to face Ian, Alyssa tried to see through the shadows that cloaked his expression. "Perhaps if you tried to speak with your grandfather, if you make him understand you have no wish to be controlled, you might be able to build a relationship with him."

"Your fanciful imagination astounds me," Ian murmured.

"But how can—"

His hand covered her mouth, cutting off her words

of protest. Leaning closer, he whispered in her ear. "I thought I heard something coming from my study."

As soon as she nodded in understanding, Ian released her and levered himself up from the stairs. In his stocking feet, he made his way across the dark foyer to the open door of the study. Slipping off her shoes, Alyssa followed, pressing a hand to Ian's back so he knew she stood behind him.

A window remained open wide, an invitation Ian had issued after Alyssa had made her final curse. Peeking over Ian's shoulder, Alyssa could see a slight figure slide into the house through the open window. Dressed all in black, the person leaned over the sill and grabbed hold of a rope. Propping his feet against the wall, the man leaned back, tugging on the cord, until a large bag fell into the room. From the squealing coming from the burlap bag, it was easy to tell what was inside.

Alyssa felt the muscles in Ian's back tense and she knew he was about to charge into the room, but before he could move, another hand clamped onto the window sill. A muffled exclamation ripped from the figure in black as he dragged his bag over behind Ian's desk and ducked down.

The furtive actions led Alyssa to believe that the two men weren't connected. The situation kept on getting stranger and stranger. A booted foot swung up through the window, and with considerably less grace than the first intruder, this fellow landed on the floor with a loud thud. Rising to his feet, the second man brushed himself off before pulling his bag in through the window.

Suddenly, there was another loud squeal from the first man's bag. "Who's there?" hissed the second intruder.

Apparently Ian had seen enough. Flicking a match, Ian lit a nearby taper and strode into the room. "Who the devil are the two of you and what are you doing in my house?"

The second man staggered backward, catching himself against the wall, while the slighter man squeaked again from behind the desk. "Stand up over there," Ian ordered the first man, waiting while the intruder slowly got to his feet. "Pull off your masks, sirs, and reveal yourselves."

When the larger man yanked off his mask, Alyssa couldn't believe her eyes. "Mr. Meiser!"

Glumly, the man nodded. " 'Tis I, Lady Alyssa," he confirmed.

"But . . . but *why?*"

"The earl and I didn't wish for the ton to think you weren't truthful."

"So you let frogs and geese loose in Mr. Fortune's house," Alyssa concluded.

Meiser shifted on his feet. "It was either that or everyone would know you hadn't a drop of Gypsy blood."

Nodding, Ian glanced over to the figure crouched behind his desk. "And who is this, then?"

"I have no idea," Meiser returned with a shake of his head.

"Out with you." Walking over to his desk, Ian grasped the slight figure and pulled him over to the light. "Let's have a look at you now."

Tugging off the low-slung hat, Ian started as a wealth of long, blond hair tumbled from beneath the cap.

"*Calla?*" Alyssa couldn't believe her eyes.

A defiant expression tightened Calla's features as she lifted her chin and met Alyssa's gaze. "I'm sorry, Alyssa. But I didn't want anyone to know that you weren't a Gypsy. After all, it was our livelihood. You went out night after night and entertained the ton, so collecting a few frogs while you were gone was the least I could do."

The thought of her young sister roaming the streets of London gathering frogs made Alyssa feel ill. "And did you collect geese as well?"

Nodding, Calla explained, "The birds were more difficult to catch, but I managed. But when I came to let them free in your house, Ian, there were already some running around."

"Those would have been my geese," Meiser offered. Pressing a hand to his chest, he looked at Alyssa. "I only acted in your best interest."

Hearing the sincerity in the man's voice, Alyssa softened toward him. "I believe you, Mr. Meiser." She turned toward Ian with a smile. "See, Ian. No one meant me any harm. In fact, both Calla and Mr. Meiser were convinced they were helping me."

Ian glared at Meiser. "You may leave now. I shall have a word with the earl in the morning."

Sparing a glance at Alyssa, Meiser nodded and clambered out the window. Immediately, Ian turned his gaze upon Calla. "And as for you, young lady, I shall speak with my aunt in the morning to ensure she keeps a closer watch on you." Reaching out, he tugged on Calla's hair. "Do you have any idea how dangerous it is to roam the streets of London alone at night?"

"Ian's quite right," Alyssa agreed. "Just the thought of you wandering about makes me shiver."

Slanting her a pointed look, Ian reminded her without words that he'd lectured her on this very topic a number of times. She glared at him right back. "I'm not fourteen years old," she muttered under her breath.

Ian smiled at her. "There are times, my dear Alyssa, when I wonder."

Lady Eleanor's hand shook as she lifted it to her face. "Thank you for telling me about Calla's nighttime activities, Ian." She offered him a grateful smile. "I shall have to ensure the safety of both Calla *and* Alyssa in the future." She reprimanded Alyssa with a stare. "Don't believe for one moment that I feel any better about you roaming the streets at night simply because you are the elder. If anything, I am far more disappointed in your behavior, Alyssa, as you are old enough to know better."

"I'm sorry, Lady Eleanor," Alyssa murmured softly, "but I did what I felt needed to be done."

Reaching forward, Lady Eleanor patted Alyssa on the back of her hand. "I understand, dear, but I would have been more than willing to help you. After all, that's what family is for."

Feeling a rush of love, Alyssa nodded, uncertain of her ability to speak.

"I do hope you can stay and join us for the noon repast," Lady Eleanor said on a bright note. "I would so enjoy your company."

Ian hesitated and Alyssa was certain he would refuse, but then, much to her surprise, he accepted. "That would be delightful."

"I'm glad you stayed, Ian," Alyssa murmured as she strolled around the rear gardens at his side. "You made your aunt happy."

"I'm thankful I stayed as well." What surprised Ian was just how *much* he enjoyed the dinner. "I never knew my father was such a mischievous lad."

"From the sound of it, he often slid from mischievous into just plain naughty," Alyssa said with a laugh. "I well understand where your bedeviling nature came from now."

"Bedeviling nature?" He lifted his brows. "I have never behaved as anything other than a gentleman toward you."

"Ha! Have you forgotten how we first met? You felt compelled to torment me while I was simply trying to make an honest day's wage."

"Ah, yes, there was that," Ian replied, flushing slightly. "I should be heading off for my offices now. I have a few investments I need to investigate." Clasping her hand, he bent over and pressed a kiss to the back of her fingers. Straightening again, he asked, "Will I see you at the Athertons' ball this evening?"

"Yes . . . I mean, no," Alyssa stammered.

A side of Ian's mouth quirked upward. "What's it to be, Alyssa? Yes or no."

"Both," she said, before explaining. "What I mean is *yes*, I will be there, so you will probably see me, but *no*, I will not be conversing with you or even dance with you while there."

"Why the devil not?"

"Because it would defeat the whole purpose of issuing all of these blasted curses!" She set her hands upon her hips. "We've finally convinced everyone that we have no intention of marrying, so now we should avoid one another in public to reinforce that idea."

"Bloody hell," Ian murmured, thrusting a hand through his hair, before allowing it to drop to his side. His gaze shone with an intense light as he looked at her. "I've grown rather accustomed to your company at these affairs," he admitted.

"And I yours," she replied, praying her voice didn't reveal how deeply his words affected her. "I suppose we'll both have to return to suffering through the evenings alone."

"Oh, joy."

Alyssa would have smiled over Ian's wit if she hadn't been too busy holding back tears.

Lifting his hand, he brushed the tips of his fingers along the curve of her cheek. "Be happy, Alyssa."

"Same to you," she murmured in a tight voice.

He smiled at her before turning on his heel and leaving her alone in the garden. Watching him leave pained her and Alyssa wanted to do nothing more than to call him back.

May God help her; she'd fallen in love with Ian.

When had it happened? From the first she'd been attracted to him, but ever since they'd become friends, she'd slipped quietly and solidly in love with him.

And now she had to watch him walk away.

21

~❧~

The Athertons' ball was in full swing when Ian arrived. Though he'd wanted to stay away, he'd been unable to resist the urge to see Alyssa. He'd been with her just this afternoon, but somehow the knowledge that he was no longer free to call upon her, to speak with her privately, made him yearn for her company.

Accepting a drink, he sipped quietly and searched the room for Alyssa.

"She's over speaking with Lady Wirth," Peter said as he moved next to Ian.

Not even pretending a lack of interest, Ian leaned forward to catch a glimpse of Alyssa. Just the sight of her calmed his raging emotions.

"Earlier this evening, everyone was speaking of her intent to never again tell a fortune or issue a curse." Peter patted down his vest. "Naturally, everyone was dismayed . . . especially the gentlemen."

Ian looked sharply at his friend. "What do you mean by that, Peter?"

"Nothing untoward," he hurried to assure Ian. "All I meant was that most of the gentlemen seek Lady Alyssa's advice with regard to their financial investments."

"Fools," Ian scoffed. "Alyssa may be many things, but a seer she is not."

Shrugging lightly, Peter tugged on the sleeve of his shirt. "Perhaps not, but you've managed to do a wonderful job of convincing everyone that she does indeed possess Gypsy magic."

"That's true," Ian returned, "but as long as Alyssa ceases reading fortunes, people will soon forget about her supposed abilities."

"I wouldn't accept that wager regardless of the odds," Peter scoffed. "I doubt if anyone will ever forget that Lady Alyssa Porter is also Madam Zora."

Before Ian could respond to Peter's assertion, he was hailed by Lord Wirth. "I say, Fortune, just the man I wanted to see."

"Lord Wirth," he murmured in greeting, bowing to the older man. "What can I do for you?"

"I wondered if you might speak to your aunt on my behalf."

The unusual request surprised Ian. "On what matter?"

"Regarding Lady Alyssa . . . or more specifically, Madam Zora." Glancing around, Lord Wirth stepped closer and lowered his voice to a whisper. "It is my understanding that Lady Alyssa will no longer be telling fortunes, so I was wondering if you might speak with your aunt and ask her to convince Lady Alyssa to grant me an audience."

Taken aback, Ian was at a loss for words.

"Privately, of course," Lord Wirth rushed to reassure Ian. "It is perfectly understandable that Lady Alyssa would not wish to tell fortunes anymore . . . especially after that incident the other evening when someone tried to accost her. Why, I thought—"

"Someone tried to *accost* Lady Alyssa?" Ian asked fiercely, interrupting Lord Wirth.

"I-I-I don't know any more about it, Fortune," Lord Wirth stuttered, taking a small step back. "I had just finished speaking to Lady Alyssa about a small business matter when I heard her cry out. Naturally, I hurried back to see if she needed my aid. Lady Alyssa was shaken and she told me someone had reached out from behind a large floral arrangement and grabbed hold of her arm."

"She never mentioned a word to me," Ian said grimly.

Lord Wirth shook his head. "I don't believe she wished to speak of the incident. She even asked me to hold my silence." A distressed expression shifted his features. "I do hope she won't be upset with me for betraying her confidence."

"Don't fret, my lord. I'll see to it that she doesn't hold it against you," Ian said as he turned from the older gentleman. "Now, if you'll pardon me, I'd like to have a word with Lady Alyssa."

Stepping away from Peter and Lord Wirth, Ian started toward the opposite side of the room, only to pull up short when he noticed that Alyssa was no longer speaking with Lady Wirth.

Where the devil had she gotten off to now?

"Good evening, Lady Wirth, Lady Alyssa." Bowing to them, Lord Atherton smiled engagingly. "Pardon for the intrusion, but I was wondering if I might have a moment of your time, Lady Alyssa."

Lady Wirth raised an eyebrow, but she excused herself nonetheless.

Immediately, Lord Atherton launched into his question. "Is it true that you are no longer telling fortunes?"

The slight edge to his voice disconcerted Alyssa. "I'm afraid so," she replied softly.

"Surely you can aid me . . . just one last time," he implored her.

"I'm sorry, my lord, but I must remain firm to my decision."

Reaching out, Lord Atherton grabbed hold of her arm. "But I need—"

"My lord, please!" exclaimed Alyssa, pulling back her arm. Had it been Lord Atherton who'd reached out for her the other night? Disturbed by the notion, Alyssa hurried away, ignoring his pleas.

Glancing behind her to make certain no one watched her, Alyssa slipped out the door into the cool night air. She took a deep breath, trying to calm her racing nerves.

"The Gypsy emerges."

Startled, Alyssa spun around to face Lord Hammond. "Your grace," she murmured. "I hadn't noticed you when I came out for a breath of fresh air."

"I'd say not," he retorted. "You rushed outside as if the devil himself were on your heels."

"No, merely one of his disciples."

The duke's lips twitched. "I've always admired your spirit, gel. You would have bred strong sons and strengthened the line . . . if only you hadn't gone and ruined all of my well-crafted plans," he finished on a gruff note. "Now I shall have to begin my search for a suitable bride all over again." He glared at Alyssa. "You've made my life exceedingly difficult."

"*Your* life?" she repeated, incredulous. Suddenly, it all seemed too much to take. "How dare you!" she raged, stepping forward to glare at the duke. "First you try to trick me into a marriage by proxy and because of you, I am forced to curse Ian." She waved her finger at him. "Those curses cause people to fear me. And, as if that isn't bad enough, I've been cornered and grabbed by gentlemen wanting me to tell their fortunes." She shook with anger as she cut off her tirade. What she refused to tell the duke was that worst of all, she'd gone and fallen in love with Ian, who would have nothing to do with her because of the pompous, controlling man standing before her.

Stepping forward, she poked the duke once with her finger. "So, don't tell me that I've made *your* life difficult, your grace, for you've completely turned mine upside down."

"Yes, I can see that your life was so much better before I offered the marriage by proxy," Lord Hammond said dryly, looking pointedly at her new gown. "You have no idea how much effort I must expend in order to find a suitable bride."

And as quickly as the fight consumed her, it left her. Alyssa allowed her hand to drop to her side. "Why bother then? You should trust your grandson to make a suitable match for himself. Ian is a fine man; he'll choose well," she said, ignoring the pain sparked by her reassurances.

"You don't know what you're talking about," the duke retorted.

"Indeed, I do. Your grandson entered society in order to find a titled bride." She smiled sadly at the realization that it would never be her. "If you'd only left him alone, he undoubtedly would have already chosen one."

Lord Hammond scowled fiercely at her. "Perhaps, but would she have been suitable?"

"I assume so." Wrapping her arms around herself, Alyssa smiled at the duke. "Ian is so much like you in so many ways," she whispered. "Think of what you would do if someone tried to manipulate you into marriage."

The answer reflected clearly in the duke's stiffened carriage.

"My point exactly," Alyssa said with a firm nod. "So, by trying to order Ian to marry the person of your choosing, you are in essence encouraging him to do exactly the opposite."

Tapping a finger against his cheek, the duke

seemed to be considering her arguments. "So what you're saying is that if I wish Ian to marry one type of lady, I should try to get him to marry the exact opposite."

Lord, but the man was bullheaded. "No, your grace, that's not what I'm saying at all. You should *talk* to your grandson," she urged. "I'm quite certain that through loving guidance, you would be able to help Ian choose his bride."

For a long moment, the duke was silent . . . then he let out a bark of laughter. "Loving guidance, indeed," he sneered coldly. "I assure you I will find a way to get my grandson to honor his familial responsibilities as well as pick a suitable bride."

At least she'd tried, Alyssa consoled herself. "You shall never *force* Ian to your will," she warned him, her voice sad. "Your only hope is if you finally begin to *listen* to what he has to say."

Wearily, she made her way down into the darkness of the garden.

"Have you seen Lady Alyssa?"

Lord Allerby looked askance at Ian's question. "Lady Alyssa? Good God, man, haven't you had enough curses to last your lifetime?"

Annoyed, Ian hid his feelings beneath a polite smile. "I believe I'm safe, as Lady Alyssa has announced she no longer intends to curse me."

"Oh, yes, that's right," returned Lord Allerby.

"Now, have you seen Lady Alyssa?"

Nodding, Lord Allerby gestured toward the glass

doors that led onto the terrace. "When I last saw her she was conversing with Lord Hammond."

"My *grandfather?*" Ian didn't even wait for a response. Instead, he stepped outside onto the terrace, but found only the duke. Without preamble, he asked, "Have you seen Lady Alyssa?"

"Lady Alyssa?" murmured the duke, pausing to study the end of his cigar. "Do I know that young lady? Ah, yes, I believe she was the one in which you expressed no interest." He lifted a brow. "So tell me, Ian, do you now wish you hadn't been so hasty in dismissing the marriage proxy?"

Yes.

The instinctive response quivered on the tip of his tongue, but he wouldn't give voice to it. Instead, he shook his head. "I don't have time to play games with you this evening," Ian said, dismissing his grandfather. "I need to find Lady Alyssa." Heading back into Atherton's house, Ian had his hand upon the door handle when his grandfather spoke.

"She went into the garden," he said gruffly.

Help from the duke was the last thing he'd expected. Striding across the terrace, Ian paused on the top step, glancing back at the man who had unknowingly shaped his life. "Thank you," he said, realizing they were the first nonhostile words he'd ever spoken to the duke.

Luckily, the Athertons' garden was small, so it wouldn't be difficult to locate Alyssa. He walked around the perimeter of the yard, yet he'd seen no sign of her. On a second time around, he noticed the garden door slightly ajar. Peering out to the street, he saw

Alyssa being tugged into a carriage. Shoving open the door, Ian burst through as the carriage pulled away.

Unable to follow on foot, Ian rushed back into the Athertons' yard to find help. The first person he came upon was his grandfather. Looking at the duke, Ian tossed aside his pride.

"Grandfather, I need your help."

22

Within a few minutes, a group of men had gathered upon the terrace. "Thank you all for your help," Ian began. "I have no wish to alarm everyone, but I just saw Lady Alyssa pulled into a carriage and taken away. I was hoping one of you might have seen something."

Most of the men shook their heads. Only Lord Hamilton stepped forward. "You are asking the wrong people, Fortune," he remarked. "After all, we were all inside the house. Perhaps if we questioned our drivers, they might have seen something."

"Splendid idea," Ian replied. Following the group of men as they headed toward their carriages, Ian fell into step beside his grandfather. "Thank you for helping me round up the men who had arrived late."

"Ian, I would do anything to help."

That made two civil exchanges with his grandfather in one evening. Ian would have to tell Alyssa . . . when he found her, that is.

Various carriages lined the streets and drivers sat atop them. Calling to his man, Lord Hamilton beckoned him down from his perch. "Did you see a carriage leave in the last few minutes, Beck?"

"Quite a few," replied the driver. Beck's eyes narrowed as he thought back. "But one struck me as being odd."

Stepping forward, Ian asked, "Odd in what way?"

"The carriage was a hackney, but the driver works for Lord Covington," Beck explained.

"Are you positive it was Covington's driver?"

Beck nodded at Ian. "Indeed, I am, my lord. Jim and I play cards every other Saturday, so I recognized him right off."

"What in the blue blazes would Covington want with Lady Alyssa?" demanded Lord Hammond.

"I don't know," Ian returned, his voice darkened with anger, "but I intend to find out."

Striding toward his carriage, Ian was surprised to find his grandfather had once again fallen into step beside him. "My carriage is closer," the duke offered.

Not wanting to quibble at a critical time like this, Ian nodded and veered toward the duke's carriage.

Once ensconced within the shadowed confines of the Hammond carriage, the duke ordered them to be off. As the conveyance rocked to a start, silence fell between the two men. Concern for Alyssa pulsed through Ian and he fought the urge to shout at the driver to go faster still.

"She'll be just fine," his grandfather said in a low voice. "That girl is a tough one."

Ian nodded in agreement. "Indeed she is."

"Besides, Covington is a harmless old bird. He wouldn't harm a hair on her head."

Surprisingly enough, the duke's blunt reassurances made Ian feel much better. When the carriage pulled up in front of the Covingtons' town house, Ian didn't even wait for it to come to a complete stop before he opened the door and vaulted out.

Clapping the knocker a few times, Ian waited impatiently for a servant to open the door. While he waited, Ian felt the duke move to stand next to him. After what seemed like an interminable wait, the door creaked open.

"May I help you, my lord, your grace?" the butler asked coolly, but Ian had seen the flash of awareness in the man's gaze.

"We need to see Lord Covington on a matter of urgency," Ian said firmly, placing his hand upon the door.

Panic flittered across the butler's expression. "I'm afraid that is quite impossible, my lord."

"And I'm afraid I shall have to insist." With one push, the door opened enough for Ian to step past the butler.

"My lord," exclaimed the butler, rushing after Ian as he strode into the house and headed straight for Covington's study. "You can't go in there."

"Watch me." Sweeping the servant away, Ian entered the study . . . and came up short at the sight of

Alyssa, smiling gaily as she laid cards upon Covington's desk.

"Ian!" she exclaimed, completely unaware of the relief rushing through him. "What brings you here?"

"You," he replied in a clipped tone as anger pushed aside the feeling of relief.

Pleasure brightened her gaze as she pressed a hand to her chest. "You were worried about me," she whispered.

"Silly of me, I know," he replied dryly. "I don't know how I could have been so foolish as to be concerned after seeing you yanked into a carriage and carried off into the night."

Her eyes widened as the duke stepped into the room, moving to stand next to Ian. "Your grace!" Immediately, she turned her gaze onto Ian. "You brought your grandfather with you."

Ian could see the conclusion Alyssa was drawing. "He assisted me in locating you," Ian said briskly. "But what I want to know is what are you doing here?"

"Lord Covington has asked for my assistance."

Eyeing the cards, Ian knew perfectly well why Covington had wanted to see Alyssa. "He wanted you to tell his fortune." He leveled a stern look at Alyssa. "I thought we agreed—no more fortunes."

"I know," Alyssa returned, "but Lord Covington hasn't felt well these past few days due to lack of sleep. He's been anxious about an investment he made that has taken a turn for the worse."

"It's true," Lord Covington said, wringing his hands together. "I know I was a bit . . . overenthusiastic in my efforts to have Lady Alyssa read my fortune. I was hoping she might be able to tell me if the mining company would turn around again."

"The Electrolytic Marine Mining Company?" Ian asked briskly.

Lord Covington's brows drew together. "Yes, how did you know."

"That company's name seems to be coming up a bit too much for comfort," Ian remarked, before shaking his head. "Still, that has no bearing upon why you felt the need to remove Lady Alyssa from a ball, Covington."

"I know . . ." Lord Covington looked at Alyssa. "And I'm sorry."

Reaching out, Alyssa patted his hand. "It is quite all right, my lord, but in the future why don't you send me a note asking me to visit? It is far preferable . . . not to mention less shocking to my system."

Suddenly, Ian remembered the reason he'd sought Alyssa in the first place. "Were you the one who accosted Lady Alyssa the other night?"

Frowning, Lord Covington shook his head. "Absolutely not. One night quite a while back, I saw her on the streets and called to her, but she ran away from me and I was unable to catch up with her."

Ian remembered the incident clearly. "Very well, Covington, but I don't ever want you taking liberties as you did tonight." He gave Covington a hard look. "Do we understand each other?"

"Perfectly," Covington hastened to say. "You have my word of honor it won't happen again."

Holding out his hand, Ian beckoned to Alyssa. As he led her from the house, she murmured, "Really, Ian.

There was no need to be so . . . forceful with Lord Covington."

"Sorry if I displeased you, my lady. Perhaps next time I should look the other way when I see you being abducted."

Behind them, the duke made a strangled noise that sounded suspiciously like a laugh.

23

The carriage ride back to the Athertons' ball was a tense one. Alyssa shifted on her seat as Ian glared at her from the opposite seat. Looking toward the duke who sat next to Ian, she saw he wore a foreboding expression as well. Delightful, she thought with an inward sigh. Ian and his grandfather finally agreed upon something—to be thoroughly annoyed with her.

"You shouldn't be so upset with me," Alyssa said, unable to stand their silence any longer. "It's not as if I had a choice in the matter. As you noticed, Ian, I was put into Lord Covington's carriage rather forcefully."

"True," Ian conceded, making Alyssa believe he was ready to be reasonable, "but then I ask myself what you were doing out on the road in the first place."

There went that hope. "I heard people arguing."

Lifting his brows, Ian waited for her to continue.

"That's the reason I looked out the rear gate. I

heard two men arguing about how they were going to get inside, so I thought I should look to see what the problem was." She lifted her chin. "There was no way I could have known that those gentlemen were there for *me*. It was an unfortunate coincidence."

"One that would not have occurred had you remained at the party," Ian retorted sharply.

The vehemence in his voice startled Alyssa. "I truly don't understand why you are so annoyed with me, Ian."

While Ian remained silent, his grandfather didn't. "As well he should be upset with you," the duke snapped. "Good Heavens, girl, you hear two men arguing and you decide to investigate the matter!" He shook his head. "Have you no sense?"

Crossing her arms, Alyssa glared back at the two men. "I refuse to explain myself any further," she said firmly. "Might I remind you that nothing untoward happened to me?"

"Only by a stroke of fate, as your behavior was positively reckless." Leaning forward, Ian held her immobile with his penetrating stare. "Don't forget, Alyssa, that we still don't know who tried to grab you at the Wirths' affair the other night."

She waved her hand. "It was probably someone who simply wished to have their fortune told." Breathing a sigh of relief as the carriage came to a stop, Alyssa moved to the door and held out her hand, allowing the footman to hand her down. Pausing at the door, Alyssa glanced back into the carriage. "The two of you are far too much alike for comfort."

As soon as she walked away, Ian looked at his grandfather who was looking right back.

"Rubbish," Ian pronounced.

The duke nodded firmly. "Utter nonsense."

Leaning his head back against the cushioned seat, Ian closed his eyes. "I suppose I should follow Alyssa to ensure she reaches Aunt Eleanor safely."

"True enough," the duke agreed. "With that girl, you're never quite certain what will happen, are you?"

"Never." Ian rubbed a hand against his forehead. "I'm just so infuriated with her at the moment I'm afraid I won't be able to control my temper if something does go awry."

"If that's how you feel, then I'll go," the duke said tartly. "Lord knows the last thing we need is yet another scene."

Whatever the reason, Ian was glad for his grandfather's help. "Thank you," he said as the duke stepped out of the carriage.

With a regal tilt of his head, the duke accepted Ian's thanks before turning on his heel and following Alyssa. After ordering his driver to head home, Ian wondered at the fury still pulsating within him. While Alyssa's actions had been foolhardy, they certainly hadn't warranted the level of anger he felt.

Slamming his fist against the leather seat, Ian imagined what *could* have happened to Alyssa. How could she take a risk with her life like that? Didn't she realize how much danger she put herself in every time she roamed the streets? Lord, if anything had happened to her, he'd . . .

Ian straightened on his seat as he finished the thought. If anything happened to Alyssa, he'd lose part of himself. Stunned, Ian pressed a hand against his chest.

He loved her.

From the moment he first saw her, she pulled at his senses, teased his emotions, and made him yearn for more. His grandfather's words taunted him as Ian realized that he wished he *hadn't* been so hasty in rejecting the proxy.

Now he faced even bigger problems. Not only would he have to endure his grandfather's gloating, he'd first have to convince Alyssa that he *wanted* to marry her. Since he'd just expended so much energy trying to convince Alyssa and every member of the ton that he *didn't* want to marry her, he would have a devil of a time assuring her he'd fallen in love with her.

One thing was for certain: around Alyssa, life was never easy.

Unable to sleep, Ian decided to lose himself in his work, so he headed to his offices at first light. Unlocking the door, he stood on the threshold . . . unable to believe his eyes. Papers lay strewn all over, his chair listed to the right, and his books had been tossed onto the floor.

Why would anyone want to ransack his office? It wasn't as if he kept money here. Perusing the room again, Ian noticed a piece of paper pinned on the wall with a large knife. Stepping gingerly around the mess, he made his way toward the missive.

Convince the Gypsy to tell her fortunes and play at
curses or when next we grab her, we'll keep her.

Ripping the page off the wall, Ian ran from his
office.

Alyssa awoke to the sound of knocking.

"My lady?" The maid's soft call urged Alyssa to roll
over and bid her to enter. As soon as Erin stepped into
the room, she began to apologize profusely. "Beggin'
your pardon, my lady, but Master Ian is here and he's
insistin' that he speak with you right off."

Undoubtedly to lecture her again on the dangers of
wandering about the streets of London. Yawning,
Alyssa climbed out of bed and, with Erin's assistance,
got dressed. As she headed downstairs, Alyssa
squelched the excitement swirling inside of her.

"Good morning, Ian," she said as she stepped into
Lady Eleanor's parlor. "It's a bit early for a social call,
isn't it?"

"I'm sorry for the early hour, but I had to see you."
Leaving his position by the window, he held out a note.
"When I arrived at my offices today, I found them ran-
sacked and this missive was staked to the wall."

Blinking, Alyssa accepted the note, read it swiftly,
then looked back up at Ian. "Convince me to tell my
fortunes? The next time they grab me?"

"Covington's clearly not the author; he knows
we're watching him. When we find who wrote the
note, we'll find who reached for you at the Wirths'
ball," Ian said, his expression grim.

Questions slammed through her, but only one made it to her lips. "Why?"

"I don't know," Ian admitted. "So, we need to try and piece everything together." Walking over to his aunt's secretary, he retrieved writing implements and began to jot down notes. "The first thing we can gather from that note is that it has to be someone who knew that all of the curses were simply a ruse."

"Otherwise they wouldn't have approached you to convince me to continue 'playing,' " Alyssa concluded.

"Precisely."

"It must also be someone who benefits from my fortunes," Alyssa pointed out. "But I can't even begin to think who it might be."

"The note also warned me to remain silent." He tapped the quill against the desk. "What could I possibly say about your fortunes that would cause someone to warn me off?"

Trying to piece together the clues, Alyssa paced across the room. As she neared the window, her golden ring caught the morning sun, causing the metal to wink brightly at her.

Golden.

Spinning on her heel, she faced Ian. "I have the connection," she said in an excited rush. "Most of the gentlemen who sought my opinion inquired about one company in particular. Even Lord Covington had questions about that specific company."

Ian's gaze sharpened. "Electrolytic Marine Mining Company."

"That's the one," Alyssa agreed. "You were most

vocal about your lack of trust in the company and even managed to convince a number of gentlemen *not* to invest." As she made the connection, all the pieces tumbled into place. "In fact, Lord Wirth questioned me about that company right before someone tried to grab me."

"But wasn't that after you'd made your announcement that you would no longer tell fortunes?"

"It most certainly was," Alyssa confirmed.

"Perhaps the Electrolytic Marine Mining Company wanted you to continue with your fortunetelling. After all, you simply told those gents what they wanted to hear . . . and most of them wanted to believe that gold could be mined from the ocean."

"Who wouldn't want to believe in that lovely idea?" Alyssa asked softly.

"Ah, but that was the beauty of Jennings' scam," Ian began, setting down the quill and rising to his feet. "The mere idea of his company tempted even the most savvy investor. Think on how vast the oceans are, then imagine the wealth you would obtain if the seas could be mined."

"A very clever scheme," Alyssa agreed.

"And now it is time to confront Jennings with our theory."

"Let's be off, then."

Clasping Alyssa's arm, Ian pulled her to a stop. "I believe it might be best if you remain here, Alyssa."

She laughed, then reached up to gently pat Ian's cheek. "You simply must rid yourself of this habit of deciding what is best for me, Ian." Walking across the foyer, Alyssa retrieved her shawl. "Let's not waste time arguing about whether or not I am accompanying you."

Ian's fierce scowl did little to dissuade Alyssa. "And you have the nerve to call *me* stubborn," he grumbled as he followed her out the door.

24

The ornate exterior of Caleb Jennings' home made both Alyssa and Ian pause. "I'd say the Electrolytic Marine Mining Company is profitable for Jennings," Ian murmured as he rapped with the heavy brass knocker.

When no one answered immediately, Alyssa glanced at Ian. "It *is* awfully early to call upon someone."

He stared at her as if she'd lost her mind. "We believe this man is behind the tossing of my office, your near abduction, and cheating half the ton out of their monies . . . yet you're concerned about waking him?"

And Ian was perfectly correct, Alyssa realized. Tilting her chin up, she reached out and slammed the knocker down four additional times for good measure.

"Now *that's* the Alyssa Porter I like to see."

Before she could reply, the front door cracked open. "Wot are ye doin' bangin'—"

"We need to see Mr. Jennings immediately," Ian stated firmly.

"Now see 'ere—"

"It's all right, Albert," said a voice from inside the house. "You can show Mr. Fortune into my study."

Grumbling about the peculiarities of nobility, Albert shuffled ahead of Ian and Alyssa, before jabbing his hand toward an open doorway. "Get in wi' ya."

The butler's poor manners were at odds with the flawless interior of Jennings' home. As Alyssa stepped into the study, she immediately noticed Jennings standing in front of the window with his back toward them. Though he still wore his elegant evening clothes, they were now rumpled and looking worse for wear. Jennings swirled the amber liquor in his glass once before lifting it to his mouth and draining the contents with one swallow. "I've been expecting you, Mr. Fortune," he admitted before turning to face them. "Ah, and Lady Alyssa as well. Now you *are* a surprise."

"Unfortunately, not a pleasant one," she murmured softly.

"Most unfortunate." Heading toward the sideboard, Jennings poured himself another drink. "Have you sent for the magistrate yet?"

"For whom?" Ian asked. Alyssa could tell by the wary note in Ian's voice that the question had caught him off-guard.

"Why, Arthur, of course." Jennings lifted the decanter. "Care to join me in a drink?"

"No," Ian refused bluntly, before heading back to

the conversation at hand. "Why would I send the magistrate to Ryan?"

Surprise widened Jennings' gaze. "Because he destroyed your office . . . as well as tried to snatch this lovely lady out of a crowded ballroom."

"That was Ryan behind the flowers?" Alyssa asked.

He nodded sadly. "I'm afraid so, and I can only offer my apologies for not seeing his true nature until it was too late." Moving toward his desk, Jennings picked up a slip of paper. "This is Arthur's address." His hand shook as he held it out to Ian. "Please be kind to him," Jennings pleaded.

"I shall do my best," Ian promised. "Shall we leave this gentleman to enjoy the morning, Alyssa?"

Hearing the false note in Ian's voice, Alyssa wondered what he was up to now. Still, she trusted him enough to play along. She'd almost reached the door when Ian touched her elbow, bringing her to a stop.

"There is just one thing that troubles me, Jennings," Ian said, his brows drawn together in confusion. "You see, I had an opportunity to hear Mr. Ryan speak the other night, and he struck me as not being particularly bright." He smiled pleasantly at Jennings. "Certainly not clever enough to have conceived this scheme all on his own."

Jennings' lips twisted in derision. "The man ruined your offices," he reminded Ian. "That is hardly what I'd call the move of an intelligent man."

"Agreed," Ian said without a moment's hesitation. "But then you should consider the fact that he wouldn't even have been in that position if someone hadn't carefully placed him there."

"To take the blame," Alyssa finished with a flourish, noting with satisfaction the expression of panic flickering across Jennings' features.

"Precisely," Ian said succinctly. "And I'm quite certain that a search of this house would uncover a second set of books. This new set would, of course, reflect that the entire company was a clever swindle."

Jennings dropped his façade. "And what if it did? What if a thorough search would even turn up a draft copy of the note left in your office?" Smirking, he shrugged in completely disregard for his crimes. "I've nothing to worry about, for by the time you or your lovely companion fetch a magistrate, my books and I will be long gone," he finished with a triumphant laugh.

At that moment, they heard a loud demand to be allowed into the town house. Turning toward Jennings, Ian murmured, "Did I mention that *before* I arrived I sent a note around asking the magistrates to meet me here?"

Raw fury shifted into Jennings' expression.

Ian drove the point home. "I'm certain you and the magistrate will find much to talk about, don't you?"

"Damn you, Fortune," he ground out in raw anger. "You just had to stick your nose into my business, didn't you?"

Unfazed, Ian simply smiled. "I suppose I did."

After Ian escorted Alyssa home, he explained all that had transpired to his aunt. Standing there, listening to him bid Lady Eleanor farewell, Alyssa knew it was their last good-bye as well.

"I shall keep you posted on the magistrate's case against Jennings and Ryan," Ian promised them. "After speaking with Sir Connor, I feel confident those two won't be free to cheat anyone else for a very long time."

"Let's pray so." Glancing at Alyssa, Lady Eleanor leaned forward to press a kiss upon Ian's cheek. "Please excuse me, Ian. I really should see what is keeping Calla this morning. It wouldn't do to allow her to become a lazy bugabed."

"No, it wouldn't," Ian agreed with a grin. "And I want you to know that I am agreeing with you even though I don't have any idea what a bugabed is."

His aunt laughed as she headed upstairs. Alyssa smiled fondly after Lady Eleanor. "You make her happy."

"As do you and Calla," he replied without a moment's hesitation.

"Thank you." Looking at him, Alyssa felt her heart tighten. "Thank you for all you've done, Ian. Just knowing you has enriched our lives."

His smile dimmed as she finished her statement. "I shall call upon you in a few days to bring you the latest news about Jennings."

What Ian failed to realize was she would be long gone.

It had taken him the better part of yesterday and today, but Ian felt his offices were finally back to normal.

"Excuse me, sir . . ." Ian's assistant said as he peered around the door. "But there—"

"By God, I'm his grandfather."

And with that, in strode the Duke of Hammond. To hide his shock, Ian leaned back in his chair. "I never thought I'd see the day when your esteemed personage would darken my door."

"I expected your brash comments, so no need to waste your breath upon me." The duke wandered farther into the room. "Most impressive," he murmured reluctantly.

"Thank you," Ian said. "Though I must admit, I'm uncertain as to why you're here."

"Can't a man express an interest in his grandon's business?" he said in a low, gruff voice. Peering over Ian's shoulder, the duke pointed to the figure at the bottom of the ledger. "Pounds? You make this many *pounds* in a month?"

"No, in a week," Ian corrected.

The duke sucked in a swift breath. "Good God!" He looked at the figure once again. "Maybe there is something to this working for a living, after all."

Ian smiled at his grandfather's reaction. "And that was a slow week."

"*Slow?*" Respect glinted in the duke's eyes. "What did you say your business is again?"

Before Ian could reply, he heard a commotion out in the foyer. "This is odd," he began, "I've been in these offices for over five years and in all that time I've only had a handful of visitors." He glanced back at his grandfather. "Now I have two in one day."

"Business must be booming."

Fighting the urge to laugh, Ian rose to his feet when Lady Eleanor burst into the room.

A derisive scoff escaped the duke. "It's not a business associate at all." He waved a hand toward Eleanor. "It's only family."

Only family. Warmth pierced Ian as he rounded his desk and pressed a kiss onto his aunt's flushed cheek. "Aunt Eleanor," he murmured politely. "What a pleasant surprise."

Flustered, she straightened her hat. "I just wish my visit were under more pleasant circumstances."

"Is something amiss?" Ian asked, hearing the distress in his aunt's statement.

"It's Alyssa."

A groan broke from the duke. "What's that girl gone and done now?" he demanded.

His aunt's hand fluttered toward her chest. "She's leaving."

Ian froze. *Leaving? For where?*

"For the country . . . and she doesn't plan to return to town." His aunt fixed her gaze upon him. "You simply *must* do something, Ian."

"Don't worry, Aunt Eleanor," Ian reassured her, the warmth inside of him gone at the thought of losing Alyssa. "She won't be going anywhere."

"Ah, so you like my choice after all, do you, Ian?"

Wincing at the gloating tone in his grandfather's voice, Ian turned to face the duke, but before he could utter a word, his aunt replied first.

"Do be quiet, Regis," she snapped. "You're not help-ing the situation."

Retrieving his jacket, Ian shrugged into it. "Is Alyssa at your home?"

"No, she and Calla went to Lady Heath's garden party," his aunt explained. "I pleaded a headache and rushed over to your house as soon as they'd left. Your butler directed me here."

"Would you care to accompany me to Lady Heath's?" Ian offered.

"We're all going, Ian," pronounced the duke as he stepped out the door. "This is, after all, family business."

If he hadn't been so terrified at the thought of losing Alyssa, Ian was quite certain that pronouncement would have struck terror in his heart. But at the mo-ment, he had far more important things to worry about.

Disgruntled, Ian sipped at his punch, prepared to wait all afternoon if need be to speak privately with Alyssa. The moment he'd arrived, he'd approached her, but she'd evaded him, flittering from one group of ladies to the next. Though the urge to separate her from the pack and claim her for his own pulsed through him, he fought for control. The last thing he wanted was yet another scene.

Instead, he settled back in his chair and prepared for a long wait, comforting himself with the thought that she couldn't avoid him forever.

"Why the devil is he just sitting there?" demanded the duke.

"Because Alyssa rebuffed his efforts to speak privately with him," Eleanor pointed out. "She undoubtedly knows why he wishes a word with her and isn't in the mood for an argument."

"Too bloody bad for her." Glancing around the lawn, the duke fixed his gaze upon Lady Covington.

Noticing his attention shift, Eleanor placed a hand upon the duke's arm. "What are you planning to do?"

"Motivating my grandson into getting off his backside and fixing this situation."

Her fingers tightened. "You will cause a scene," she warned.

"If I end up with a granddaughter, I believe it a small price to pay." The duke shrugged off Eleanor's hold. "Wouldn't you agree?"

"Lead the way," Eleanor replied, slipping her arm through his.

Lady Covington smiled at them. "Your grace, Lady Eleanor, how delightful to see you both."

"The pleasure is ours," the Duke replied smoothly. "In fact, I'm relieved to see you here."

Lady Covington caught the hint. "Relieved?"

"Indeed," he said, leaning forward to inspire confidence. "I felt it necessary to tell you that this morning Lady Alyssa mentioned she needed to speak with you."

"She did?" Lady Covington pressed a hand to her cheek. "Whatever for?"

"I'm not quite certain, but I believe it has something to do with her tea."

A slight frown drew Lady Covington's brow downward. "Her *tea?*"

Lady Eleanor eased into the conversation. "More specifically, her tea leaves. Gypsies, as you know, often see messages in the residue of tea leaves."

"And she saw something about *me?*" squeaked Lady Covington.

The duke nodded. "I'm afraid so," he said regretfully. "Perhaps you should go speak with Lady Alyssa and ask her to read your palm. After all, palm reading is far more reliable a source for fortunetelling than tea leaves."

Lady Covington bit her lower lip. "But I thought Lady Alyssa announced she would no longer be telling fortunes."

"That's true," the duke responded. "However, since this is a most unusual circumstance, I believe you should be most insistent when you ask her to read your palm."

"You might also want to wait until Lady Alyssa mentions the tea leaves," suggested Eleanor. "I wouldn't want her to think I betrayed her confidence. But since her tea revealed something about you, my dear friend, how could I do less?"

"Thank you." Lady Covington's gratitude was heartfelt.

They both watched Lady Covington rush over to Alyssa and thrust a palm under her nose. "That was wicked of us," Eleanor admitted.

The lack of remorse in her voice made the duke smile. "True," he murmured, smiling in satisfaction as Ian caught his first glimpse of Alyssa telling Lady Covington's fortune, "but highly effective."

As they watched Ian charge across the lawn with an annoyed expression, Eleanor conceded the point. "Is it a burden to always be right?"

The duke simply chuckled in response.

Eleanor smiled up at her brother. "Might I help you plan the wedding, Regis?"

25

"Pardon me, Lady Covington," Ian began the moment he neared Alyssa, "but Lady Alyssa has decided not to tell fortunes anymore." Smiling politely at the older woman, he murmured, "I'm certain you understand why, with all the trouble it's brought her."

Pulling back her hand, Lady Covington looked upset. "I would never wish to bring harm to Lady Alyssa."

"And you won't," Alyssa said immediately, pausing to glare at Ian. "If it would relieve your mind, I would be more than happy to read your palm."

"I thought we agreed that your fortunetelling days were over, Lady Alyssa," Ian said through clenched teeth.

"Since Lady Covington is distressed and firmly believes everything will be set to rights if I read her palm, I'm happy to indulge her request." Studying Lady Covington's palm again, Alyssa began to trace the lines running across her hand. "When I look into—"

"I'm dreadfully sorry," Ian murmured an instant before he tugged Alyssa away.

She allowed Ian to drag her a few steps before her shock wore off. In the middle of the lawn, Alyssa jerked her hand from his clasp, refusing to budge another inch. "Allow me to point out, Mr. Fortune, that you have no say over what I can and cannot do."

"Since I'm the one who helps you out of trouble, I believe it does entitle me to some say over your actions," he countered.

"Helps me out of trouble?" she gasped. "If not for you, I wouldn't have been in a mess in the first place."

"No, you'd still be hiding your true identity from everyone, living in a hovel, and collecting pittances for weaving your fortunes." Vibrating with emotion, Ian moved closer to stare down at her. "Forgive me for offering you a better life."

"*You* didn't offer me anything," she said firmly. "Your grandfather arranged for us to stay with Lady Eleanor, then she graciously extended the invitation after we agreed I wouldn't sign the proxy."

"More the fool am I," he muttered, thrusting a hand through his hair.

Ian's sentiment made her catch her breath. "What was that?" she asked.

"I said I was a fool for refusing the proxy," he admitted gruffly, sounding more like the duke than ever. "I allowed my desire to thwart my grandfather blind me to the fact that you are everything I want in a bride."

Her heart swelled as he pledged himself to her.

"You have a fine lineage, are well-mannered, and pleasant company," Ian pointed out, each item killing the spark of hope within her breast.

"Would you like to check my teeth?"

Ian blinked twice. "Excuse me?"

"Since you seem so determined to break down my assets, I was wondering if you would like to take my teeth into consideration."

Scowling at her, Ian shook his head. "You are determined to misread everything I say, aren't you? Then let me state my feelings plainly so there are no misunderstandings between us." His gaze roamed over her face. "I'm in love with you."

For an instant, one beautiful instant, Alyssa savored the pledge, before she forced herself to look at the situation honestly. Slowly, she shook her head. "You're not in love with me, Ian."

Frustration darkened his expression. "If I weren't in love with you, why would I so desperately want to marry you?"

"Because marrying me is . . . convenient," she returned fiercely.

"*Convenient?*" Ian exclaimed, his expression incredulous. "Nothing about you is convenient, Alyssa." He placed his hands upon her shoulders and drew her closer. "Did you know I had a pond built on my property a month ago?"

Alyssa shook her head.

"Now ask me why."

"Ian—"

"*Ask me why.*"

Narrowing her gaze, she indulged him. "Why?"

"To provide water for my frogs and my geese." He held her against him. "That's right, Alyssa. I've kept them as pets because every time I see a bloody frog, I think of you, and whenever I look at those blasted birds, I remember how I chased you in the park that evening."

She opened her mouth to respond, but he cut her off before she could utter a word.

"Is it the most romantic way to prove my love to you? Not at all, but it's my way." He molded her against him. "Are you convenient? Absolutely not. In fact, you have managed to turn my life into one crazy, chaotic, utterly wonderful mess that I wouldn't trade for the world. I don't need any Gypsy magic to see into my future and know it can be more than I ever dreamed possible . . . as long as you're a part of it."

Hope, so sweet and fragile, grew within her. "You kept the frogs for me?"

"And the geese." Gazing down into her eyes, he pledged himself once more. "I love you, Alyssa."

She'd come to trust this man implicitly. How could she doubt his word in this?

"I love you too, Ian," she whispered.

Lifting her in his arms, Ian swung her around as the garden exploded with clapping and exclamations of delight. But Ian ignored it all and sealed their avowals of love with a kiss.

To the side, Lord Hammond looked on in satisfaction. "I shall have a great-grandchild within the year," the duke predicted, watching his grandson kiss his future bride.

Eleanor, his ever practical sister, asked, "How soon can we have this wedding?"

The music swelled, filling the church, as Calla made her way down the aisle. Smiling at Ian, she stood to the side and turned to watch the bride come down the aisle.

Ian's breath caught in his throat when he saw Alyssa. His bride. Once Fortune's Lady, now Fortune's Bride.

His grandfather escorted Alyssa down the aisle while Peter stood at his side. His life, once so empty, had suddenly become full and complete.

And the reason was heading toward him at this very moment.

Stepping forward, Ian accepted Alyssa's hand from his grandfather and led her the remainder of the way to the altar. The Archbishop intoned Mass, but Ian heard not a word of it. Instead, he listened to the beating of his heart, to the music he heard in his bride's smile, to the joy whispering all around him.

Finally, the moment of true joining came. Turning toward Alyssa, Ian pledged himself to her. "I, Ian Howard Fortune, Marquess of Dorset, do hereby take you, Alyssa, Madam Zora-Porter as my bride, in sickness, in health, and in craziness 'til death us do part."

Her laughter spilled into his soul. "And I, Alyssa, Madam Zora-Porter, do hereby take you, Mr. Ian Fortune, the reluctant Marquess of Dorset, for my lawful husband, to honor, cherish, and occasionally obey, 'til death us do part."

As the Archbishop sputtered over the unconventional vows, Ian lifted Alyssa's veil and, cupping her face in his hands, sealed their future, their magical future, with a kiss.

"There were times when I feared this moment would never arrive," Ian murmured as he leaned back against the door to his bedchamber.

Desire rushed through her at the sight of Ian's sensual smile. "Our wedding night," she whispered. Three words that evoked such imaginings of promised delights.

"Tell me, Lady Dorset," Ian began as he tugged off his cravat. "Do you have any objections if we plan on staying in our chamber for a few days?"

"How can I make a decision like that without knowing all of the facts first? You must remember I'm uncertain of what actually happens behind closed doors."

Ian's lips curved upward with a decidedly sensual tilt. "Very well then, my lady. I will be more than happy to demonstrate the pleasures found within the marriage bed . . . before you make your decision."

As Ian gathered her into his arms, Alyssa tilted her head back to smile into his face. "I am all yours."

"Yes," he rasped, "I know."

Lowering his head, Ian touched his mouth to hers, sealing their vows with a kiss. Alyssa's lips parted, offering him access to her inner warmth, and he accepted the invitation without hesitation. Passion flared between them as Ian deepened the kiss, wrapping them in a haze of desire.

He slid a hand along the curve of her neck, over the

mound of her breast, and around her back, molding her against him. Alyssa entwined her arms around his neck, pulling him closer still.

Breaking off their kiss, Ian began to trail his lips along the line of her neck, nibbling at her collarbone, as he undid the buttons running down the back of her dress. Eager to help him, Alyssa turned slightly, giving him better access to unfasten her wedding gown. He rewarded her efforts with another arousing kiss.

The moment all the buttons were released, Ian tugged her dress downward, exposing her corset and undergarments. He pressed soft kisses along the line of her chemise as he loosened the confining corset. Freedom from the tight garment felt wonderful as Alyssa took a deep breath, unconsciously lifting her breasts toward Ian's waiting mouth.

Accepting the offer, he opened his lips over the crest of her breast, laving the nipple through the chemise. The sensual torment swept through Alyssa and she closed her eyes to savor each emotion, each sensation he created within her. She rejoiced when he pulled the chemise down as well, ending the separation between her aching flesh and his skillful lips.

The touch of his mouth upon her bare breasts only made her yearn for more. Wanting to feel his skin against hers, she tugged at his shirt, letting Ian know she wanted to touch him as he touched her. Shifting back for a moment, Ian shrugged out of his jacket, pulled his shirt over his head, and paused to tug off his boots and hose as well.

When he gathered her back into his arms, the hair

on his chest brushed against her sensitive nipples, bringing a cry of satisfaction to Alyssa's lips. Eagerly, he swallowed the sound with a kiss.

Trailing his hand along the curve of her waist, Ian pushed her gown and chemise over the curve of her hips, allowing them to fall into a white puddle of silk upon the floor. He curved his arm beneath her knees and, with a lift, cradled her in his arms.

Tenderly, he carried her over to the bed and placed her gently upon it. Kneeling at her feet, he reached up and slid off her slippers and stockings, pausing to press kisses upon her legs. Sitting before him in naked abandon, Alyssa reveled in Ian's desire. His gaze roamed over her as he slowly slid his hands up the curve of her legs, onto her hips, up over her breasts.

Standing before her, Ian quickly shed his pants, giving her a glimpse of his naked glory, before pressing her back onto the bed and settling upon her. Wrapping her arms about his neck, Alyssa urged him downward to claim another ravenous kiss.

Desire exploded between them as Ian angled his head to kiss her deeply once more. After a long exchange, he broke free to nibble at the nape of her neck. Closing her eyes, Alyssa arched upward into his touch. Slowly, Ian began to work his way down her body. Pausing to nuzzle her breasts, he wedged his knee between her legs, opening her to the weight of his body. The feel of his flesh pressed against her most intimate part brought a cry of desire from her lips.

Wrapping her fingers in the silken strands of his hair, Alyssa lost herself to the delights of passion.

Curving his hand over her hip, Ian combed his fingers over her womanhood, cupping her heat, making her burn for more.

"Ian," she cried, lifting her lips to his hand. "Oh, Ian."

Slowly he slid one finger into her moistness. A gasp rippled from her as raw need engulfed her. When Ian began to move his hand, Alyssa grew certain she would explode beneath his touch.

Desire pulsed through her, winding higher and higher, burning deep into her very womb, until she needed more, needed him, needed . . .

Glorious warmth flooded her as she crashed over the pinnacle, all golden and light. The only solid reality in this world of passion was Ian. Little tremors racked her body as she settled back from the heights of desire.

Ian smiled against her skin as he slid further down her body, kissing the underside of her breasts, nipping at her waist, gently scraping his teeth upon her hip. Much to her surprise, desire began to build within her again, burning away the haze of contentment.

"Ian?" she whispered, lifting her head to look down her body at him when he shifted between her legs.

The smile he gave her promised sensual pleasure. Holding her gaze, he lowered his mouth, shocking her. Instinctively, she tried to close her legs, but his shoulders held them open. One touch and any thought of resistance left her.

Spreading her legs wider, she offered herself up to him. Ian's hands curved beneath her buttocks, arching her up to his mouth. The stroke of his tongue against her womanhood sent raw desire soaring through her once more. Slowly, he licked at her, paused to press gentle kisses against her aching flesh, and tormented her with his tongue.

Pressing her feet into the bed, Alyssa lifted herself to his mouth, rushing along on a flood of desire. Explosions rocked through her when he pulled her sensitive flesh into his mouth.

Limp, Alyssa let her legs fall back onto the bed. Gently, Ian pressed kisses against her womanhood, easing her downward from the heights of passion. When her body stopped shaking, he moved back up her body, pausing to kiss her breasts again.

He shifted upward until he now lay atop her. Wrapping her arms around him, Alyssa welcomed his hardness against her. Slowly, Ian pressed his manhood against her moistened flesh.

"Let me make you mine," he rasped as he lightly scraped his teeth along the nape of her neck.

"Yes," she whispered, digging her nails into his shoulders. "Oh, yes."

A groan of satisfaction rumbled in his chest as Ian reached down between them and positioned himself at her opening. Lifting himself up onto his hands, he paused, capturing her gaze with his. "My wife."

The raw possession in his voice touched a chord deep within her and created an echo. Reaching up, she stroked a hand down the taut planes of his face. "My husband."

Passion flared in his gaze as he shifted forward,

melding their bodies into one. Gasping at the unexpected pain, Alyssa remained very still until she slowly adjusted to the feel of him inside of her.

They were one.

The thought caused Alyssa to arch into Ian, bringing them closer still and creating renewed desire within her. Eager to embrace more of the tantalizing sensations, she swirled her hips upward once again and deepened the burning need inside of her.

Withdrawing slightly, Ian pressed forward again, bringing a gasp from Alyssa as the movement sent a wave of hunger through her. Ian's mouth tilted upward in pleasure as he began to move within her, sliding into her with sensual abandon until she felt herself race toward the brilliant sensations shimmering just out of reach.

Close, so close, Alyssa held onto Ian as he sent her over the edge of passion. But this time it was far more intense, far more satisfying. A cry of desire ripped from Ian as he buried himself into her one last time. Shudders racked through his body as he poured himself into her, giving all of himself to her, accepting her warmth in return.

Slowly, he lowered himself onto her, molding her against him. Cradling her arms around Ian, Alyssa held him close, feeling their hearts beat in unison. Ian levered himself up onto an elbow and smiled down at her.

"Well?"

"Well, what?" she asked, knowing full well what he wanted to hear.

"Shall we stay locked in our chamber for a few days?"

Shaking her head, Alyssa smiled at him. "No," she murmured in a low voice. "I'll accept nothing less than an entire week."

Ian's husky laughter filled the room as she drew him down for another kiss.

Epilogue

Three months later

Their country estate overflowed with people as everyone came for their first glimpse of the most entertaining couple in society.

"I must congratulate you on your feat, Lord Dorset," Peter murmured as he drew back his bow and sent an arrow shooting toward the target. "You've managed to do precisely what you set out to accomplish when you entered society. No, to be more accurate, you've *exceeded* your goals."

Ian took aim. "And how is that?"

"Not only have you married a titled lady and earned your grandfather's respect, but you've also come into a title all on your own."

Releasing the string, Ian watched as the arrow lodged itself near the heart of the red circle. "I've always had a title, Peter. All I've done is acknowledge it."

"True, but I'll wager you prefer being the Marquess of Dorset as opposed to Mr. Fortune."

Did he prefer it? Ian truly didn't care about the title, but what he did enjoy was being part of a family again. "There are certain advantages," Ian replied.

"I'd say." Peter notched his next arrow. "I've always enjoyed the leisurely life of a titled gentleman."

"Not so leisurely these days though," Ian pointed out.

Laughing, Peter nodded in agreement. "So true, my friend. I always thought I'd despise earning a living, yet I find working with you quite interesting." He sent the arrow flying. "My fortunes are recovering nicely . . . thanks to you."

"And in a steadier fashion than all of your investment schemes."

"You do have a point." Putting down his bow, Peter gave Ian his full attention. "Speaking of investment schemes, what ever happened to Jennings and his company?"

"Jennings was sentenced to prison for twenty years, as was Arthur Ryan. What few assets that remained from their company were divided up among the investors." Shaking his head, Ian clapped a hand upon Peter's shoulder. "I'm just happy that you weren't one of the men who lost money."

Before Peter could respond, the duke's voice boomed out at them. "Ian! What in the blazes are you doing out here and not entertaining your bride?"

Setting down his bow, Ian turned to face his grandfather. "I believe that time apart is healthy for a marriage."

A snort of derision left the duke. "Then how the devil am I supposed to get my great-grandson?"

"I'm sorry, grandfather, but I'm simply not up to an argument today."

Ian had to smile when the duke began to sputter. "Not up to it," he grumbled beneath his breath. "Out here playing with a bow and arrow instead of acting the husband."

Learning to ignore his grandfather's orders had helped Ian keep a kind of peace between them. "I believe I shall take your suggestion, your grace, and see what my wife is up to."

"I'll tell you what she's up to," the duke retorted. "She's in your parlor with that crystal ball of hers."

Ian's head jerked upward. "She's telling fortunes?"

"To any lady who wishes," the duke confirmed.

Moving to stand next to the duke, Peter watched Ian stride toward the house.

The duke's smile was one of complete satisfaction. "At least the boy's blood is heated now."

"And anger so often leads to passion," Peter concluded. Crossing his arms, he nodded in admiration. "You are a wily fellow, aren't you?"

Stroking the tips of her fingers over the crystal ball, Alyssa began a low chant that brought twitters of laughter from the ladies sitting in the room. "I see a handsome fellow who is completely enamored of you," she intoned.

"My Archie," said Lady Sanders with a sigh. "He simply *adores* me."

Closing her eyes, Alyssa tilted her head back. "I see . . ."

". . . a husband who is most displeased with his new wife."

At the sound of Ian's voice, Alyssa sat upright. "Ian," she exclaimed, rising from her chair to press a kiss onto his cheek. "I thought you were enjoying a bit of archery with Peter."

"I was . . . until my grandfather informed me of your pastime." Looking around the room, Ian smiled at the ladies. "Would you mind if I had a moment alone with my bride?"

Within a matter of minutes, the room cleared, leaving Ian alone with Alyssa. "I thought you'd put away your crystal ball. After Covington became obsessed with your gift and then Jennings tried to use you for his advantage, I thought you understood why it is dangerous for you to tell fortunes," he said firmly.

"I fully understand, Ian. But this was different. The ladies and I were merely amusing ourselves."

"Let me assure you, Alyssa, I would not find it amusing at all if someone were to take your fortunes to heart and suddenly wish to claim you for their own personal seer."

"It's sweet of you to worry about me, Ian, but you must trust me, darling; my fortunes were quite ridiculous."

He looked skeptical.

Laughing, Alyssa sat down again and began to run her hands along the crystal ball. "Shall I tell your fortune, Ian?"

Taking the chair across from her, Ian lounged against the wooden seat. "I do hope my future holds many, many days spent with you."

"Ah, but you don't need magical powers to know that," she remarked lightly. "What do I see here?" Leaning closer, Alyssa peered into the crystal ball. "First there was Fortune's Lady, then there was Fortune's Bride, . . ." She met Ian's gaze. ". . . and soon there will be Fortune's Baby."

The look upon her husband's face was priceless. "Fortune's Baby?" Ian rasped, before slipping onto his knees in front of her.

The reverent note in his voice touched her. "Yes," she whispered as she reached out to stroke Ian's hair back from his forehead. "I expect our child will arrive early next summer."

Enfolding her in his arms, Ian pressed his face against her still flat stomach. "I adore you, Alyssa, and I shall be a good father to our child."

"I know that," she said without hesitation, running her fingers through his hair. For a long while, they sat wrapped around each other, rejoicing in the moment.

Ian lifted his head. "I only have one request, Alyssa."

"Anything," she said softly.

"Don't tell my grandfather until he notices." Ian's grin was pure mischief.

"You do enjoy to torment that poor old man."

"Poor old man?" Ian asked. "Are we speaking about the same person?"

Alyssa began to chuckle. "You can be so very wicked at times, Ian."

"Ah, yes," he murmured, leaning forward to kiss her neck. "But you enjoy my wicked ways so very much."

Their laughter mingled together . . . and filled their home.